T0083499

WATERCOLOURS

WATERCOLOURS

A Story from Auschwitz

LIDIA OSTAŁOWSKA
Translated by
Sean Gasper Bye

zubaan

ZUBAAN
128 B Shahpur Jat, 1st floor
New Delhi 110 049
Email: contact@zubaanbooks.com
Website: www.zubaanbooks.com

First published by Zubaan Publishers Pvt Ltd 2016
Published by arrangement with Wydawnictwo Czarne, Poland

10 9 8 7 6 5 4 3 2 1

ISBN 978 93 85932 03 8

Printed at Gopsons Papers Ltd

Contents

Translator's Preface   vii

1937. Christmastime in Hollywood   1

1943. In Birkenau, on Another Planet   9

1946. In Paris with Remus   96

1973. From Hollywood to Auschwitz and Back   111

1999. On the Banks of Zayante Creek   175

Bibliography   240

Select Glossary of Historical Figures and Terms   247

A Guide to Polish Pronunciation   250

Contents

Translator's Preface

In Polish, the word *historia* means both 'history' and 'story'. Lidia Ostałowska's *Watercolours* is both history and story. It is the story of one woman's persecution, survival, and struggle for her rights. It is also a history of the Auschwitz concentration camp: the factory of death. It is a story of the people who passed through that camp, victims and perpetrators, the survivors and the dead. It is the history of how their fates have shaped our memory of the Holocaust to this day. Above all, this book is about when stories and history come into conflict. What happens when a person's story becomes caught up in history against their will?

Dina Babbitt was a teenager when she was deported from Prague, first to the Theresienstadt Ghetto and then to Auschwitz. She was a talented artist, fascinated by animation. In Auschwitz, her artistic talents were spotted by an SS officer, and she was sent to work for Dr Joseph Mengele, the camp doctor. Mengele was overseeing horrific experiments on prisoners in the camp, and forced Dina to paint portraits of his test subjects. Her models were the Roma prisoners who fascinated Mengele. The Nazis had marked the Roma, like the Jews, as sub-humans fit for extermination. Hundreds of thousands of Roma were killed at Nazi hands – but Dina, and her paintings, survived. These paintings, first lost and then found again, became the subject of an ownership dispute between her and the Auschwitz Museum that would continue, unresolved, until Dina's death in 2009.

At the heart of the dispute was a simple fact: the paintings were some of the very little surviving documentation of the Romani Holocaust. After the war, many Roma survivors refused to cooperate with the non-Roma historians gathering evidence of Nazi crimes. Much of the German documentation had been lost or destroyed. Evidence from non-Roma, such as Dina's paintings, therefore became essential to reconstructing the history of the Romani Holocaust. Decades after the war, a Romani consciousness movement led to greater awareness of Nazi crimes against the Roma, and eventually a Romani exhibition was opened at the Auschwitz Museum. Dina's paintings became the centrepiece of this exhibition – unique evidence not only of the crimes committed, but of the individuals who lost their lives in brutal fashion at Nazi hands.

To the museum, the paintings were historical documents. To Dina, they were works of art and her personal property.

In interweaving these two narratives – story and history – Lidia Ostałowska sets herself a larger task than simply recounting the twists and turns of this complex dispute. *Watercolours* is an exploration of the moral question at the heart of this conflict. The book gives us a close, personal portrait of Dina and her struggle for her paintings. But Ostałowska understands we can only assess Dina's story through the lens of our collective memory of the Holocaust. This memory is not fixed, but has evolved over the decades since the war to emphasize different aspects, different experiences, and even different sets of victims. Ostałowska shows us how Holocaust memory has been shaped by cultural factors and manipulated for political purposes. Since the war, there have been a number of official and unofficial narratives of the Holocaust that have evolved and changed, sometimes gradually, sometimes abruptly. Those changes have always been contentious and often very painful – for survivors and their descendants, but also for the citizens of Germany, Poland, and other countries directly affected by the Holocaust.

Ostałowska shows the failings of the Nuremberg trials, the official lies told in the Communist world to exploit Auschwitz as a symbol of martyrdom, and the ignorance and neglect which some Holocaust survivors encountered in the West and in Israel after the war. She also shows the brave struggle of Polish historians, young Germans, Roma activists, and above all the Jewish community around the world to make sure that the true story of the Holocaust – in all its horrifying depth and breadth – is made plain for the world to see. Often this action has played out at Auschwitz itself, a place not only of tremendous symbolic value to tens of millions around the world, but which is above all, a vast cemetery.

For the translator, Ostałowska's writing presents certain challenges. She is part of the famous Polish school of literary reportage, exemplified by Ryszard Kapuściński. These writers employ a technique known as 'little realism' – taking an individual's story as a microcosm to address larger social or historical questions. Key to the technique is a warm, honest, human focus, linked with a straightforward, concise prose style that allows the story to speak for itself. While Ostałowska's prose is plain, it is anything but simple, and it required tremendous work to recraft it into English. I hope my efforts have been successful.

To me, this book is a unique history not only of the Holocaust, but how it has rippled through time up to the present day. Ostałowska's focus on Dina (as well as other individuals affected by this story) reminds us these ripples are primarily a human phenomenon. Ostałowska's focus is less on how the Holocaust and the memory of it has affected politics, ideologies, or grand concepts of history. Most important to her is how it has affected individual lives. In the long, complex process of investigation, commemoration and justice, it is easy to lose sight of this individual dimension. And in a world where history is increasingly used as an ideological and political tool, it is essential not to overlook the individual lives from which it is composed. Ostałowska encourages us to embrace the tension at the heart of the word *historia* – to see stories and history as not contradictory, but complementary. "History," she writes, "lives through memory. It dies when the two no longer speak."

Watercolours is a history that is vibrantly, assertively alive.

Sean Gasper Bye
New York, 22 October 2016

In the window of his shop in Montreal, Abraham Botines displayed a bar of beige soap with a swastika on it and the caption 'Polanad 1940'.

Botines, a 73-year-old Jew, has run his shop selling souvenirs and curios since 1967. He admits he's not sure if this soap really comes from a concentration camp. He says he's been collecting souvenirs of the Holocaust for many years, because he 'belongs to that generation'.

'My children aren't interested, so I decided to sell the souvenirs. It's my soap and I can do what I like with it.'

The police have launched an investigation to determine, among other things, if the soap is made of human fat. Trading in objects bearing swastikas is not illegal in Canada, but selling soap made from human beings would violate the ban on desecration of corpses. On the other hand, if the soap is not of human origin, Botines could be punished for false advertising.

Gazeta Wyborcza newspaper, 31 March 2010

1937. Christmastime in Hollywood

Once upon a time in winter, when a fine snow was falling from the sky, a queen was sitting by a black ebony-framed window and sewing. But because she was gazing out the window, she pricked her finger on the needle, and out fell three drops of blood. The red blood looked so beautiful on the white snow that the queen thought to herself: 'I would like a child as white as snow, as red as blood and as black as this window's ebony frame.' Soon, she bore a daughter with skin as white as snow, with cheeks as red as blood, and hair as black as ebony.

Walt Disney invited his guests to the premiere of *Snow White and the Seven Dwarfs* just before Christmas. On 21 December 1937, Charlie Chaplin (then preparing to film *The Great Dictator*), a young Judy Garland, Douglas Fairbanks, Carole Lombard and Marlene Dietrich all came to the Carthay Circle Theatre, the most famous cinema in the golden age of Hollywood.

> Someday my prince will come,
> Someday we'll meet again,
> And away to his castle we'll go,
> To be happy forever I know.

Some of the journalists spotted John Barrymore (a star since playing Hamlet) hiding his tears behind dark glasses.

There wasn't a single child in the auditorium.

But the audience reacted like children, spontaneously. 'The audience [...] applauded after individual sequences, just as though they were watching a stage play. I've never seen anything quite like it since,' recalled the Disney animator Wolfgang 'Woolie' Reitherman.

It was the first feature-length animated film. It had been predicted that nobody could possibly sit through such a thing – the colours would hurt their eyes. But instead, there were cries of delight and a standing ovation. Sergei Eisenstein, the director of *Battleship Potemkin*, would soon call *Snow White* the best film in the history of cinema.

The biggest, the greatest, the best. Seven hundred and fifty artists worked for that success. To be precise: 32 animators, 102 assistants, 107 inbetweeners (who filled in between phases of motion), 20 composition specialists, 25 for backgrounds, 65 for special effects (clouds, dust, smoke; anything that moves but isn't a live figure) and as many as 158 to paint the characters on transparent celluloid. They made heaps of drawings and sketches, a quarter-million of which went into the film. The chemists in Disney's laboratories explored innovative technology and the cameramen perfected a brand-new invention – the multi-plane camera, which created the impression of three dimensions.

The story of Snow White has been retold for centuries in many languages. It was written by the Brothers Grimm: Romantics searching for the roots of the German soul. The designer Ken Anderson recalls Disney being obsessed with Snow White. One night, when the animators returned to the studio after dinner, he'd called a few dozen of them onto the set.

'We all sat in folding chairs, the lights went down, and Walt spent the next four hours telling us the story of Snow White and the Seven Dwarfs. He didn't just tell the story, he acted out each character [...]. It was a shock to all of us'.

No one could conceive of a project on such a vast scale. Besides, the screenplay was risky: one character kills another, which wasn't done in cartoons. But Disney was so adamant they would succeed that everyone came to believe him.

In 1934, the graphic artist Art Babbitt organized informal workshops for the animators, and then work was transferred to the studio. Don Graham from the Chouinard Art Institute was artistic supervisor for the animation. He was keen to make sure the characters moved smoothly, naturally and gracefully. He brought movable artists' mannequins to his classes and explained the mysteries of the science of motion.

The celluloid Snow White also had a real female prototype. Marjorie Belcher (who would soon become famous as Marge Champion, of the dancing team Marge and Gower Champion) would tap her heels, eat from a bowl, wield a broom and fasten buttons in Snow White's place. The Prince was meant to look like Douglas Fairbanks.

In Hollywood the film was derided as 'Disney's folly'. The greatest madness was the amount of money poured into it. The cost had originally been estimated at $250,000, and production time at eighteen months. Ultimately it took three years and consumed $1.5 million dollars.

Walt Disney put up his house as collateral. 'There could be no compromising on money, talent or time [...] and this at a time when the whole country was in the midst of a crippling depression,' he recalled in an interview. 'As the budget climbed higher and higher, I began to have some doubts too, wondering if we could ever get our investment back. [...] Then came a shocker. My brother Roy told me that we would have to borrow another quarter million dollars'.

Who would offer a loan based on some scraps of film? Joseph Rosenberg from the Bank of America watched some excerpts from *Snow White*. When the lights came up, Disney was unable to discern anything from the banker's expression. Rosenberg got up and left the screening room without a word. Finally, he declared: 'That thing is going to make a hatful of money.'

In spite of the Depression, it made nearly $2.5 billion.

Bang, bang, ugh, oh!

Europe. Two days before Christmas and a day after the American premiere, Reich Minister of Propaganda Joseph Goebbels wrote in his journal: 'I gave the Führer twelve Mickey Mouse films as a present. He was very pleased, he found the precious gift delightful.'

Although Mickey was the symbol of a foreign power, he was also familiar. Hitler had been 17 in 1906, when the very first cartoon was made: *Humorous Phases of Funny Faces*, in which the animator James Stuart Blackton urged smokers to fight their addiction. Four years later, in the Lithuanian city of Kaunas, then under Russian rule, a young director called Władysław Starewicz was experimenting with insects. 'When I was trying to film live stag beetles battling over a female, I found that as soon as I turned on the lights they would freeze stock-still. So then I thought, what if I euthanized my little knights? I separated their limbs and horns from their bodies, then reattached them in the right place using very thin wires. I dressed the dead beetle puppets I'd prepared in costumes and cavalier boots, and put rapiers in their hands.' Then Starewicz filmed them frame by frame. 'They're moving – they're moving like they're alive!' He had invented the first puppet animation.

But audiences preferred cartoon stories, even the earliest examples, such as one about a dog who keeps eating a sausage until he bursts. The plots were simple, and have remained so ever since. Heroes were crushed, stretched, thrown from great heights, drowned, fried, chopped up and smashed with whatever came to hand. Bang, bang, ugh, oh! But none of them ever died.

Hitler loved these films, and his army was brought up on them.

Aryan Snow White, Doc the Jew

For every joke that made it into the final version of *Snow White*, the animators received five dollars. During the Great Depression, you could eat your fill for thirty-five cents. The Dwarfs provided the best opportunities for jokes: Doc, Grumpy, Sneezy, Happy, Sleepy, Dopey and Bashful. But what about Burpy, Baldy and Lazy? The list of potential names was long, and their personalities changed as well.

The gnomes in the Grimm Brothers' version were indistinguishable from one another. They worked underground all day long without a moment's rest. Disney decided against portraying them that way – he predicted the dwarfs would enchant the audience if each was unique. Most distinctive was Dopey – the young one, with ears that stuck out and great big feet, carefree as a child, and with no beard.

The dwarfs were painted in muted tones so they wouldn't outshine Snow White. She glowed with a then-fashionable

Aryan beauty – pale skin and a neat little nose (and in modified form, Snow White would still be reigning years later as the Barbie Doll). But her cheeks were too red, so the women working in the colour department corrected this flaw by painting a more delicate pink straight onto the film reel.

An 80-piece orchestra played the music. For the first time in the history of cinema, the soundtrack was released commercially on 78s. It included sound effects and dialogue in addition to the music. Once again, Disney was a pioneer.

The film was a record-breaking success: in three months, twenty million Americans had bought tickets. Then *Snow White* conquered Europe, where distributors granted the voice-overs to popular actors, and skilled poets translated the songs.

> I chased a polecat up a tree
> Way out upon a limb
> And when he got the best of me
> I got the worst of him!
> Ho hum, the tune is dumb, the words don't mean a thing,
> Isn't this a silly song for everyone to sing?

Children were laughing their heads off and people were soon humming the hit tunes in one European country after another. It premiered in London in February 1938 (and the rest of the United Kingdom a little later); in France in March; in Belgium and the Netherlands in May; in Italy in August (at the Venice Film Festival); in Czechoslovakia, Sweden and Denmark in September; in Finland in October; and in Hungary, Portugal and German-speaking Switzerland in December.

Germany didn't import the film, probably because of the harsh currency restrictions in place at the time. The Austrians did instead. They cast their compatriot Paula Wessely, a star of the Nazi-controlled UFA film studio, in the role of Snow White.

One of her co-stars was Otto Wallburg, a superb actor. The son of a Jewish banker, he was the first to lose his contract with UFA and later his position at Max Reinhardt's theatre in Berlin. He and Reinhardt both left Germany – Reinhardt went via France to the United States, and Wallburg to Vienna.

Wallburg played Doc.

The Germans had planned that the annexation of Austria in 1938 would also include Snow White and the Seven Dwarfs. But the performers' racial origins stood in the way. No films with Jewish actors were shown in the Reich, nor in Austria after 12 March.

The Austrian version of Disney's super-production wasn't shown in Germany until 1950. (To West Germans, that is – those in the East had to wait another 35 years.) By then Snow White-Wessely was banned from plying her trade. She'd been brought down by her role in *Homecoming* (*Heimkehr*), a 1941 National Socialist extravaganza about the suffering of the ethnic German minority in Poland. It showed old women being whipped and mothers with children in their arms being beaten with rifle butts. It was a portrayal of Polish degeneracy. The Polish actors had been recruited by Igo Sym, the manager of a Nazi-sanctioned theatre in Warsaw, a collaborator and a Gestapo agent. It was an infamous affair. The underground resistance assassinated Sym in March 1941; in retaliation, the Germans shot 21 Varsovians in Palmiry, a village outside the city where mass killings were conducted.

Doc-Wallburg fled the Nazis to the Netherlands. In March 1939, when 11-year-old Shirley Temple was presenting Disney with an Oscar (along with seven miniature Oscar statuettes), Wallburg was in Amsterdam, performing at the Jewish cabaret Joodsche Schouwburg. But only until May 1940, when he went into hiding. Someone informed and he was arrested.

Then came a transit camp for Jews in Westerbork, deportation to the Theresienstadt ghetto, and from there to Auschwitz. Then came Selection.

He died in a gas chamber.

1943. In Birkenau, on Another Planet

Just before Christmas 1943, 20-year-old Dina Gottliebová stood in Birkenau facing a wooden barrack wall. She held paints and brushes. She was wondering what to paint.

In the future, her mural would be drawn in pencil, traced in ink, then preserved in computer animation. People on YouTube and fans of Disney educational programmes would discuss it at length. Dina would refer to it in testimonies, reports and interviews before cameras and microphones.

We never met. In 2001, I wrote to her asking for an interview, but she didn't respond. At that time her dispute with the Auschwitz-Birkenau State Museum was ongoing, so perhaps it was difficult for her to trust a Polish journalist. Yet she spoke to many other people about her fate, and as can happen when telling stories about the most significant moments in one's life, she would sometimes add new details. She died on 29 July 2009.

I have recorded Dina Gottliebová's words faithfully. The source she drew on was memory – not always in line with historical fact (that's the nature of wartime accounts), and probably incomplete, for in memory there is much we keep for ourselves. Does that make it any less believable?

History lives through memory. It dies when the two no longer speak.

'I thought I'd paint a balustrade, as though we were in a Swiss chalet gazing out at a meadow. So I painted green grass and a blue sky, and little clouds. On the balustrade I painted stylized flowers in pots, but they were so artistic that they looked real. The children watched me. I wanted to paint the most joyful scene I knew. I had already started on some cows and sheep, but I asked them, "What would you like in the meadow?" They answered unanimously, "Snow White and the Seven Dwarfs." That was a film I'd seen seven times in Prague before we were deported, because I was interested in the animation techniques. It was also the last one the children had seen. They chose the pictures themselves. I remember the figures well: I painted Snow White dancing with Dopey, and the other dwarfs jumping up and down and clapping. It was so the children could have something to look at, rather than just blank walls. Fredy Hirsch asked me to paint the interior. My first question was "with what?" but he assured me he'd organize something.'

Fredy was a German Jew with an athlete's physique, a sportsman, a would-be Olympian, and a leader of the Zionist youth movement. The girls were crazy about him, but they never got anywhere, because he was gay. After the race laws came into force, he moved to Czechoslovakia and became an instructor at the Prague athletic club Ha-Gibor. In 1941, he was deported to the ghetto in Theresienstadt.

Dina had met him two years earlier in her hometown of Brno when she was at art college. She studied graphic design and sculpture. After two terms, she had to cut her education short – Jews were no longer allowed to study. Then Professor Lichtak, who taught sculpture, hired her as his assistant under the table. When working illegally also became impossible, she went to Prague. Petr Kien, a Jewish artist who had been thrown out of the Academy, was teaching young people in a synagogue in the Vinohrady district. Dina once again enrolled in graphic design.

'One day we had to start wearing stars. You had to sew the star neatly onto your jacket. The first time I went out to college like that, I wasn't sure what I should do or where I should look. And suddenly I saw a man – he was coming towards me, and he had a yellow star too. We smiled at one another. That made it a little easier for me.'

Dina studied for a year. When she had some spare time she would surreptitiously unstitch the star and sneak off to the cinema. Until one day, news came from Brno: her mother was going to the ghetto. Then Dina left Prague to join those people who were now cargo, crammed into trains and carriages marked with a letter *U*. She'd been four months old when her parents, Richard and Jana, divorced. Her father was raising another family with a second Mrs Gottliebová.

'When I was born, he named me Anne Marie, and his second daughter Marianne. I suppose so he wouldn't get mixed up. "Dina" is my Jewish name, I changed it myself.'

Her first day in Theresienstadt was also her 19th birthday. Dina soon fell in with Hirsch and some other acquaintances.

Brundibár the evil organ-grinder

Theresienstadt was a claustrophobic town that 'the Führer had granted to the Jews'. There were flower beds, a concert pavilion, and signs reading: 'To the Baths' and 'To the Park', and there was a playground in the park. There was a menu in a clean canteen, and luxury goods in shop windows.

But all that only happened once, when a delegation from the International Red Cross came in 1944, concerned about the Jews of Eastern Europe (for not only Czechs were being deported there). The performance in the ghetto had to be good, so some of the child prisoners were coached for the occasion beforehand. They were to surround Kommendant Rahm in the street and say, 'Uncle, play with us.' He would answer, 'Not today, today I have no time, but tomorrow for certain,' and pull a tin of sardines from his pocket, at which the children would groan, 'Sardines again?!'

Normally, this is what Theresienstadt was like: no shops at all, rationed food, a cup of thin milk had to last a week. There was a constant shortage of water, so you couldn't wash potatoes before cooking them. Conditions in the barracks were cramped, there was a plague of lice and bedbugs. There was diarrhoea, typhus, and freezing cold, because the stoves weren't lit.

There were 15,000 children wandering about in the ghetto. They would see their parents only in the evening, on their way back from forced labour in the kitchens, bakeries and workshops. At night they would return to the crowded rooms of the children's quarters. The teachers looking after them taught drawing and singing legally, and maths, history and geography on the sly. Hebrew was optional. One pupil would always stand guard.

The tutors did what they could to add colour to the children's lives. There were concerts, performances and exhibitions, even children's operas. The biggest hit was a production of *Brundibár* with music by the composer Hans Krása, who had also been sent to Theresienstadt. The little heroes, Pepíček and Aninka, arrive at the village market. They're selling milk to earn money for their sick mother. Helping them are a clever dog, a nimble cat and a brave swallow. The troupe are driven away by the evil organ-grinder Brundibár (which is a Czech nickname for a bumblebee). Everyone knew how to interpret it, and the show was performed dozens of times. (Years later the American director Hilary Helstein found some of the actors when she was making a documentary about the Holocaust from the perspective of artists. Her film, *As Seen Through These Eyes*, came out in 2009. Dina Gottliebová was one of those featured.) Fredy Hirsch would organize competitions for the children of Theresienstadt. He looked after their physical fitness, and, in the process, their moral strength too, for a strong mind needs a strong body. He made them do gymnastics, taught them to keep clean, and would inspect their ears, throats and legs.

Poets, artists, journalists, writers, professors and Nobel Prize winners all locked up in a tight space: it was a frenzy of activity. Anything to forget, anything to distract from what was coming. The ghetto sang, exercised, went to lectures, made films and argued over Communism and Zionism. And fell in love. Dina confessed years later that she'd had her head in the clouds in Theresienstadt. She'd met her first love there. Her sweetheart was Karel Klinger, five years her senior.

'He came from the country and he turned up for the transport with his animals. He explained to the SS officers that he hadn't known what do with them. He made the SS-men laugh and they put him in charge of the stables in the ghetto. He had a room in the attic there, and knocked a hole in the roof for light. We got engaged. During our secret meetings we would lie in bed and look at the stars and think of names for the babies we planned to have.'

She left Karel behind in the ghetto.

Transports 'to the East' had been departing from Theresienstadt constantly, jointly organized by members of the Nazi-controlled Jewish Council that governed the ghetto.

In September 1943 they deported as many as 5,000 people – once again they were identified on their transfer papers by the letter *U*. The town was too crowded to be smartened up in the event of a visit from international inspectors. The journey took three days.

'On the train, I didn't care where I was going or why. I sat there and cried. I climbed onto the blankets and suitcases people were taking from Theresienstadt, and sat by a small window, which was letting in a little bit of air. I must confess something. There was a bucket down on the floor where people were relieving themselves. But I was sitting up there and crying, and I couldn't stop to pee and then go on crying, could I? So I went right there. I'm glad I did, because afterwards the SS got all of those things. I peed on those blankets and suitcases, very quietly up there.'

The tracks led to Auschwitz. The cattle wagons stopped at night and people were unloaded amid shouting.

'The whole time I kept thinking about my mum, I kept looking round to see if she was there. Other than that I couldn't understand what was happening. I still had my clothes on, my riding boots, my riding breeches and a shirt. I asked everyone if they'd seen my mum. A girl came up and told me the first transport was right there with us.'

Then suddenly – like a dream, an illusion, or a mirage – Dina was transformed.

'My mum appeared. She smiled to me and said I looked like a Franciscan. I had long hair, a brown dress and a rope for a belt.'

Together they trudged from the ramp to sector BIIb, the *Familienlager Theresienstadt*, meaning the family camp for the Theresienstadt Jews in Birkenau.

'I'd found myself on another planet.'

The commandant steals some barbed wire

Commandant Rudolf Höss was taking part in a grandiose project: laying the groundwork for the *Generalplan Ost*. Once the war was over, the Germans intended to reintroduce the previous millennium's system of slavery. At the top of the hierarchy would be Nazi grandees and members of the SS: the new pharaohs and high priests lording over the serfs, prisoners and slaves in the camps. Just below them would come the German colonists, Wehrmacht soldiers and the ethnic Germans from the conquered lands. In *The Slave State*, Albert Speer calculated the colonization of the East would cost the lives of 29 million prisoners – each one working to death for the benefit of the Thousand-Year Reich, building modern railway lines, giant canals linking the rivers of Europe, motorways, factories and farms.

The Polish town of Oświęcim – known by its new German name, Auschwitz – was chosen as a testing ground.

Höss came to Auschwitz in the spring of 1940 and immediately found something amiss. 'I still didn't even know where I could get a hundred metres of barbed wire. In Gleiwitz there were mountains of barbed wire in the engineers' depot in the harbour. But I could not get any of it [...]. I could not convince [the Concentration Camp Inspector] to help me in this matter, so I had to steal the urgently needed barbed wire from various places. [...] We even took old bunkers apart just to get the armour plate from them.'

Somehow, he managed.

The plan picked up steam. Otto Ambros, a board member of the chemical firm I.G. Farbenindustrie, arrived in Auschwitz to examine sites where a rubber and plastics factory might be constructed. He chose the village of Monowice. The Auschwitz civilian authorities were hoping for a large investment, so they assured Ambros they would create a reserve of Jewish labour in the town, to be replaced by German settlers after the war was won. Ambros listened to what they had to say and remarked, 'it's just a shame Auschwitz is so ugly.' But the prospects excited him enough that in 1941 he wrote to company headquarters saying 'our new friendship with the SS is very fruitful.'

Hans Strosberg designed a model town for I.G. Farben's workers. He had a keen eye for detail and planned every aspect carefully. Each estate of single-family homes would have four butchers, bakers and hairdressers, five cobblers and three tailors (one with a shop). There would also be one laundrywoman, one saddler, one garage, one chemist and seven greengrocers. For all the town's citizens there would be three cinemas, six preschools, five primary schools, two secondary schools, a stadium, a German settlers' museum and four Party offices. The learned professions would be represented by three GPs, two dentists, a solicitor and a notary public, plus one midwife. For the children there were to be seven playgrounds, a Hitler Youth centre, a football pitch and two tennis courts. It was to be cheap, comfortable and very clean. Strosberg's drawings included small figures, hard at work in grey overalls and wielding hammers – on each of their backs was the letter *P*: Poles.

Beyond the houses there were barracks: no trespassing. Beyond the barracks lay the Auschwitz concentration camp, featuring the largest parade ground in Europe, for 30,000 slaves. It had monumental gates, not yet bearing the unassuming inscription *Arbeit Macht Frei*, but instead with Germanic symbols signifying the power of the SS.

But the concept of slave labour in the town was never implemented. Höss had promised the prisoners would achieve

75 per cent of the productivity of a German worker, but in the event they never managed above 30. Interests diverged: the company needed hands for work, but the camp had its eye on the Final Solution and was wagering on extermination. The single-family homes came to naught and there was not a single *pfennig* for the Germanic symbols.

On 11 December 1944, representatives of the German chemical giants gathered at a conference in Kattowitz (Katowice). After some discussion, it was suggested that productivity was low because the prisoners were likely hungry. It was decided the more productive ones would receive more food at the expense of the less productive. However, no one was ever able to test the theory, and less than two months later Katowice found itself in Russian hands.

The Bulldog is in charge

The prisoner number tattooed on Dina's forearm was 61016. She played those numbers in the lottery after the war, although by then a surgeon had erased them. She wasn't given a striped uniform and kept her hair – the men's heads weren't shaved either, the barber simply gave everyone a small trim. Theresienstadt was under a so-called six-month quarantine in Auschwitz. The prisoners were supposed to look like civilians, as proof that the 'east' wasn't a killing field. They expected the Red Cross might show up even here.

Robbed of their possessions, their ragged clothing marked with a number and a star, wearing clogs or bare feet, they crowded into windowless stables. The men and boys went into the even-numbered ones and the women and children into the odd-numbered ones. Inside they found plank beds, straw pallets, filthy blankets and a dirt floor – 600 by 130 metres, barrack after barrack. There were three latrines, each consisting of a concrete cover with 396 round holes in two rows. In the morning, each barrack was taken there for a few minutes, and the prisoners would sit back-to-back. There were three washrooms, consisting of inflow pipes over a rusty trough. Often the water wouldn't even dribble out. Further along, there was barbed wire, a trench, guard towers – and beyond that, more sectors, each one like a neighbourhood. On one side of them was a sector for Jews – mostly from Hungary – and on the other, a quarantine camp.

Fritz Wilhelm Buntrock (nicknamed 'Bulldog') sat in the barrack at the gates of the Theresienstadt Familienlager holding a pair of binoculars. From this perch, he ruled the camp. No one was ever sure when they might cross him. He boasted: 'No grass grows where my fist lands.' He'd dispense thrashings, join in on Selection and torment people being led to the gas chambers. (After the war, he was sentenced to death. They hanged him in Montelupich, the Nazis' notorious prison in Kraków.)

Day-to-day decisions in sector BIIb were taken by Arno Böhm, the *Lagerältester* or 'camp elder' – the highest position a prisoner could have. Thirty years old and with a camp number of eight, he had arrived on the first transport of German criminals. They were the prisoners who made up the 'staff'.

Böhm kept himself well fed by stealing from other prisoners. He forced women into having sex with him, would often walk about drunk, and on several occasions he struck someone so hard it was like a kick from a horse. The Polish author and Auschwitz prisoner Tadeusz Borowski mentioned him in his book *Auschwitz, Our Home*: 'an old-time Block Elder, a Kapo and Camp Kapo, who used to kill men for selling tea in the black market and administered 25 lashes for every minute you were late and every word you uttered after the evening gong; he is also the man who always wrote short but touching letters, filled with love and nostalgia, to his old parents in Frankfurt.'

But Dina knew how to deal with him, and they even became friends.

'On Böhm's suggestion, I started out painting numbers on the barracks. Then some SS officers came to the family camp and gave me photos of their wives, fiancées or girlfriends, which I would use to paint portraits. So Böhm gave me my own room where I could work freely.'

A brief description of a typical morning in the family camp, according to an account by the prisoner Ludek Klaser: 'Reveille was at five in the morning, accompanied by plenty of noise and inevitable beatings with a baton. You had half an hour to get dressed, go to the washroom to get a few drops of water from the dry pipes, make your bed and drink a few sips of a bitter, lukewarm liquid, so that at a quarter to seven you could be in your place in line for roll call. It was all chaos and confusion with constant shouting and beatings. Finally, it was six o'clock, and we the living would be standing in even lines, side-by-side, in groups of five. The bodies of those who'd died overnight would be laid on the ground by the entrance to our block. We shifted our weight from one foot to the other, freezing and starving, waiting impatiently for the signal that roll call was over, and then we'd form up into teams assigned to work in different places.'

Some of them worked on building the camp road. (They would drag heavy stones from a few kilometres away. Whoever didn't bring enough over got whipped and was forced to lift stones so heavy that their friends would have to carry them home afterwards.) Some worked in the textile plant (sewing rifle belts from scraps of fabric), and some worked splitting mica.

But to the surprise and envy of the others in Auschwitz-Birkenau, they kept on living.

Don Quixote is here

Officially, Dina was painting propaganda signs and warning notices in her studio: 'No entry!', 'Cleanliness is your obligation!', 'Lice are deadly!' Unofficially, she was accepting private commissions.

She shared her small bit of good fortune.

'I met Miša Grünwald, an 11-year-old boy from Prague who'd come into the camp on the second transport from Theresienstadt. Watching him from my window, I fell in love and decided to make the most of my situation to help him as well. He was my *pipel*. He brought me firewood, lit the stove and watched me sketch and paint. I painted his portrait in the camp, but I don't think I kept it,' she told the staff of the Auschwitz Museum. 'I ought to explain *pipels* were most frequently young boys, usually the objects of homosexual attention from the other prisoners. The *Lagerältester* Arno Böhm had a *pipel* too.'

He was Erich Fischer, an impudent little Viennese street urchin.

One day, a certain Dr König entered Dina's room.

'He reminded me of Don Quixote. He was tall and thin with long arms and he was wearing a poorly-tailored uniform that was far too large for him. I thought to myself he was the first scrawny SS officer I'd ever seen. He asked to sit down.'

From then on, he would stop by again and again.

'He'd watch me paint and Miša Grünwald would light his cigarettes. Dr König was an addict, he smoked the cheapest, most foul-smelling cigarettes. It matched his ill-fitting uniform. When we talked, he was funny and polite, on the whole he behaved like an ordinary human being. We would joke and tell stories, though never about the camp.'

But now and again he mentioned his university friend Josef Mengele.

'Dr König said he was a king.'

On another occasion, Fritz Buntrock came to Dina's room brandishing a picture postcard of a nude woman standing before a waterfall. She was to paint it life-sized by morning. All night long she toiled away at top speed. In return, she got some cigarettes, which she traded for bread – one piece for one cigarette, the usual rate. The next day, Bulldog brought the picture in for improvement. Where the woman's ginger-haired pussy had been, now there was a hole.

On the playground

The mural of Snow White dancing with Dopey gave inspiration to new games.

The children's block had a small stage that hosted performances twice a week. Jiří Fränkl wrote a play for the six-year-old boys about Robinson Crusoe, featuring a song that went: 'Though we are the first to set foot here, I'll never lose faith in my Lord God dear, for home He will bring us safe from harm, into our mummy and daddy's arms.' The preschoolers built puppets from rags their mothers smuggled out of the camp textile mill. Each week, they also held drawing and poetry competitions. The children wrote using charred wooden sticks on scraps of paper dug out of the rubbish.

In one show, Snow White and the dwarfs found themselves in the camp. There was singing and the obligatory happy ending. A 14-year-old girl with an amazingly beautiful voice played Snow White and the littlest children played the dwarfs. The children's block in Barrack 31, which included a youth club and a school, had become the spiritual heart of sector BIIb. Fredy Hirsch was the barrack chief, and the children adored him.

Yehuda Bacon, who acted in the original Theresienstadt production of *Brundibár* and who today is an eminent Israeli artist, recalled: 'I don't know how Fredy managed to get the Germans to consent to all his plans. I assume he took advantage of them wanting to boast we were being treated humanely.'

Either that or he convinced camp headquarters the children would only get in the way of the labour. One way or the other, he managed to construct a false reality in Barrack 31 that was nothing like being in a camp.

Yehuda Bacon: 'Being there felt like a dream – it was paradise. They cared for us there. Best of all, in winter we didn't have do roll call in the rain: we'd gather in the barrack for a headcount. Early in the morning, Fredy would get us all together in the snow and we'd do gymnastics stripped to the waist. Normally people were afraid of being cold and wet. Fredy just wanted to toughen us up, which was a good thing.'

And just like in Theresienstadt, they once again had official lessons in arithmetic and handicrafts. Then they had illegal ones, in Czech grammar and speaking, English, Latin, history and geography.

Yehuda Bacon: 'We had a physics teacher who explained what would happen if we could fly to the moon, meaning if we left Earth's gravitational pull.'

One of the older boys would stand guard as before. The younger children were told the conspiracy was a game and they cheerfully joined in. But it was risky. They'd be questioned by SS-men and any of the children might snitch for a piece bread, or because they didn't know any better.

A playground was built between the block and the ramp. The prisoner Klára Nová mentioned it in her testimony:

'What a place for children to play! There was an electrified barbed-wire fence on one side, and the gas chambers and chimneys on the other, belching out smoke day and night. In that shadow of suffocating death, children played and sang Czech folk songs in their young, bright voices.'

The children understood plenty, though. Block 31 got special rations made for it. Yehuda Bacon:

'Once I was put in charge of cooking them on the hob. We'd say: "All right, the first batch of soup is ready." Then we'd look out the window at the crematorium and say, "The first batch is ready there too." When we saw white smoke, we could tell what it was from: whether it was human flesh or documents burning.'

In the meantime, preparations were underway for a festive show about Snow White.

Dina: 'I made the wig for Snow White out of paper I'd painted black, and I wound the curls round a pencil.'

The staff liked to drop in for the Sunday concerts and performances. Johann Schwarzhüber, the director of the men's camp in Birkenau, even invited his friends: he was bursting with pride. Franz Lucas, an SS doctor in the Theresienstadt

Familienlager, was also in the audience. (After the war he was sentenced to three years and three months in prison.)

Yehuda Bacon: 'The SS-men wanted some variety as well.'

They sat the children on their laps and got choked up thinking of their own little ones. Arno Böhm stood out – giving a whistle as though something displeased him. The children thought it was odd.

Finally, the performance began. The children sang and acted out an allegory set in a Disney film. Snow White ate the poisoned apple her stepmother gave her and fell asleep. Maybe she was having a nightmare: her legs were like cotton wool and her throat was tight. It was a long dream with no escape, but in the end she awakened in the sunshine and fresh air of the forest, with a handsome prince beside her.

The camp was only a dream: you'd wake up and all would be well.

Dina: 'It was a wonderful thing.'

A few days later, Dr Franz Lucas asked her if she could paint portraits. She replied:

'I think so.'

Through the lens

In February 1944, a Jeep pulled up in front of the camp.

Dina: 'When I got in the car I was sure they were going to kill me. The driver didn't say a word.'

They drove along a bumpy road to the gates of section BIIe. They passed a whipping post and stopped in front of the infirmary.

Josef Mengele, the doctor of the Gypsy camp, was leaning over a tripod in the freezing cold, examining prisoners through the lens of a camera. The prisoners were brought in small groups of six or eight.

'I had no idea who he was or what experiments he was doing. I watched him taking pictures of the Gypsies and could tell he wasn't pleased. Afterward, Dr Lucas introduced me. He said I was a painter and could do really good portraits. He explained to me that colour photography was imprecise, but here it was essential to capture the natural tones of skin colour.'

Then Mengele cut him off and ordered Dina to look through the lens. Could she paint portraits of the Gypsies that were equally faithful?

'I can try.'

Before long, the silent driver brought her back to the Familienlager.

The wheeler-dealer

In September, the Jews from Theresienstadt finished their six-month quarantine. Everyone was nervous, asking what might come next.

There was very good news: they were under the care of the International Red Cross, soon a prisoner exchange would take place and they'd go abroad.

There was very bad news: a Polish prisoner who'd registered their transport remembered an incident with an old woman. The woman had dementia and couldn't give her personal information. 'Don't worry,' said Oberscharführer Chustek from the political department, with a wave of his hand. 'She'll go to the gas in six months anyway.'

The gas chambers were a closely-guarded secret, but rumours confirmed their existence. First, crystal pellets would poison the lower layer of air, just above the floor. Slowly but surely, the Zyklon-B gas would rise. When it was all over, the Sonderkommando would get to work. Through the open door, they would find a mountain of trampled corpses. At the bottom were the infants, above them, the children, then the women and old people, and on top the strongest men, their bodies scratched and bloodied in the struggle.

Dina started preparing herself.

'I wanted to get my hands on some poison, so I could die quickly if I had to and not suffer.'

She knew an SS officer named Rennfahrer, who did business with Böhm and his deputy, Willy Brachmann.

'He was sort of a wheeler-dealer. He was always going off making arrangements somewhere or other. Once he told me he was going to Prague. I asked him to visit some friends of mine. When he came back, he told me they'd said to wish me luck and had given him a little present for me, but he'd thrown it out on the way. After the war, I found out he really had been to see them.'

Once he proposed helping Dina escape.

'He was going to drive me out of the camp on a motorbike, wearing an SS uniform. I gave it some thought, but in the end I said no. I didn't trust him and I was afraid he'd shoot me out on the road. Besides, I didn't want to leave my mum on her own.'

A wish

For the poison, she turned to Brachmann.

'Rennfahrer provided him with three envelopes of poison, which of course Brachmann paid him a tidy sum for. There was one portion for me, one for my mum and one for him. We hid them in the barrack.'

At the end of February, Filip Müller from the Sonderkommando spotted a letter SS officer Chustek had carelessly left out. He froze. A crematorium had to be prepared for 'special treatment,' for the Czech camp. He informed Kapo Kamiński, who was in the Resistance, who told him the ovens in Crematorium II were already warmed up.

They sent word to sector BIIb.

Dina: 'Soon, news went round the latrines that our whole transport from Theresienstadt was going to be gassed.'

Killing so many at once was a complex operation for the staff. Director Schwarzhüber (sentenced to death after the war) was wondering how best to go about it. He ordered a list to be made of all the prisoners, and to tell them they were going to a new camp in Heydebreck (now called Kędzierzyn-Koźle), where they would live with their families.

Dina: 'Some people were even happy.'

But she knew. The criminal Arno Böhm had just been released from the camp.

'He'd promised his girlfriend that as he was leaving, he'd show us what was in store. We watched him through the barbed wire. He held up a closed hand with his index finger pointing upwards.'

Smoke.

They waited a week for what would come next.

'Meanwhile, Dr König came to visit and saw how disheartened I was. I told him we were waiting for a transport, and he knew exactly what that transport would mean.'

He protested. Nothing was going to happen, he begged her to believe him. To prove it, he gave her an assignment – a photograph of his wife and children. It would take a month to paint their portraits. That gave Dina hope. If these photos were found on her when she went to the gas chambers... König was taking a big risk.

Four days later, she was summoned to the hospital block, where a large registration was underway. Under Mengele's direction, a nurse was recording the names of twins. They were accompanied by a clerk and a Jewish prisoner, Dr Hellman. Dr Hellman smiled at Dina and declared, 'At Dr Mengele's wish, you will not be sent on the transport to work.'

'I told him, "I want to live, but what about my mother? I won't stay here without her." Everyone looked at me as if I'd gone mad. Dr Hellman started to explain my mother was young and fit to work. Mengele ordered me to give him her camp number. I couldn't remember it, so he sent the clerk for my mum. She came and showed him her number, and he added it to the list. But I still didn't believe we were safe.'

Envelopes

One day, Fredy Hirsch sat down on the warm, enclosed brick channel that ran from the fireplaces down the middle of the barrack, and chatted with Zuzana Růžičková, a fellow-prisoner. Talking more to himself than to her, he said 'Remember how in Theresienstadt we were so obsessed with Zionism? Look at the people here. Who are they? Zionists? Assimilationists? Radicals? Communists? Everything we thought was so important makes no difference anymore. We're just people – poor and naked. Masaryk was a great man. Humanism is the only way.'

President Tomáš Masaryk was the father of independent Czechoslovakia. He was a philosopher, a humanist and a freethinker. He often said, 'getting worked up isn't a political programme.' He was an enemy of German idealism and Marxism: 'history teaches us that all countries have fallen because of chauvinism, no matter whether racial, political, religious or class-based.' His birthday fell on 7 March, so the children's block were gearing up for a celebration.

But early that morning it was announced that prisoners from the September transport were to relocate to sector BIIa, the quarantine camp adjacent. Time to move: there was chaos and confusion everywhere. Now it was time for the poison from the wheeler-dealer, Rennfahrer.

Lagerältester Willy Brachmann had duties to fulfil and was racing to and fro. Dina went up to him: 'Willy, don't lose your head. Let's go to your room and take it.'

She wanted to die by his side – but why? When they'd released Arno Böhm from the camp and Brachmann took over, the prisoners had heaved a sigh of relief. He was gentler, especially with the children. But was Willy's kindness reason enough to die together? She was living with Brachmann, or rather – as she put it – she 'belonged to him'. Was she in love? Was their secret pact so significant? Or when the end is near, perhaps it makes no difference anymore?

'Yes, yes, we'll go to my room,' he said to Dina, 'but right now I have to take care of these people.' She thought he meant he didn't want to take the poison, so she tracked down her mother and they hid in Willy's room.

'We opened the envelopes, but there was nothing in them! I looked again, I thought maybe it was strong poison and you only needed a tiny bit. But there was nothing. Willy arrived and I said, "look here, on this piece of paper". Willy looked into his envelope, which didn't have anything in it either.'

He was furious, though he may have been making a show of it.

'We crossed over to the quarantine camp. I couldn't stop shaking. I sat on a top bunk with my mum. I was shaking and thinking this was the last time we'd be together. There was another prisoner sitting with us who had a beautiful singing voice, and she suddenly started to hum *Wenn der Herrgot net will, nutzt es gar nix*, "if the Lord doesn't want it, then nothing will help". It wasn't exactly soothing. There was a young mother from Prague with us too. She'd been the first from our transport to have a baby, and was sitting there with him.'

The transfer finished at five in the afternoon. The men and women had been separated. There was a bugle call: *Lagersperre*, camp lockdown. No one could leave their barracks. All night long, they heard lorries growling in the direction of the gas chambers.

'We waited until the lorries pulled up in front of our block – but then a Hungarian transport arrived and they drove off to meet it. I was still alive. I climbed down from the bunk and that young mother was sitting there nursing her child. She smiled at me. She was wearing a blue headscarf and looked like the Virgin Mary. Her child was lovely and strong, already two months old.'

The next day, 8 March, Rapportführer Fritz Buntrock made his way through the quarantine barracks.

'That afternoon he arrived with a piece of paper and read out some names, mainly those of twins. My mother and I were the last two. When he read our names, I remember collapsing on the bed. I hadn't fainted, though I did lose consciousness for a moment. Then he went on to the next block, but told us to line up and go.'

Those who remained were condemned to die – 3,790 people.

Those who'd been reprieved marched towards the gate. There were around 70 of them: first, the identical twins, then, the less similar fraternal ones, behind them a handful of doctors, Dina and her mother Jana. They crossed from the quarantine camp back to the Familienlager. Fredy Hirsch was no more – he lay on the ground, unconscious. He probably could have saved himself, but alone, without the children. He'd swallowed Phenobarbital. His friends tried to find milk to use as an antidote, but he died.

Dina remembered an incident at the gate:

'Out of nowhere a Romanian SS officer showed up waving a bit of paper. He gave it to Buntrock, who called out Erich Fischer's name.' Fischer was the insolent little street urchin from Vienna who had been Böhm's *pipel*. 'The SS-man said, "Come on, you're coming with us." Erich said he wouldn't go without his mum and dad. The SS-man knelt down in front of him and pleaded. "Come on, you know where that transport is going." Erich began to cry, and Buntrock started looking uncomfortable. Erich pointed up in the air, turned round and went back into the quarantine camp.'

He died that night: 3,791.

Dina and her mother returned to sector BIIb.

'Someone said my hair had turned white.'

Little Pipe

From then on, Dina spent little time among her own people. Each morning Oberscharführer Ludwig Plagge, a.k.a. Little Pipe, would come to collect her on his bicycle. (In 1947, the Supreme National Tribunal in Kraków sentenced Little Pipe to death.) From the Theresienstadt camp, they headed for the

Gypsy camp – known as the *Zigeunerlager* – then continued on
to the so-called Sauna, which contained a few showers, a room
for shaving the prisoners' heads and Dr Mengele's surgery.

This barrack was almost at the edge of the sector. It was a
long ride through the most secret area in Birkenau.

Nettle-pickers and Hottentots

The Gypsies had already been in sector BIIe for a year, though
not every prisoner knew that. Once, some women picking
nettles had stumbled upon them. Every day, the women went
to a different place outside the camp, then took a different route
back with the food. Suddenly, they saw through the barbed
wire 'Gypsy men in their big hats, high boots – with traces
of their Gypsy beauty: curly hair, black moustaches; and with
short pipes. Nothing was taken from them when they entered
the camp [...]. With the men are their women in full-gathered
flowered skirts, in bright, tightly laced bodices, with strands of
beads and gold coins threaded on chains and earrings tinkling
gaily in their ears,' wrote the Auschwitz survivor Seweryna
Szmaglewska in her book *Smoke Over Birkenau*.

Two worlds. Us – in striped uniforms and clogs, with
shaved heads, stripped of any signs of individuality, solitary in
the great swarm. And them – exotic and unreal, in theatrical
costumes, their bracelets clinking and their skirts rustling.

A human zoo.

The history of human menageries is as ancient as the great
sea voyages. They were created in the nineteenth century to
make money, and in the twentieth, out of love for eugenics.
Savages in ethnographic displays, darkie villages inhabited by
Nubians and Samoans. At the circus in London, for a shilling
you could see the 'Hottentot Venus' paraded about on a chain.

In the Bronx Zoo, there was a Pigmy in a cage with an orang-utan and a sign reading 'The Missing Link'. These 'curiosities' were adored from Marseille to Antwerp, from Stuttgart to Warsaw. At the 1931 International Colonial Exhibition in Paris, 34 million people bought tickets to see a display of Africans who'd been stripped naked.

Back in Birkenau, Szmaglewska wrote that the nettle-pickers noticed the Gypsy women 'are incredibly filthy. They most likely don't take off their damask and silk garb when they lie down beside their husbands to sleep; they don't wash their dark bodies or brush their ebony-black hair. Children run about amongst them, quite small, half-naked with a thicket of black curls, some are bigger and dressed up like their parents. The Gypsies are children of the forest.' Their behaviour was innocent. 'Ignoring the SS officers' orders, the Gypsies walk right up to the barbed wire to watch the women walking by. In their mysterious language, they explain or ask questions, their expressive faces reflecting many emotions.'

But what emotions were they?

The commandant of the Auschwitz concentration camp, Rudolf Höss, pondered this in his autobiography: 'In spite of the adverse conditions, the majority of the Gypsies, as far as I could tell, had not suffered psychologically very much because of the confinement; if one overlooks the fact that they could not travel around anymore as they were accustomed to doing.'

(Sector BIIe was within view of the crematoriums that belched with fire, and the ramp, where the Jews endured Selection. The barbed wire was electrified at night, and some-times during the day as well – though prisoners could never be sure when. There were no trees. Through the middle of the sector ran a track of wet or dry mud, lined with wooden barracks. Converted back into stables, each barrack could have held 50 Gypsy horses. The walls had gaps in them and when the weather was bad, rain and snow would come lashing in. Inside was a bricked-in channel from one chimney to the other, dividing the space in two. There was a table, but no stove, because even in winter there was no heat. There were three levels of bunks on either side, one bunk for an entire family. The women made the bunks more comfortable by padding them with a red blanket.)

But in Höss's view, the Gypsies' 'previous primitive lifestyle had accustomed them to close living quarters, poor hygienic conditions and poor nourishment. Even illness and the high death rate were not taken seriously by them.'

(There were over 900 deaths in the Gypsy camp month on month: from typhus, diarrhoea due to starvation, scarlet fever and diphtheria. Children there had the highest mortality rate in Birkenau. Unaccustomed to eating, they stopped asking for food – they all wanted something to drink. Threatening and pleading were not enough to stop them drinking filthy water. When they were no longer able to walk, they would slip out of their beds at night and secretly crawl to the buckets to drink up the bathwater.)

Commandant Höss: 'I have never seen a scowl or a hate-filled expression on a Gypsy's face. Whenever I arrived in their camp, they immediately ran out of their barracks, played their instruments, let their children dance, and performed their usual tricks.' 'For the most part,' he wrote, 'they still behaved like children. They were still spontaneous in their thinking and behaviour.'

In other words, they were different from Western people – not on the same evolutionary level.

But they had their own talents, which sometimes were put to good use. Tadeusz Borowski wrote: 'Either it's Christmas

Eve or it isn't, and you're asleep! Hey, musicians, play, dammit! The shrill squeak of the Gypsy choir burst through the open door. Two young Gypsy women tied together at the shoulders with colourful scarves started to dance at the threshold, shaking their bracelet-covered hands over their heads.'

Höss had a great deal of trouble with the Gypsies. 'Even though they caused me a great deal of aggravation when I was Kommandant of Auschwitz, they were my favourite prisoners, if one could say something like that. [...] The job they wanted the most was the transport Kommando because it allowed them to move around everywhere and satisfy their curiosity and also get a chance to steal. This urge to steal and to roam around is born into them and cannot be stamped out. Also, they have an entirely different moral viewpoint. They do not believe stealing is absolutely bad. They cannot understand why a man should be punished for it.'

A scene from *Smoke Over Birkenau*: a delousing operation is taking place in one sector. The women leave their barracks, but hold on tight to their valuables. An SS doctor shoves his way in among the ranks. He 'tears all these things out of their hands and throws them in the ditch. Bowls and spoons fly with a clash, bread, rations of margarine and sausage end in the ditch. You dare not make any attempt to recover them. The doctor is big and husky and has a heavy hand. From behind the barracks gypsies cautiously creep out. They are not included in today's delousing programme. Swift as an arrow they reach the ditch, filch what they want, then flee. The doctor hits hard but the nimble gypsies evade the blows.'

A flock of magpies.

The Gypsy women never offered their account of what it was like to creep out, dash into a ditch, filch something and flee. After the war, their men, dressed in brimmed hats, kept silent about the Zigeunerlager too. It fell to others to testify on their behalf.

Tadeusz Joachimowski, a Polish prisoner, spent a few weeks working in the Gypsy camp. He noticed something peculiar and mentioned in it in his account: the SS officers did not treat the Gypsies the same as the other prisoners.

'Completely indifferently, as though they were an indistinct mass. They didn't force them to work or beat them, they simply paid them no mind or passed them by. Of course it was different for the SS-men who'd been given special duties.'

Bloodlines

Joachimowski was a clerk in Auschwitz I, as the main section of the camp was called. In spring of 1943, when the Gypsy sector was under construction, he received an order: he and the other clerks were to compile a register of the new arrivals. They entered a barrack chosen at random. Almost no one had shoes, people were walking about on the cold, filthy dirt floor in bare feet. The stench was powerful, suffocating. The clerks couldn't stand it.

The registration tables were set up outdoors. The barrack chief lined the Gypsies up in 45 rows, with 10 in each row. Then Joachimowski examined them more closely.

'They were all different ages. In the bright sun, every one of them looked truly awful. One reason they looked so terrible was they hadn't been able to wash since the day they'd arrived from the Reich, when they'd bathed in the men's camp in section BIb. More than a week had passed since then. Besides that, none of them had slept or eaten enough.'

1943. In Birkenau, on Another Planet • 37

The clerks' work turned out to be challenging: there was no information on more than half of the children, and their parents were playing dumb. But the forms needed to be filled out. What was sent to the political department and the main office was mostly nonsense.

There were spaces on the registration forms to record military service and medals. The clerks discovered First World War veterans among the Gypsies, as well as Wehrmacht soldiers freshly decorated for bravery in Crete, Crimea and Sevastopol.

The camp resistance movement sent news to the outside world of these *Zugangs* – new arrivals. 'Recently, when a transport arrived from Germany and an SS officer treated a Gypsy man too roughly, the man leapt at him, shouting abuse: "You coward, here you are fighting women and children instead of out at the front! I was wounded at Stalingrad, I've been decorated, I outrank you! How dare you insult me!" The SS officer soon backed off.'

These assimilated sergeants took pride in their Iron Crosses. They despised the ordinary Gypsies, and even more so the prisoners of other nationalities who'd been given positions in the camp. Bit by bit, they took over their jobs. These Gypsy men knew the language, understood discipline and knew how to really make people suffer. At first, each of them swore he'd been arrested by mistake and would be released after a few days. Some actually were released. In those early days, even the camp Gestapo didn't know what they were meant to do with this bewildered lot.

The confusion was because the Gypsies had previously been considered Aryans.

In 1936, Himmler hit on an idea: to segregate the Gypsies. Separate the wheat from the chaff and lock up the racially pure ones in reservations. There, they could live as they wished, as relics of the past and research subjects. The rest were of no use and had to be exterminated. All that remained was to develop criteria for separating them. For this task, the SS Reichsführer turned to Robert Ritter. While a whole army of German scientists had written about Jews, only he had studied Gypsies. A neurologist, psychiatrist and anthropologist from the university hospital in Tübingen, he researched Gypsy genealogies going back 10 generations.

Ritter founded two different institutions: the Centre for the Study of Racial Hygiene and Social Biology, and the Institute of Criminal Biology. He began by getting hold of 19,000 files from the Munich city police. These files were the fruits of a 1926 anti-Gypsy law in Bavaria (which said to expel the foreign ones, imprison the local ones in workhouses and put their children in correction centres). Implementing the law had required data: personal information, proofs of identity, places of residence, paths of migration, property records, and family and clan connections. By 1942 Ritter knew the ancestry of 30,000 Gypsies from so-called Greater Germany. That was nearly every one of them. It was a Herculean task, but at last everyone had a category.

Z – pure Gypsy blood
ZM+ – more than half-Gypsy
ZM1 – half Gypsy, half German
ZM2 – half ZM1, half German
MZ – more than half-German
NZ – non-Gypsy

Assisting Ritter was the slim, modest daughter of an official from Dresden. Until recently, Eva Justin had been an ordinary nurse with a secondary-school education. Like many girls, she'd joined the Young German Order. She worked at St Joseph's Orphanage in Mulfingen, where she was put in charge of the young Gypsies. She'd started working for Ritter as a trainee racial analyst. Apparently she spoke a little Romani. She went into fields and forest clearings to measure Gypsies' heads and smile at their children. She protected them against deportation, so long as she was studying them.

She was an average woman, but she quickly worked her way up to being Ritter's assistant. She began working on her PhD. 'The Gypsies are incapable of integration with German society because of their primitive way of thinking,' she wrote. 'Even if we attempted to integrate them into society or influence them by improving their education, they would nonetheless remain an asocial people.' She concluded: 'To preserve racial integrity we must insist the men are completely sterilized.'

She was obsessed with sterilisation. Ritter had a different fixation. For him, the most dangerous thing was intermarriage between Germans and Gypsies – the children of such unions would grow up to be illiterates, criminals and harlots. To make matters worse, the ill were crowding out the well: in the Austrian town of Oberwart, from 1890 to 1933 the Gypsy population had grown by 40 per cent, while the local population had only grown by 20.

Werner loves and searches

It was now forbidden for Gypsy men to marry German women. Pupils were ejected from schools, craftsmen from workshops, workers from post offices and railways, and soldiers from the military. Magicians, dancers, musicians, circus performers and dance hall owners had their horses confiscated. Gypsies were forced to go to special shops, and only during certain hours.

They were castrated. If they resisted, they ended up behind barbed wire in Ravensbrück and Dachau.

When war broke out, the German Gypsies were driven into the so-called General Government in occupied Poland. Homeless and left to their own devices, they roamed a land terrified of hearing German spoken. Finally, they were captured and locked up in Jewish ghettos or hastily built camps.

During this period, Private Werner Soetebier was conquering France. When he returned to Hamburg on leave from the front, he was unable to locate his beautiful Gypsy fiancée, Berta Bamberger. She had been deported. So he composed a letter to Governor-General Hans Frank: 'I know my fiancée very well, and she stands equal in her nature to a German woman. I myself despise the majority of the Gypsies, who are parasites sucking our nation dry. By happenstance this woman was married to a Gypsy man whom she never loved. That man received a just punishment, and died in a concentration camp after two years of imprisonment. At the age of 31, my fiancée has not grown at all ugly, which is rare among the Gypsies.'

He asked the Governor-General for help and gave all of Berta's details, as well as her address. Frank responded: 'It is inexcusable for you as a German to describe a woman of lesser racial value and of alien blood as your life companion.' This was a well-worn formula. Town councils had long been writing to German men in mixed marriages asking: 'How can you imagine remaining married to your current wife?'

Werner and Berta's love story was described by the Polish poet and Gypsy researcher Jerzy Ficowski. This is how it ended. Once Soetebier understood Hans Frank's letter was a fatal denunciation, he went to rescue Berta. He searched for her in numerous transit camps and in the winter of 1942, he found her in Kozie Górki near Siedlce. It was a small camp where heaps of frost-covered corpses lay around a water pump in the courtyard. Berta had died of typhus. Apparently right to the end, she believed her fiancé would rescue her. Once Werner saw the extermination camp with his own eyes, he shot himself by the roadside in the forest.

This story was quite unusual, because the German public had been prepared for the Final Solution. Himmler played the part of Eichmann in the 'Gypsy question'. As time went on, he abandoned his pipe dream of reservations where the Gypsies would subsist like bison. He accepted Ritter's view: that anyone with Gypsies or Gypsy half-breeds in their grandparents' generation was genetically contaminated.

In February 1943, a telegram from the Criminal Department of Himmler's Reich Main Security Office reached the Auschwitz Commandant. It informed him of the arrival of many thousands of Gypsies, but only vagrants with no fixed abode and no work.

Pery Broad, a Gestapo camp functionary: 'That provision existed exclusively on paper and was never enforced, because the Gypsies who were easiest to catch ended up being the largest share of prisoners in the camp. Girls working as stenographers in Wehrmacht units, workers in the Nazis' Todt engineering firm, conservatory students and other people who had led stable lives and had worked honestly for years suddenly landed in a concentration camp with a prison number tattoo. But that wasn't enough. Hundreds of soldiers who didn't even know they were part Gypsy were brought right from the Front. They'd all believed they were being sent to a Gyspy settlement.'

In Auschwitz, their uniforms were marked with a black triangle – meaning 'asocial'. Their numbers started with a *Z* for *Zigeuner* – Gypsy. Babies' legs were tattooed – the numbers extended from the groin to the knee.

Céline sings

There was a small room in the Sauna next to Mengele's surgery.

Dina: 'I'd call it a studio. Mengele gave me watercolours, a brush and a drawing pad. I'd never painted with watercolours before, though – we'd only had oils and tempera paints in school. There was no easel – I got two chairs instead. I sat on one and propped the drawing board up on the other. And I got started.'

She began with finding a model, because the doctor hadn't chosen one, he'd only said, 'go and pick someone.' Dina walked out of the barrack.

'I chose the first person I saw – a girl wearing an elaborately tied, very colourful headscarf.'

The painting took two or three days. It was a left-facing three-quarter view, with a caption underneath: *Zigeuner-Mischling aus Deutschland*, 'Gypsy Half-Breed from Germany'.

'I instinctively signed it in pencil: "Dinah". Mengele noticed, but didn't order me to erase it. The portrait didn't come out very well, but he was happy. Nowadays I think the first portrait was the worst. I hadn't done separate sketches.'

The technique of watercolour painting is only simple on the surface. Dina knew how much skill and practice were required. The pigment (bonded together with gum Arabic) is mixed with water, and this water is what alters the intensity of the color. There's no white paint on the palette, the artist uses the white of the paper to give the effect of light. You can't spoil the paper with pencil marks – a few coloured dots, and that's your sketch. There's no question of making corrections. Each stroke of the brush must be perfect, because it is final.

She must have been frightened, although she never admitted as much in her testimonies. All the while she was clinging to life. Had she been saved by the all-powerful Mengele, the scrawny Dr König or Snow White? It didn't matter, now she was totally dependent on her artistic talents.

After the success of the 'Gypsy Half-Breed', she went out among the stables with a new commission.

It was chaos, a jumble of Gypsies in ragged clothing. How can you do laundry with no water, how can you mend clothes without needles or thread? The SS officers would march men up and down the gravel Lagerstrasse 'for punishment', bellowing orders. Turn in a circle, do a squat, roll about on the ground, sing. Most often they would sing *Das kann doch einen Seeman nicht erschüttern*, 'That Can't Shake a Seaman'. Hollow-cheeked children wrapped their arms round their instruments, and the violins and guitars seemed larger than the children themselves.

In this wretched throng, a young Gypsy girl with a blue scarf tied round her neck stood out.

'I removed that scarf and draped it over her head. I asked her to smile a little. She told me her two-month-old daughter had just died because she couldn't breastfeed. After that I stopped asking people to smile.'

(All the children born in the Zigeunerlager died. There were 378 of them.)

This girl, Céline, was suffering from diarrhoea.

'She couldn't digest swedes or black bread. So I asked for some white bread for her and, on Mengele's orders, I actually got it. There was this tall, handsome man there, a Czech in a white uniform. He worked as a waiter for Dr Mengele. Every day he brought me a little bread. It helped her.'

Dina whispered to Céline.

'I tried to sing a French song, but I couldn't remember it. She helped me along. She knew the words, so she must have been French. She looked like a porcelain doll or a prima donna.

Gazing into her eyes was like gazing into her soul. You can see that in the painting.'

Now and again the doctor would check on her. Although he usually avoided physical contact with the prisoners, he himself pushed the blue scarf behind the Gypsy woman's ear to reveal it: the ear was considered important in the study of race.

But it damaged the composition.

'That ear makes the picture look odd.'

Mengele accepted the portrait of Céline, but declared he would select the next subjects.

'The ones he picked were older and less attractive. They were men. I chose women.'

Now Dina took her time at her primitive easel.

'When I was working in the Gypsy camp, I didn't have to report for roll call, I didn't have to do anything, just paint. When Mengele went for his mid-afternoon meal he'd bring something back for me to eat as well. It was the only time I felt human in Auschwitz. I took my time.'

This was her new routine. Two weeks – one watercolour.

Beppo defends Nordic blood

Joachimowski had been a record-keeper in the Zigeunerlager for some time. But so far he hadn't seen the new doctor, who had taken over the hospital there in May 1943. At last, a friend pointed him out.

'He was walking along the side of the path with his head down, as though counting the stones under his feet.'

He cut an elegant figure. He had a striking bearing and gaze. On the surface he seemed amiable and human. That didn't fool Joachimowski.

'It was often the case that the kinder an SS-man looked, the more of a killer he actually was.'

Curious, he followed after the doctor.

After several months of efforts on his part, Josef Mengele had been transferred to the camp to conduct his research. He was ambitious and passionate about his work. He was young – barely 32. He was the eldest son of the owner of a farming equipment factory. His father's dream had been for Josef and his younger brothers to build a family industrial empire.

It wasn't engineering that attracted his son though: he preferred nature, music and art. He wrote: his plays were performed during a charity campaign for orphans in his native Günzberg. People raved about his talent, intelligence and polished manners. Charismatic Josef came to outgrow his small-town surroundings. Not sharing his father's scepticism of Hitler, he joined the Stahlhelm.

The Stahlhelm was an organization, but before that it had been a helmet, a steel one. This helmet had been so important to the soldiers of the Great War of 1914 that they came to adopt it as one of their emblems. They'd been defenceless in their Prussian-style spiked helmets: shrapnel tore open their skulls, the backs of their heads were blown apart. So Captain Friedrich Schwert (in civilian life a professor at the Hannover Technical Institute) constructed a new head covering. He used a single piece of chrome-nickel steel and gave it a shape that would also protect the back of the neck and the eyes.

The Stahlhelm went into service in the German army at the Battle of Verdun in 1916. Many innovations were to come, and the M1935 model was exported to conflict-torn Spain and China, where the Kuomintang nationalists were at war with the communists. It was so unique and distinctive that it became a symbol of German military might. (This was precisely the reason West Germany later abandoned it.)

During the Weimar period, when Josef Mengele was in his 20s, the steel helmet expressed pride and hope. So in 1918, an organization of war veterans – nationalists opposed to the republic – adopted its name. Soon the veterans opened membership to others as well. By 1930, the Stahlhelm numbered half a million members and was the largest paramilitary group in the country. Three years later, the organization was merged into the Nazi Stormtroopers. The Mengeles' pride and joy was among the Nazis, in the service of terror.

Well, it couldn't be helped. At home they loved him anyway, and tenderly called him Beppo. This was the Italian nickname for Giuseppe, which cultured people recognized as the title character of Byron's Venetian epic poem.

After passing his exams in 1930, Josef studied medicine in Frankfurt and philosophy in Munich. He encountered lecturers fascinated by eugenics, who had adapted the views of the British scientist Francis Galton to new ends. It was no longer a question of eliminating hereditary illnesses, fighting alcoholism, improving occupational health and athleticism. The goal was racial genetics, and its Gospel: the sanctity of Nordic blood, which was never to be mixed with any other.

A Black Wound Badge

European eugenics societies called on the healthy, talented and wealthy to multiply. But in Germany, they didn't rely on persuasion. At the University of Munich, Dr Ernst Rüdin taught that doctors should destroy lives of no value, first and foremost the lives of Jews, who were a bizarre hybrid of Negroes, Arabs and Whites. Professor Theodor Mollison could reveal Semitic ancestry using photographic analysis.

These devotees of human perfection wished to work on a grand scale. They knew the state was the supreme tool for breeding, because it alone could ensure the well-adapted reproduced, and not the worthless. So they needed politicians, and the politicians needed scientists, to make this work in practice. The two came together in Hitler's Germany. Their theories were taken as dogma, and legislation raced to catch up with them.

The Institute of Genetic Biology and Racial Hygiene at the University of Frankfurt took the lead on this fashionable subject. It unified research and clinical practice. Mengele, with a newly-minted doctorate in philosophy and soon to have one in medicine, joined the Institute on Mollison's recommendation. In 1937, he found himself on the team of one of Europe's most eminent geneticists, the passionate Nazi Professor Otmar von Verschuer. Mengele became his assistant. Verschuer supported him, predicting he would have a marvellous career, and sent him to anthropology conferences in Tübingen, to meet Ritter. In Tübingen, they remembered him as quiet and dignified.

Mengele would visit Verschuer at home, and it was thanks to him he developed his passion for twins. Imagine if every German woman had more than one child every time she gave birth! Together, they wrote reports for special tribunals prosecuting Jews for having sex with Aryan women.

(In Frankfurt after the war, one Jewish researcher refused to work with Verschuer, but since he was too eminent to sack, he continued his academic career, now investigating the effects of radiation on the human body.)

Mengele was already in the Nazi Party and wanted to join the SS. His family tree was investigated and he was accepted. In 1940 he joined the Wehrmacht. He transferred to the Waffen-SS, where he served as a field doctor in the *Wiking* panzer division, fighting in France and the Soviet Union. He received an Iron Cross First Class for dragging two soldiers from a burning tank under enemy fire, as well as a Medal for the Care of the German People and a Black Wound Badge, for sustaining injuries in the Ukraine. His wounds were so serious that Hauptsturmführer Mengele was declared unfit for active duty. He hoped to return to research.

He found Baron von Verschuer at the Kaiser Wilhelm Institute of Anthropology, Human Heredity and Eugenics in Berlin (one of the institutions later incorporated into the Max Planck Institute). Verschuer was complaining of stagnation due to a lack of clinical cases. But they found a solution. After all, there was one place where it was possible to do unlimited analysis and measurement: the concentration camps. The camps were an unrestricted research environment, a never-ending reservoir of afflictions and disorders.

His superiors despatched the promising SS doctor to Auschwitz, the largest centre of the Holocaust, and granted him the Zigeunerlager. But he also remained on duty in clinics and hospitals in other sectors of the camp, and soon was made head doctor, *Lagerarzt*. He oversaw all of Birkenau.

Joachimowski observed him in secret. The new doctor was walking along the side of the road with his head down, as though counting stones. He went up to barracks 20 and 22. He ordered 1,700 Gypsies from the Białystok region to be led out. He sent them to the crematorium.

It was a preventative measure: they were carrying typhus.

Hobbyhorse

Sessions in the sauna began with the same ritual: every morning a team of outstanding doctors and nurses would gather together. Mengele was able to pick out experts from the ramp. In mid-May 1944, he identified Miklós Nyiszli, a pathologist who'd studied in Germany, on a transport of Hungarian Jews. Mengele engaged him to perform autopsies on his test subjects.

Nyiszli on the Sauna: 'The Gypsy camp offered one curiosity: the experimental barracks. The director of the Research Laboratory was Dr Epstein, professor at the University of Prague, a paediatrician of world renown […]. His assistant was Dr Bendel, of the University of Paris Medical School.'

(Professor Epstein testified at Höss's trial: 'I remember what my first impression was when I arrived in the Gypsy camp. It seemed like I was not in Europe any longer but in the Sudan, somewhere deep in Africa.')

The lab had use of modern equipment: the German Research Foundation and the Kaiser Wilhelm Institute – where it had the support of the eternal Nobel Prize candidate Ferdinand Sauerbruch – made sure of it. The army and pharmaceutical firms took advantage of research in the camps, and every doctor in Auschwitz could devote themselves to their passion. Professor Carl Clauberg, an expert on treating female infertility, was developing a method for non-surgical sterilization on a massive scale. He eagerly injected women with an irritant discovered by a colleague in the camp, Johannes Göbel from the drug company Schering Werke. Afterwards, Dr Horst Schumann would irradiate or simply excise their ovaries.

Mengele's hobbyhorses were twins, dwarfs, people with one blue eye and one brown eye, and the disabled. He studied the differences between Jews, Gypsies and the rest of the human race, as well as their resistance to contagious diseases. (He infected pregnant women with typhus to see if the disease would transmit to their children.) The doctor was obsessed with all sorts of anatomical oddities.

Sara Nomberg-Przytyk, a Polish Jew who worked in the hospital in Birkenau said, 'He loved seeking out people who hadn't been made in God's image. Once he brought in a woman with two noses, another time a girl with sheep's wool on her head instead of hair, and yet another time he came in with a woman who had donkey's ears.' Or a Ukrainian man with an incredibly long penis. The man was examined and then shot, having provided a moment's entertainment for those watching.

Prisoners transferred into the sauna were handed over to specialists. Precise instruments measured the length and width of their heads, noses, hands, shoulders and feet. After the anthropometry came morphology: analysing blood and trans-fusing it from one twin to the other, spinal taps, x-rays. Lastly came a dentist (to make a plaster cast of the jaw and teeth), then finally a laryngologist, ophthalmologist and a surgeon.

Dina: 'Mengele's assistant was a tall, young, pretty Polish girl. She was cheerful. I think her name was Zosia. She recorded all the data, whatever Mengele told her. It was her job to take fingerprints as well. First she'd wash the Gypsies' hands with ether – she had to take special care with the bottle, she told me once they'd stolen the ether and drunk it.'

The doctor would often call Dina over to teach her something. 'He showed me the differences between types of Gypsies: how in the Aryan type the hairline matched the line of the eyes, how the blue of the Gypsies' eyes was different from the Aryans' blue, and which colour was deepest. He was using these experiments to gather material for a book on the physical similarities and characteristics of Gypsies from different countries. He talked about it constantly.'

She presumed her paintings would be illustrations in the book. Mengele examined each watercolour carefully. Sometimes he'd order her to make some finishing touches and then take the painting away with him. He kept these treasures in a locked safe, to guard against competition. He insisted on a precise representation of reality.

'He used books and charts when working on his test subjects. He had templates to work out their eye and skin colour, which he'd hold up to make a reading. One of his descriptions for the shape of someone's lips was the letter *M*.'

She noticed Mengele's lips had that same shape. It was a minor detail, but before long it would prove useful.

Watching a performance

She observed everyday life in the barrack. 'They maintained a peculiar kind of courtesy, which made it feel like you were in an animal testing facility. It never seemed as though Mengele thought of the Gypsies as people. Sometimes he'd offer them a friendly smile, sometimes tell a joke, usually to Zosia or me.'

He kept bringing people in for portraits. A grey-haired woman, a grown man, a boy… They don't usually look the viewer in the eye in the paintings, so it's impossible to return their gaze. There is no communication between us, we are not permitted into the mind of the sitter. And this is significant – in the Renaissance, when portraiture was flourishing, its creators took the humanist stance that the face expressed the movements of the soul. The Gypsies' faces are dead.

They sat on stools before Dina. She never mentioned stools for models in her testimonies, but today art critics can determine it from the pictures. The Gypsies are portrayed like suspects on an arrest warrant. Gunslingers in the Wild West looked the same on nineteenth century 'Wanted' posters, and so did Al Capone when he was arrested in 1931. This technique is called a 'mug shot'. The well-known American private investigator Allan Pinkerton invented it for his famous detective agency. Mug shots aid in police investigations and are employed to this day, including in Europe. (That being said, nowadays human rights activists oppose their use. They make everyone, no matter how innocent, look like a criminal.)

Joseph Mengele was taking advantage of Dina's artistic skill to attain photographic perfection.

This was a tried and tested approach, since watercolours were for more than misty, impressionistic landscapes. Before anyone had reproduced an image using a light-sensitive emulsion, naturalists, geographers and anthropologists on expeditions would pack a light wooden case in their trunk, containing watercolour paints, a sketchpad, badger-hair brushes, pencils, knives to cut the paper and sharpen the pencils, and a water dish. Oil paints dried too slowly to be of any documentary use. Watercolours were cheaper and simpler.

On the eve of the First World War, the anthropologist Bronisław Malinowski brought a new invention on his voyage to New Guinea: a hand-held camera. But he also invited an artist, the famous painter and author Stanisław Ignacy Witkiewicz. None of Witkiewicz's paintings from that trip have survived, but we know of others, published in textbooks of zoology, botany and medicine, in atlases and monographs. Books the future *Lagerarzt* would have leafed through.

Mengele aspired to a professorship so he paid special attention to the illustrations for his thesis. He'd made Dina his private artist (and that's how she was presented after the war), but he wouldn't have entrusted his career to a single prisoner. He made the most of Auschwitz's mechanisms. Marianne Hermann, Ludwig Feld, Vladimír Zlamar and Janina Prażmowska all painted the Gypsies or parts of their bodies. Mengele personally photographed the stages of his experiments, as well as instructing others to do so.

One of those photographers was the young Pole Wilhelm Brasse (subject of the well-known film *The Portraitist* by Ireneusz Dobrowolski). Brasse had trained in a stylish studio in Katowice. In the *Erkennungsdienst* – the camp Gestapo's photo studio in Auschwitz I – he photographed naked Jewish children. He found it upsetting. He cobbled together a makeshift partition so they had somewhere to undress. This was a final gesture of humanity: when it was over, they were murdered with phenol. In one of the surviving photographs, Gypsy girls sent in by Mengele stand naked in a row: four small children's faces, terrified, their hair cropped down to the skin.

There are also other interpretations: that these weren't girls, but castrated Gypsy boys.

Dina painted the Gypsies as Mengele saw them – did she realize that? Or perhaps, as she moved her brush across the page, she decided to soften the portraits?

What does an artist feel under that sort of pressure? Art should not be in the service of genocide. What if it is, and is still a source of pleasure? Even when degraded to photography, to a craft, art makes life possible. How can a person accept that?

Dina had no memory of Mengele's Gypsy experiments, that's what she said. But she admitted to hearing of one in the women's camp.

'A forty-year-old woman from Berlin, who illustrated fashion magazines and sketched models, was subjected to electrical shocks of different intensities. He wanted to see how much she could withstand. So far as I know, she didn't survive.'

The people she was painting in the Zigeunerlager were vanishing. Prisoners from the medical team secretly passed on information about the doctor's experiments, making particular note of some.

Vera Aleksander was a Jew who worked in the twins' barrack. After the war she recalled: 'An SS man came and took two children away on Mengele's orders. They were my two favourites, Guido and Nino, about four years old. Two or three days later he brought them back in a dreadful state. They'd been sewn together like Siamese twins. Their wounds were so filthy they were festering. I could smell the stench of gangrene. The children screamed all night. Somehow their mother managed to get her hands on some morphine and used it to put them out of their misery.'

Vera said the veins in their wrists had been sewn together.

Psychiatrists believe that to survive the camp it was necessary to find a way to distance yourself from it. Those who succeeded in this were present, but not with their whole selves. They were deaf, blind, not taking in the complete experience. They didn't remember, because they'd banished some part of themselves, condemned it to oblivion. The so-called 'Muslims' – those who were completely destroyed, with no will to fight for their lives – truly saw Auschwitz. They perished because no one could survive such a thing. But the mad saw nothing. They retreated into fantasy.

Forty years after the war, the painter Mieczysław Kościelniak admitted on a radio programme: 'I can't understand this in myself or in others, but there you have it. Human nature commands you to pass into a fictional life. Fiction was how we survived in the camp. When an audience sits in a theatre and watches a performance, they lose themselves in the story. In the same way, we moved into fiction. Although death was raging around us, we believed we'd make it out.'

Dina believes she preserved 10, perhaps 12 Gypsy faces in watercolour.

Where did these Gypsies come from?

What were their names?

Were they frightened?

What happened to them?

There are no details in her mind.

'I don't remember anything exceptional about my subjects. They never asked for anything and I wouldn't have been in a position to answer anyway. Instead, they were stoic. They sat there and didn't speak to me. The only one to complain was the girl in the headscarf.'

The Führer doodles dwarfs

Each evening on Wilhelmstrasse in Berlin, and later in the new, monumental Reich Chancellery building on Voss Strasse, a private group would gather. After dinner they would settle into comfortable armchairs in the salon, and Hitler would unbutton his jacket and stretch out his legs. The lights would slowly dim and a film would start. After that would come another, then sometimes another. In his memoirs, the architect Albert Speer shared his impressions of these screenings. 'At about one in the morning, we stood up stiff and dazed. Hitler alone seemed sprightly; he discoursed on the actors' performances'.

Officially, Walt Disney was banned. He'd made a series of anti-Fascist propaganda films showing the Führer as a Valkyrie, with so many of his Hitler Youth boys dying onscreen that they transformed into a forest of cruciform grave-markers. On top of that, Disney sent Donald Duck, Mickey Mouse, Pluto the Dog and Dumbo the Elephant to war against the Germans. The Reich Chancellery's idea of emphasizing Disney's Germanic heritage (through his maternal grandmother) suddenly fell to pieces. Accordingly, the critics received their instructions. They wrote, for instance, that *Fantasia* was defiling a treasure of German culture – the music of Bach – or that Disney was famous for films about a mouse, and mice symbolized Jews, shit, and pestilence. But Goebbels could provide copies, so on 35 mm reels Hitler would watch what was banned for everyone else. He also watched films with Marlene Dietrich, who'd renounced her German citizenship.

And he saw *Snow White* many times.

(In 2008, William Hakvaag, the director of a small World War II museum in northern Norway, announced he'd found four of Hitler's drawings. They include characters from *Snow White* and *Pinocchio*. Reportedly the drawings were hidden behind a painting signed 'A. Hitler'. Hakvaag had bought it in Germany at an auction. One commenter in a forum wrote: 'I work in medieval studies, not 20th century history, but my historian's intuition does not permit me to believe that in 1940, in the middle of a war whose goal was to conquer Europe, Hitler was doodling dwarfs.')

The Krcz house on Kolejowa Street

The Auschwitz concentration camp had extraterritorial status and was hidden from the eyes of anyone unauthorized.

The camp's 'zone of interest' stretched 40 kilometres beyond the barbed wire, and was patrolled by armed military police and Gestapo officers. The Poles who had lived there earlier had long since been expelled, and the Jews (more than half the town's population) were imprisoned in the ghettoes. Command ordered the houses neighbouring the camp to be demolished. Eight villages were razed to the ground, only a few ramshackle cottages survived. When, in the spring of 1942, the ever-expanding camp swallowed up the town of Brzezinka, which had been renamed Birkenau, a gas chamber was set up in an abandoned farmhouse. They called it the red house. A few months later, a similar white house was constructed.

Secrets. Crimes with no witnesses. Bilingual signs with a skull and crossbones in the centre: 'Auschwitz Concentration Camp Zone. No Trespassing! Violators Will Be Shot at Sight!'

The Commandant wanted to ensure the prisoners had no contact with the outside world and could expect no help in the event of escape. But by autumn of 1940 (in other words at the very beginning), the town already knew about Auschwitz.

There were strange men carrying poles on Kolejowa Street. The schoolteacher Janina Kajtoch gazed at them in wonder. 'They were wearing strange clothes with blue and grey stripes, and round caps with the same pattern on their shaved heads; they were walking stiffly in noisy clogs, their heads down, guarded by stern SS men with rifles.'

Who were they? The women weighed their options, took their kids by the hand and approached. The men in strange clothes gave curt answers. They'd been sent here from Tarnów, they were political prisoners, more than 700 of them, from the first transport, in June. They were building a camp, and the poles were for measurement.

From then on, the Polish town of Oświęcim kept a secret eye on the German camp of Auschwitz.

The railwayman Józef Krcz lived at 24 Kolejowa Street, opposite the train station. Repairmen were in short supply, so for the time being, the camp authorities tolerated him in the restricted area. Józef came from Czechoslovakia, and his wife was Polish. He and Karolina had two children – mischievous Staś and tiny Genia.

Staś's testimony for the Auschwitz museum:

'I was just a little boy then, so it didn't occur to me what might be going on inside the camp, given that people in striped uniforms were being beaten and killed on this building site outside of it. You could tell just by looking at them what they were going through. I'd hide in the attic and watch. One day, I saw an SS-man beating a prisoner. When he was finished terrorising the man, he ordered him to flee. Then he shot at him, but he missed his target. He murdered the prisoner by laying a bar he'd found on the ground across his neck. He stood on the bar and killed the man. His calm as he did it was terrifying.'

His mother Karolina gave this account:

'Often, and almost daily in 1943 and 1944, I witnessed huge transports of people arriving. The shouting and screaming would wake us up at night. I heard crowds of people begging for water, and often gunfire. Whenever someone escaped the camp, they'd give our house and flat a thorough search. We lived in constant fear of being evicted or even thrown into the concentration camp.'

Contact with the prisoners touched the hearts of women from Oświęcim, Babice, Grójec, Stare Stawy, Dwory and Monowice. At night they left bandages and food in places where the prisoners worked, and also in the train carriages they were meant to unload every morning: a bottle of milk, bread with lard, and garlic. And during the day (the SS officer could sometimes be bribed or would turn a blind eye), they fed the prisoners soup.

'*Eintopf:* a soup with everything in it – meat and bacon, buckwheat and potatoes, vegetables and hard-boiled eggs' – recalled August Kowalczyk in his book *A Barbed Wire Refrain.* Kowalczyk was a prisoner who became an actor after the war, spending 30 years playing SS officers. It was those very women who saved him when he escaped from the camp in 1942, including Anna Lysko, Helena Stupkowa and their families. It began with them giving him a headscarf and a dress.

A smuggled letter from Bogusław Ohrt to Janina Kajtoch: 'My sincere thanks for the sugar, onion, pork cutlets and apples. In truth, I do not know if I shall ever have the chance to give you my heartfelt thanks. I feel much stronger. If it would be possible to get some Famel syrup or cresolene, or some milder decongestant medicine, I would be very grateful.'

It became harder to help as time went on. New prisoners kept coming and the German authorities introduced ration cards for bread, potatoes, beetroot marmalade and salt. Pasta, buckwheat and eggs were the stuff of dreams. In the towns, many families couldn't buy these items anyway, because they had no money to spend. The Germans controlled the mills and poured concrete into privately-owned quern-stones. They announced it was forbidden to grind grain and bake bread independently.

Fear and hunger were pervasive. People were subjected to forced labour, displacement and draconian punishments for the most trifling offences. It was cold – there was no coal or oil, matches, soap or shoes. They had carbide lamps instead of electric lights, and apple-skin tea sweetened with saccharine.

Tuberculosis spread. But in spite of everything, some meagre help still got through, and not only to Polish prisoners.

The Czech Bohuslav Fikr, from a surveyors' work unit: 'I saw with my own eyes the houses in Oświęcim that sent packages of medicine and food. And I became acquainted with the kind hearts of the Polish people, especially miners' wives and daughters. Not one asked my name: they helped us and believed us. I only remember "Maria", "Hela", "Wanda" and "Bronia".'

The women organized themselves, foregoing rations and getting hold of false ration cards. The black market flourished as well.

The railwaymen joined in, arranging contact with the outside world and the underground government, bringing bandages and typhus medicine on their steam locomotives, and gathering information about transports arriving and departing. They smuggled fugitives from the Reich over the border into the General Government, and on the way back, loaded up with illegal loaves of bread. In 1942, railwayman Krcz's family was moved to Konarski Street. Then his luck ran out.

Staś: 'During the move Genia took ill, and because we didn't have a doctor, or food, or – most importantly – medicine, my dear sister died. It's hard to describe how devastated my mother was. I was in pain along with her, and I could find no way to comfort her.'

Keeping strangers far away

The prisoners in the Zigeunerlager from Heidelberg, Cologne or Essen were German Sinti. They held their heads high – because to them, being a Sinti was much better than being a

Roma. Józef Merstein, a musician born in 1960, was a Sinti too. His family had lived as artists going back generations.

'They played the concert halls and palaces of Western Europe. My grandfather and his brothers were living in Switzerland, after escaping the German army by fleeing across the Bodensee. Later on, they went into business there: owning cinemas, restaurants, blocks of flats. But they couldn't settle down in one place, so they travelled with the circus. They did cowboy acts: lassos, knives, stunt riding. Sometimes they sold musical instruments. They'd all graduated from secondary school and knew how to make violins.'

The troupe stopped off in Germany again. This time, anti-Gypsy laws drove them away. Hitler even confiscated the Mersteins' horses. So they headed for Poznań, bought new horses at the market and commissioned impressive wagons carved in the shapes of dragons and crocodiles. They ordered the wagon poles to be hollowed out and hid money and gold inside. The circus performed in Poland because the atmosphere there was much friendlier.

According to Józef Merstein: 'But they didn't fraternize with the local Gypsies. They thought that lot of frying-pan salesmen, illiterate blacksmiths and village musicians were like savages.'

The Polish Gypsies were as peculiar as Orthodox Jews were to their progressive brethren – and just as uncivilized. But they'd shared the same fate, ever since the end of the Middle Ages, when the first caravans arrived on the highways of Europe. Back then, they'd been greeted with curiosity, and nobles even invited the Gypsies to dine with them. Chronicles recorded visits from princes and lords of Lesser Egypt. These were the Gypsies. They passed themselves off as pilgrims or exiles because of their Christian faith, and borrowed titles to lend themselves gravity. At that time, nomads were treasured, because any penitent, no matter how poor, might be a saint.

But before long, alms-giving stopped leading straight to heaven, and poverty was no longer an ideal. No longer could a poor man save the soul of a wealthy one. Instead, the poor were meant to make themselves rich – by working, working, and working some more. Such was the commandment of Holy Scripture.

The authorities wished to rein the Gypsies in. No one was interested in what kind they were, a Gypsy was a Gypsy. So long as they stopped roaming from one country to another and abandoned their bizarre language and colourful dress.

But they might be French or Spanish Gitans, German Sintis, Polish Roma, Romanian Kalderashes, Hungarian Lovaris, Balkan Egyptians or Ashkalis, Belgian Manushes…. They spoke different dialects, settled disputes their own ways, and held fast to distinctive customs. They borrowed a number of habits and religious principles from the nations they found themselves mixing with. But they weren't tied to a state, had no interest in politics, ignored borders and only married amongst themselves. The had their own word for non-Gypsies – *gadjo*.

Fear followed their caravans as they travelled. The peasants were frightened of Gypsy magic and trickery. The nobles were frightened because the Gypsies were a free people. So from time to time, an edict or law would be handed down ordering that they were to be terrorized and expelled. At such times they'd disappear into inaccessible areas – mountain caves, or deep into the forest – only to emerge again once their fortunes had improved.

They wanted to settle, but had no luck there either. In the sixteenth century, any Gypsy who dared to enter the city of Frankfurt could be killed with impunity. In Spanish and Italian cities, Gypsy ghettoes were built to keep these strangers far away. In the seventeenth century, English authorities allowed the Mayor of Haddington to dispose of any Gypsy he caught. Men were hanged, childless women were drowned, and those with children were branded with hot irons and flogged. In the eighteenth century, the King of Prussia allowed for the hanging of Gypsies, regardless of sex, so long as they'd reached 18. In Austria-Hungary, the Gypsies were deterred from travelling by having their children taken away from them and given to peasant families. In the German-speaking lands, such measures proved quite effective. In the nineteenth century, the Gypsy slave trade was suppressed in Romania. It had lasted 400 years, until 1855. Decades later in Munich, the police created a Gypsy register – the same one Dr Robert Ritter would use in the twentieth century. Z – Gypsy, ZM+ – more than half-Gyspy, and so on.

The Zigeunerlager held 23,000 people. They'd been captured in Austria, Belgium, Czechoslovakia, France, Germany, Hungary, the Netherlands, Norway, Poland, Spain, the USSR and Yugoslavia, from a variety of groups, clans and families. Some lived in elegant houses and ran fashionable variety theatres, while some made their homes in caravans. Under other circumstances, they'd never have crossed paths.

Rudolf Höss said of his favourite prisoners' inclinations: 'There was fierce feuding among them. Their hot blood and quarrelsome natures made this inevitable because the many different tribes and clans were forced to live in close association. Within their clans, however, they stuck together as if they were glued and they were very devoted to one another.'

It was a world segregated by blood – but for a Gypsy, blood was not enough.

Adolf Szmyt-Rachy, born in 1956 and raised in a caravan of Gypsies from Kalisz, spoke of his parents' generation: 'To their minds, everything non-Gypsy was threatening, and everything Gypsy was good. My generation learned this principle the way a child learns to speak. We lived and breathed the *Romanipen* code. We weren't allowed to reveal Gypsy things to the *gadjos*. We weren't allowed to snitch on another Gypsy. Gypsies were to speak to one another in Romani. Elders were to be shown respect, because they would hand down the language and laws to us. Anything *gadjo* was unclean.'

Józef Merstein: 'You had to know how to behave, showing strict discipline or else put your reputation at risk. As a child, I was told again and again to stay away from the Bergitka Roma. They're dog-eaters from the Carpathian Mountains. Because they'd forgotten the teachings, you wouldn't eat, drink or sit at the same campfire with them. And if you touched one of them, you'd be cut off too.'

The Gypsies' daily torture in Birkenau was staying pure.

Shipment essential for war purposes

The Zigeunerlager was like a leper colony, but instead of leprosy spreading it was cheek gangrene, water cancer, or noma: three names for one illness. It attacked the jaw – the flesh would start to decay and fall off, exposing the bone. The phenomenon had never been encountered in the camp, it was a mystery.

Dina: 'Once, Dr Mengele kept me until late evening. We went to another barrack.' There they showed him a small child – at first glance Dina thought it was a baby. It was all skin and bones, and evidently in a coma.

'Mengele asked if I'd be able to paint the inside of the boy's mouth. Someone opened it up and there was a white substance built up around his gums. His throat and palate were completely black. The little boy shook, his head fell back. I quickly turned away. Then Mengele said to take the child away. There would be no painting, we didn't need it.'

No painting because it wasn't an interesting case?

No painting because it would upset Dina?

The photographer Wilhelm Brasse documented the progress of noma and the twins research.

'The doctor, the children were to be treated as priceless objects.'

Mengele built a playground for them in the Zieunerlager behind Barrack 31. At one time, there had been Gypsy wagons there, but nothing remained of them. The barrack housed a playroom. The wooden walls were painted white and the prisoner Leon Turalski – a Polish painter nicknamed Kolorek – had decorated them with scenes from fables. They haven't survived, and we can only imagine what was there. *Berry-Picking* and *Johnnie the Wanderer* by the famous children's writer Maria Konopnicka, or perhaps forest gnomes? Judging from photographs, the kindergarten seemed all right. Children gobbled down buttered bread, and they had a sand pit, a swing set, a jungle gym and a roundabout in the playground. The doctor gave the little Gypsies chocolate. They trusted him and called him 'uncle'.

One by one, he took them away – as living material for his experiments. On Mengele's orders, sometimes children with noma were killed. Their corpses were taken to the SS Institute of Hygiene in nearby Rajsko, where prisoners would dissect their organs. They preserved whole heads in jars for the SS Medical Academy in Graz. Tests on the Gypsies dragged on for weeks. Despite brutal methods, the results gave no clear answers to the questions posed by Aryan science. So Mengele sought ultimate enlightenment in autopsies.

Nowhere else in the world could a researcher perform autopsies on two twin patients on the same day. The autopsy table stood in the crematorium. On it lay a row of coloured eyeballs – yellow, green, violet. Gypsy children, including infants, were given drops to change the colour of their irises. Nyiszli would then preserve the eyes in formalin. Carefully packaged, they were sent to Professor Verschuer with a stamp: 'Urgent: Shipment Essential for War Purposes'. (This monstrous collection has never been recovered. In a letter to the Nobel Prize-winning physicist Otto Hahn in 1946, Verschuer said he felt sorry for his protégé: 'My former assistant Josef Mengele was sent to Auschwitz against his will. All that is known of his work there is that he tried to be a doctor and provide help to the sick.')

Before sending it, Nyiszli would write the cause of death in the appropriate space on the report. He wrote all kinds of nonsense – it didn't matter what. After performing autopsies on five pairs of Gypsy twins, Mengele explained, almost to justify himself, that the children were infected with syphilis and tuberculosis, as Nyiszli could see himself, so therefore...

In Birkenau, they didn't treat tuberculosis using the pneumothorax technique, or syphilis using neosalvarsan. Instead, it was an injection of phenol into the heart. Nyiszli had made a note of this – and decided he was a dead man walking.

He observed the doctor closely. 'Dr Mengele was indefatigable [...]. He spent long hours in his laboratories, then hurried to the unloading platform, [which] kept him busy half the day.' Railway cars arrived one after another from Hungary. 'Dr Mengele dispensed with the customary formality of selection. He stood there like a statue, his arm always pointing in the same direction: to the left. Thus whole trainloads were expedited to the gas chambers and pyres.'

Cold, arrogant, chillingly cruel. That's how the imprisoned medics remembered him. They couldn't abide his whistling.

'You'll find that the family of Wallstones have got fewer gemstones than gallstones...' Once, when Mengele was presented with an interesting gallstone, he cheerfully sang the whole of that ballad. This put him in a mood to be generous. He gave Nyiszli permission to visit his wife and daughter.

Nyiszli had no idea where they were. Granted a special pass, he began searching for them in section BIIc, where many Hungarian women were being held. 'I headed towards the first barracks. From all sides cries and shouts greeted me. Those who had seemingly been mere bundles of rags lying on the ground or crawling on all fours revived and, leaving their places, ran towards me.' He didn't recognize them. But they were people he knew, asking after their husbands and children.

Irene Mengele misses her husband

Working with the doctor ensured certain privileges.

Dina: 'Once, I remember I'd organized myself tall lace-up boots, the sort for riding a motorbike. I was happy I'd got hold of them, because the mud in Birkenau was dreadful. Mengele noticed the boots and said they didn't suit a young girl.'

It was a nasty remark. 'Organize' meant to buy illegally. Prisoners mainly wore clogs. Dina's boots arrived at Auschwitz on the feet of a deportee, and they were the property of the Reich. Mengele was sending her a message: he knew. And he was turning a blind eye.

The Czech prisoner Alfréd Milek said about Dina: 'She painted those Gypsy portraits for Mengele and protected herself that way. She was a young, pretty woman, always well-dressed.'

Her clothes were quite nice for a camp full of 'Muslims' – the camp slang word for prisoners who had given up all hope. Dressing well must have demanded a tremendous amount of effort, and was truly meaningful. Even more so because many people had been sent to the bunker for organizing or smuggling something into the camp – a decent pair of shoes, a tin of sardines, a warm jumper – and never come out.

Nyiszli, on Dina's work: 'Dina, the painter from Prague, made the comparative studies of the structure of the twins' skulls, ears, noses, mouths, hands and feet. Each drawing was classified in a file set up for that express purpose, complete with all individual characteristics; into this file would also go the final results of the research.'

When Dina was ordered to paint an escapee's bisected heart, she nearly fainted. Mengele's private watercolourist – she must have wondered when he would decide it was time to replace her. She must have had him figured out, day after day analysing his thoughts, reactions, inhibitions and moods.

Dina: 'He worked passionately. He was always cold and matter-of-fact, just as you'd imagine a man of science. When I was sitting next to him and he was working, he was oblivious to everything beyond his work. He was completely absorbed in it, sometimes beaming with joy.'

Miklós Nyiszli: 'I had been sitting with him in the work room, looking through the records already set up on the twins, when he noticed a faint spot of grease on the bright blue cover of one of the files. I often handled the records in the course of my dissections, and had probably spotted it with a bit of grease. Dr Mengele shot a withering glance at me and said, very seriously: "How can you be so careless with these files, which I have complied with so much love!"'

Love.

Irene Mengele, née Schönbein, came to the camp for a few days. She missed her husband. She stayed longer than planned after falling ill with diphtheria in Auschwitz, but she recovered. In spring of 1944, her son, Rolf, was born. Naturally, his father wanted to see him and was looking forward to taking a holiday.

Dina: 'He came back beaming with joy, he told me all about the child. And he gave me a little pastry he'd brought from home. It was so unexpected. I also got two packets of British cigarettes. "You smoke and I don't. I can give them to you."'

Or maybe he gave her the cigarettes another time: when he returned to the camp after a short holiday, tanned and smiling.

'He asked, "Guess where I've been? Argentina!"'

The dwarfs say: your excellency

One day in Birkenau, Dina beheld a scene right out of *Snow White*. A group of dwarfs was ambling directly towards her.

'There were seven of them, I couldn't believe my eyes. As though all my drawings of the dwarfs – Dopey, Grumpy and Sneezy – had come to life and stepped out of that painting in the children's barrack. I simply had to laugh when I saw them.'

This was the Ovitz family, Romanian Jews from the village of Rozavlea in Transylvania. With seven members, they were the largest recorded family of dwarfs in the world. They became famous in Central Europe in the 1930s as the Lilliput Troupe. They played reduced-size violins, cymbals and cellos, with only the percussion being normal-sized. The women wore elegant dresses and makeup, the men, tails and bow-ties.

When they disembarked from the cattle cars in Auschwitz in May 1944, Miki Ovitz started giving out 'Lilliput Troupe Souvenir' postcards to the SS officers. Someone ran to wake

Mengele. The doctor was so excited he couldn't keep still. Such a huge family was a treasure trove, a chance to solve the mystery of hereditary height. Though he had no idea that neighbours from their village were also pretending to be their cousins.

The Israeli documentary filmmakers Yehuda Koren and Eliat Negev uncovered the Ovitzes' fate. In their book *Giants: The Dwarfs of Auschwitz*, Koren and Negev describe the exhausting, humiliating experiments Mengele inflicted on the family of dwarfs. But he guaranteed them luxury – inasmuch as luxury was possible in Auschwitz. That's why they addressed the doctor using all the titles he held both in medicine and the SS, and sometimes added one more: your excellency.

To them he was a king.

Lea Nishri, a 14-year-old prisoner, saw Perla Ovitz years later on Israeli television and remembered this scene from the camp: 'Perla was wearing a reddish-brown leather coat, lined with fur. A normal-sized woman walked behind her, carrying a bucket of potatoes. To us one potato was an unrequited dream, let alone a whole bucketful! I never saw so many potatoes in the camp. Perla walked proudly in front of the tall woman, like an elegant lady returning from the shops with her servant. Right then I thought no Jew in the camp held their head so high. It seemed these little people could have anything in the camp they desired.'

That wasn't true, but to the other prisoners they looked like fairy-tale characters brought to life. While chatting to his favourite patients once, even Mengele confessed he'd loved the story of Snow White since he was a child. (The Germans still adore her: she was ranked no. 1 in a survey from 2007. Disney drew on the world of the German imagination. The castle from the title sequence of his films was a hunting retreat in Bavaria.)

The youngest prisoners in Birkenau had grown up on stories of the dwarfs. The cartoon ones also formed a troupe and played instruments, so the children found the Ovitzes exciting. They wore top-hats, crinolines, antelope-skin boots, red lipstick, face powder and nail varnish.

Dina: 'They didn't look like us, like people caught in a trap. They seemed hopeful and in high spirits. And while we were constantly fearful and desperate, they seemed not to believe they'd be killed. They'd had decent lives as performers before the war and in Auschwitz they considered themselves exceptional as well.'

But even she fell under the Lilliputians' spell.

'I thought this magic number seven had something optimistic and encouraging in it. Such delicate beings were managing to survive here.'

So she would manage too. She was stronger.

In the mist

Six months after her arrival in the Gypsy camp, Elizabeth Guttenberger from Stuttgart was sent to the *Schreibstube*, where the clerks worked. A well-educated woman, her assignment there suited her. She was in charge of the main register of male prisoners, updating it each day with death reports from the hospital. On her eighth day, she picked up a note bearing her father's name.

'I felt paralysed, my eyes flooded with tears.'

Just then the door banged open. Oberscharführer Plagge – Little Pipe – exploded into the room and roared, 'Why's that one in the corner blubbering?'

'I couldn't get an answer out. But my friend Hilly Weiss, who was a report-writer, explained: "Her father has died." And the SS-man snapped back, "We'll all die someday."'

And he left.

Death in the Zigeunerlager: sisters, mothers, brothers, dying from hunger, from typhus, in the gas chambers. Accounts from nomadic Gypsies are scarce. Assimilated Gypsies and prisoners of other nationalities told more vivid stories.

Franz Rosenbach, a Gypsy from Austria: 'The camp road in Birkenau was full of the dead, they lay about in heaps, it's truly difficult to describe. At night, the frozen corpses were loaded onto lorries and driven away.'

Elise Baker, a half-Gypsy adopted by a German family from Hamburg: 'At eight years old, I couldn't imagine what it meant to be so evil. There were so many very sick, extremely emaciated people, some were having fits, several hung dead from the electric fences. I didn't really understand until later, when I was grown up, that it was hell on Earth.'

František Janouch, a Czech doctor: 'The children got tiny amounts of food and even that ended up getting stolen by various ruthless people whom we called "savages", and by the working prisoners as well. The mortality rate was tremendous. On the one hand, you'd have wailing mothers running up to one side of the hospital block, knowing they'd never see their children again. And on the other, you'd have mothers searching for their children among the dead.'

Stanisław Chrulski, a Pole from the fittings work squad: 'In the infirmary they had rows of pallets along the wall with chamber pots on either side of the entrance. There was unbelievable filth everywhere and it stank of festering wounds, faeces and sweat. Gypsy women in labour lay on bare, paper pallets under horribly dirty blankets. Sickly little monsters, not children, crawled around under the beds and in the passage running through the inside of the barrack. I saw a Gypsy woman with a baby on one of the beds. The woman was dying. When the child started to whimper, the nurse showing me around, a Ukrainian woman, strangled it with a blanket, saying, "*molchi, ty svoloch*" – shut up, you bastard.'

Fog from the river Vistula and nearby ponds often descended on the area around Birkenau, drifting through groves and among the meadows. Once the Zigeunerlager was built, it drifted through the barracks and over the gravel Lagerstrasse, it enveloped the mess hall and the infirmary, it worked its way into the stables through the gaps and skylights.

At times like this, were the Gypsies frightened? Did they perceive indistinct figures in the mist? When a Gypsy died in a caravan and there was no other solution, their brethren would bury them in the forest, anywhere except in a clearing, where others might set up camp. They would mark the grave for the benefit of the whole Gypsy community – because death was not the end. Death was unnatural, and it unleashed the supernatural – powerful, malevolent forces. You had to cast spells to defend against them and spend a whole year helping the deceased on the long journey to the next world.

The soul has a hard time leaving the corpse, and was even capable of changing its mind. The deceased's face would be covered with a slashed handkerchief, in case the soul wanted to return through the mouth or the nostrils. The funeral wouldn't be organized until three days had passed without the spirit coming back.

But before that, you had to tend to the body, which spread pollution. Old women would wash and dress it with great care – the impurity had no effect on them. Then friends and acquaintances would gather for the wake and each slip a couple of pennies into the dead person's pockets. That was so they wouldn't bear any grudges and were able to buy things on the other side – and also to stop them coming back. They'd be given a cigarette case, a watch, a ring, a sewing needle or a cane – whatever they might find useful. (Nowadays wealthy Kelderash don't lay bodies in coffins. They build a large tomb and do it up like a comfortable room, with a carpet, a chest of drawers, a gilt mirror, a flatscreen TV, a sacred icon on the wall and a topped-up mobile phone on the nightstand.) These bits and bobs would never include matches. The soul would hang about the house for six weeks, meaning it might start a fire.

As the soul progressed, the living had new duties. There were also a number of feasts – *pomanas*. The grandest, most joyful of these fell one year after death. A Gypsy elder would declare: 'I open his path to a new life and I free him from the bonds of my sadness. Now we will sing and dance! Let it be for him! Mourning is ended!' But no one would mention the dead person, their name would never be spoken, and everything they owned would be thrown onto the fire. The dead must never be summoned back, and it was bad to commune with them too closely. Manush even destroy photographs of the deceased.

The *mulo* – the soul – announced its presence with a delicate puff of wind that made you shiver, or a sudden howl and a violent storm. It hid in the mist. The dying had to be shown respect. If they didn't have a peaceful death, if they'd suffered an affront, they would return as an evil spirit, a ghost or a vampire to torment people. Madness, suicide, infertility, miscarriages, stillbirths, skin diseases – this was the mischief they would make. Women were at risk, they had to be careful not to get too close to death. (Even today, when Gypsy women go into a cemetery they shove a thumb into the belt of their dress and twist their hands to avoid looking too enticing.)

In a camp of spirits, those who were offended would return. How did people sleep in the Zigeunerlager? *Mulos* were most dangerous at night. That's why after sunset the caravans would set up camp and light a fire.

Anyone violating Gypsy rules was suspect. Killing another Gypsy or betraying the Gypsy language were unforgivable transgressions. The punishment was banishment with no possibility of forgiveness or amnesty.

Some other crimes were: eating a horse or a dog. Kissing a woman below the belt. Being low down, beneath a woman. (Once in the 1960s a Gypsy woman took a plane to Kraków. The Gypsy elders thundered, 'she had nothing better to do except fly over our heads. May God strike her dead.') Men's clothes were washed separately and they sat separately at the table, because the two sexes inhabited two different worlds. A woman lived only for a man. A woman's body was unclean, and her skirt and shoes as well. Childbirth was particularly detrimental, so no one assisted a woman in labour or touched the new-born. It was forbidden to shake a midwife's hand.

It was forbidden to seduce the wife of an imprisoned Gypsy man.

It was forbidden to be naked.

And there were many other commandments – so many taboos, so much faith. Breaking these rules provoked disgust or fear.

The carpenter didn't take off his underpants

The Gypsy Antonín Absolon, in the Růžička camp: 'There was a great big room in the building where we all had to undress completely. It was awful. People didn't want to undress because everyone was in there together – men, women and children. People started shouting and crying, and they beat us. I remember distinctly my older sister Bożena didn't want to undress, although many people were already naked. A woman SS officer beat her and tore off her clothes. My sister screamed, cried and defended herself.'

Tadeusz Borowski on the Gypsies from the Białystok region – the ones Mengele sent to the gas: 'A procession of spectres drifts past an improvized table: old men with grey hair and clouded eyes; women with babies at their breasts; young, dark Gypsy dancing women, their bodies burning with fever. All naked, all atrociously filthy and lice-ridden.'

The Polish prisoner Karol Czyszczoń, who worked as a carpenter: 'Before leaving the camp, we first had to bathe in the washroom – normally packed in with the women. I remember once, a Gypsy women gave birth while I was washing. Another time I got a nasty beating, because I didn't take off my underpants.'

The Polish Jew Alter Feinsilber, known in the camp as Stanisław Jankowski, who worked in the crematorium: 'Of course, other prisoners were forbidden from going into the Gypsy camp. But even so, you could get in by giving a special bribe to the SS-man in charge of their barracks. Prisoners who could afford the bribe, which amounted to a pack of cigarettes, would make the most of it. They'd get his permission to enter the Gypsy camp, where they'd have relations with Gypsy women. Half-starved with hunger, the women would offer themselves up in exchange for cigarettes or other small trifles. Their husbands and fathers would agree to this state of affairs since they too were starving and wanted to get something out of all this.'

František Janouch: 'The working prisoners (the Lagerkapo, the barrack wardens and others) would divide off one section of the block using a partition. Speaking plainly, it was a brothel. They had everything in that barrack. They invited the Gypsy men to play music. They organized alcohol from somewhere, they had sausage they'd stolen from children or sick prisoners. And which barrack was it in? The one with the sick women and children. It was all in one barrack. It was a horrid sight...'

In the camp, every Gypsy principle was trampled underfoot. It might have been easier on them if the men and women had been separated, but the Zigeunerlager wasn't exactly built for comfort. And, as Höss made emphatically clear, 'by nature the Gypsies were as trusting as children', so they couldn't distinguish good from bad. Decisions were made for them, and many prisoners envied them.

Most likely, the Commandant felt he was their benefactor. He had an image fixed in his mind and only noticed what he wanted to. In his autobiographical notes, his portrayal of the Gypsies is naïve: 'When the selection of the able-bodied workers began, it was necessary to separate and tear apart the clans. There were many emotional scenes, much sorrow, and many tears. We were able to calm and console them somewhat by telling them they would all soon be together again. For a while we kept the working Gypsies in Auschwitz proper. They did everything possible to see their clans again, even though it was only from a distance. Oftentimes we had to search for the younger ones after roll call because they had sneaked back to their clans by using all kinds of tricks, because they were homesick.'

How did the Gypsies cope? Nowadays it's too late, there's no one left to ask. Jerzy Kijowski, a writer in the camp, evoked this image: 'There was actually a very good Gypsy band in section BIIe. It gave concerts on the square in the middle of the sector. I remember the band would play whenever a Gypsy died. The corpse would be covered with a blanket and they'd throw paper flowers onto it.'

A spot on the ear, a face like a cat's

Not long after making a present of the little pastry, Mengele asked Dina to paint him.

'I was to make a "portrait for him", that's how he put it.'

By now she was a skilled portraitist. For months she'd been sketching faces – legally or under the table, *Schwarzarbeit*. The wives and children of SS officers or sometimes Polish fellow-prisoners would come to her for portraits.

But Mengele was a completely different story.

'I drew in pencil, examining him closely.'

He had a rather engaging, expressive face, his lips were M-shaped – as she'd noticed some time before – and he had a thick head of hair.

'But his eyes were dead, although you might think I'm making that up now. I saw no emotion in them. The shape of his face reminded me of a cat's. It was white, with eyebrows that rose up sharply like little roofs.'

White? Beppo from Venice – swarthy, dark-eyed and dark-haired?

'One of the women in our camp mentioned he was handsome. He was, but he was an SS-man, so…'

When he saw the portrait, the only objection he had was to the colour of his uniform.

'"Is it really that dark?" I realized he wanted it to be lighter, so I fixed it. He jokingly asked me whether I'd noticed something unusual about him, something only his wife knew about.'

She hesitated for a moment before working up the courage to point it out: a dark spot on his left ear – a distinguishing mark.

Brilliant, and the tie's the best

Portrait sessions took place every day in Auschwitz-Birkenau.

The prisoner Józef Siwek was painting Alfred Skrzypek, a barrack murderer.

'Skrzypek ordered me to do a portrait of him with hair and in a tie. I asked him to hold still for an hour while I painted it. "I can hold it, blockhead." When I'd finished his face and I was doing the tie, I told him he could move his head now. And again he said, "I can hold it, blockhead," and he kept sitting there, not blinking an eye. I finished. Looking at it he said, "Brilliant, you've done the tie the best."'

The next commission: SS officer Glaue wanted a portrait of his child. Siwek worked in the officer's private flat in the village of Harmęże.

'Mrs Glaue left. The kid was wiggling about and could have fallen off the table. I was holding him with one hand and drawing with the other, but I wasn't making any progress. I spotted a chamber pot and sat the stupid kid on it and, wonders never cease, he held still. I quickly captured the cranky look on his face.'

Mieczysław Kościelniak had cocked up, and the kapo warned him that in two weeks he'd get blown out a chimney. Desperate, he accosted a high-ranking SS officer he didn't know and promised to paint his portrait. It worked. The SS officer was impressed and sent Kościelniak to the painters' work squad, the *Malerei*.

It wasn't the worst job. They painted horses' names on signs for the stables and fire safety signs for the barracks: how to put out a fire using blankets, buckets of water, fire extinguishers and so on. They made armbands for the working prisoners, warning signs with skulls and crossbones, a plaster model of Birkenau, pictures illustrating the expansion of the camp and holiday games for the SS officers' children in time for Christmas.

Kościelniak met Franciszek Targosz in the painting studio. Thanks to Targosz, the portraiture industry in the camp was flourishing.

It had started in early 1941, when Commandant Rudolf Höss had caught him sketching horses' rumps. To save himself, Targosz timidly proposed the idea of creating a museum in Auschwitz. Höss was very impressed with Targosz's drawing, so he heard him out, and Targosz started listing the benefits. Contact with high culture would benefit the German officers. They would only see art that strengthened the Aryan soul. There would be exhibitions of coin and stamp collections, antiques, valuable objects, antiquarian books, liturgical robes and banners. These treasures, brought here by deportees from across Europe, would have to be sorted through by someone with expertise.

The Commandant took the bait. Committing genocide was proving stressful for his staff, so Höss had hired a cultural affairs officer some time before. Recreational Leader SS Unterscharführer Kurt Knittel, a teacher by profession, had brought theatre troupes to the camp from Kattowitz, Breslau and even Vienna. He staged performances of *Princess Greta*, *Gitta Goes Wild* and *The Beaver Coat*. If the show started early, the SS officers would rush to finish their work. The Lagermuseum also stirred up quite a bit of excitement. It was a brilliant stroke of propaganda, and it would please Himmler when he came on inspection.

The museum became a sanctuary for a small group of Polish artists, all men. They organized the collections, painted hunting scenes or illustrations from Germanic legends as gifts for dignitaries, made portraits of prominent Nazis for offices, and painted murals in the style of the 'German pseudorenaissance'.

Secretly, they risked their lives creating a chronicle in paintings: *Roll Call*, *Back from Work*, *Queuing for Soup*, *'Muslims'*, *Before the Gas*. They smuggled out holiday cards, booklets and postcards with fairy tales, and realistic testimonies, all made using materials stolen from the Lagermuseum.

Józef Siwek: 'Without painting I would not have survived Auschwitz. Painting put a roof over my head, I didn't have rain pouring down on me, I wasn't shovelling in a gravel pit. But above all, when I was painting I always forgot I was in the camp, though I was painting in a state of terror. One German might order you to paint, but another might kill you for it.'

Siwek made 2,000 portraits of his comrades. Some, hidden ingeniously, made it to their families beyond the barbed wire, sometimes not until after the prisoner's death.

Peek-a-boo!

The renowned Kraków sculptor and professor Xawery Dunikowski was almost 70 when he landed in Auschwitz, so his odds of survival were slim. After the war, he told the story of being warned about an imminent Selection for the gas. He hid in a giant flour drawer, but a sneeze gave him away.

When an enraged SS officer yanked the drawer open, the old man, all white and with his eyes bugging out of his head, cried out: 'Peek-a-boo!' The German burst into giggles. 'Even a beast like that can be disarmed with a joke,' explained Dunikowski with his characteristic lisp.

In truth, it was his students who protected him, gave him medical treatment and arranged work for him indoors. He built a model of the camp and secretly sketched his friends' faces as they slept. But he was sure no art could be made in the camp – it was impossible.

After the war, friends asked the painters how they could have worked for the SS-men. Some said they restrained their talent when painting for the enemy. But that was an excuse, or a joke. The blank page was liberating, it provided a feeling of infinite freedom and put them back in control of their lives. (The artists in Hilary Helstein's documentary *As Seen Through These Eyes* make that point again and again.)

Leon 'Kolorek' Turalski didn't work in the Lagermuseum, so, like other artistically talented prisoners, he had to make do on his own. He got himself a position in the hospital in Auschwitz I, where he made drawings of the stages of diseases. After the war, in a letter to Danuta Szymańska at the Auschwitz Museum, he wrote that he was very happy with his job. It was fairly safe, and it gave him the chance to concentrate and reflect on form, expression and texture. Then there were the models – some whose faces were intriguing, suffering, or sometimes imbecilic. The prisoners agreed to pose: Turalski felt people had a weakness for posing, whether they were free or imprisoned, whether they were sick, covered in ulcers, or completely emaciated.

Once after roll call, Turalski watched a prisoner pull a drawing out from under his sleeping pallet and closely examine his image in the picture. He did this every day. It made him glad to see himself, that he was still alive and he looked all right.

For this reason, portraits and self-portraits were made nearly everywhere in Auschwitz. 'In cellars, in store rooms, after roll call, on Sundays, in the lofts and rooms of barracks, even in workshops inside and outside the camp. Small ones were made in pencil, pastels, coloured pencil and even oil paints. They were made on Bristol board, cardboard or even canvas. The materials were organized from the construction office, the painters' workshop, the mess hall, from camp hospital pharmacy parcels and from "Canada", as we called it,' Turalski wrote in the letter. For some reason, the SS officers tolerated this fever of activity.

When her barrack warden was inquiring after a painter, Halina Ołomucka volunteered. (She was later a graduate of the Łódź school of fine art under Władysław Strzemiński and now lives in Israel.) Some of the wardens were competing to see who could decorate their block best, so there was a need for aesthetic expertise of any kind. Secretly, Halina made drawings of her prisoner's bowl in five positions: as a plate, a pillow, a helmet, a chamber-pot and a stool. She made portraits of her friends, since they would say to her, draw us before we go to the ovens, so something will be left behind after we're gone. She hid the portraits in gaps in the barrack wall and under bricks.

In one interview she said: 'Once I drew the troubled face of a girl, but I didn't like the drawing. I threw it out. And then I spotted this pair of huge, frightfully sad eyes gazing at me from the rubbish bin, as though they were rebuking me and saying "on the rubbish heap once again".'

It wasn't a good portrait, but it was the one Halina Ołomucka took with her on the death march. She kept it

84 • *Watercolours*

with her in Ravensbrück, then later in Neustadt-Glewe, and it survived until the liberation.

The Unterscharführer doesn't agree

The camp gong announced lockdown at seven in the evening. Everyone into their barracks! SS officers armed with machine guns drove up and ran into the stables, shouting, expecting wailing and chaos.

There was dead silence. The Gypsies stood facing the open doorway holding knives, shovels, steel rods, crowbars and stones. Not one was trembling.

Tadeusz Joachimowski: 'The SS-men were bewildered.'

Was it a revolt?

They turned round and headed out to the camp road. They conferred briefly with the operation leader. Shortly thereafter, a whistle blew. They left their posts and drove off. They didn't want a fight. The young Gypsies had maintained their physical strength and those who'd served in the Wehrmacht were trained for combat. To make matters worse, the spark of resistance could spread further.

It was 16 May 1944. The day before, Unterscharführer Georg Bonigut, chief of the Zigeunerlager, had approached Joachimowski and passed on the latest news – from a good source, Dr Mengele himself. The Gypsy camp was to be be exterminated with Zyklon gas.

Joachimowski: 'Bonigut didn't agree with the SS's tactics. He was a good man. He told me to warn the Gypsies, who I was absolutely sure "wouldn't be led like lambs to the slaughter".'

No one knows whom Joachimowski tipped off. The Gypsies themselves had been sensing the end was near; for some time, the men had been sewing long, narrow pockets into the lapels of their jackets for concealing razors and knives.

The day after the revolt, Georg Bonigut once again summoned Joachimowski: 'The Gypsies are safe for now.'

And he gave a new order: make a list of prisoners who'd served in the German army and their families, as well as a list of the relatives of soldiers still fighting at the front. It took the clerks three days and three nights. Half of the 6,500 prisoners ended up on the list. Because of the revolt, they were mainly young men – the aim was to weaken the Gypsy camp.

Before long a committee had arrived: the SS officers from the political department and Mengele. The Gypsies on the list were called to the entrance gate with all their belongings. What could they have had with them? A few old rags, blankets, pots. They were inspected. The atmosphere was tense – they argued constantly with the Doctor.

Joachimowski: 'Bonigut said for now he was in charge here, that the list had been properly made, and he simply pushed the registered Gypsies out the gate by force, over the committee's objections.'

The Germans said there would be some kind of 'transport'. Anything was better than the Zigeunerlager. Antonín Absolon, then still a kid, ran up to Mengele.

'I didn't hesitate a second, and I started talking to him in the broken German I'd learned in the camp, saying I wanted to get on that transport, that I'd been left alone, my mum and dad were dead and I wanted to go home. I guess he didn't understand it all because the woman prisoner standing behind him started explaining something to him. He said I could go.'

Was Mengele being magnanimous? Or was he showing Bonigut who was in charge there?

The prisoners were lined up in columns of 100.

Absolon: 'We marched to another camp, with red brick buildings. Now I know that was the main concentration camp in Auschwitz. The journey completely exhausted me and I couldn't believe I was getting out of there.'

No one could. The Gypsy camp was seething and rumours were going round that the young men were dead, so they were loaded onto a freight train at the main station in Auschwitz. The carriages ostentatiously rolled past sector BIIe. Then the train returned to the station, and the prisoners to the Auschwitz barracks. Later, they were sent to Ravensbrück, Buchenwald or the gas.

But the mood in the Zigeunerlager grew calm. Headquarters believed the danger was past.

The people murdering Gypsies must have been really throwing themselves into the task – especially in the occupied countries, Ukraine and Slovakia, where entire Gypsy settlements were being wiped out. In the Balkans, in Serbia and Croatia, local nationalists were assisting in the genocide. That was the situation in the notorious Jasenovac camp, where there were Catholic priests among the staff and where 20,000 Gypsies were killed. But more Gypsies died in the forests than in camps. Whoever was caught, or was ratted out by their neighbours, perished on the spot or in mass executions.

It was no secret the Gypsies would fight back. Oberleutnant Walther, a death squad commander, warned in a secret report: 'It is much easier to execute Jews than Gypsies. We must admit the Jews go to death more stoically, standing quietly, whereas the Gypsies weep, shout and are constantly moving about, even once they've reached the execution site. Some leap into the ditches before the shots are fired and attempt to play dead.'

The eternally resentful Höss said the same: 'It was not easy to get them into the gas chamber. I personally did not witness this. Schwarzhüber told me no previous extermination of the Jews had been as difficult as this. It had been especially hard for him because he knew almost every one of them and had a good relationship with them.'

Lord of life and death, he knew nothing of life or death.

In the summer, before eating the first apple of the season, a Gypsy will kiss it and say: 'Let this be for the dead'. The first bite of hedgehog (a springtime delicacy), the first ice lolly, the first flowers – these are for the souls. What better can a person give to those who've passed than the joy and flavour of life?

Recruitment

After Fredy Hirsch's death, the energy went out of the children's block, and life went on without the old rules. Helplessly, the Czech camp counted the days. The quarantine of the December transport ended in June 1944. No one had any doubt what would happen next. Some didn't care, they could only think about today's bowl of soup. Others, especially those with families, showed their love for one another.

Dina fell in love with a stepbrother.

'In the camp he was constantly hungry, I kept giving him bread.'

Petr was 11. He'd been imprisoned in Birkenau with Dina's father's new family in December, just before Christmas. Both he and his half-sister had probably been there to enjoy the play with Snow White and the dwarfs imprisoned in Auschwitz. Dina did her best to save her family, especially her youngest brother.

'Petr was too young to be a *pipel*,' she noted matter-of-factly in her testimony. But obviously her efforts were unsuccessful:

after all, there were even younger *pipels*, some as young as seven. Miša Grünwald, who'd lit Dr König's cigarettes in Dina's cramped studio, was 11 as well. Karl Stojka, an Austrian Gypsy and Josef Mengele's errand-boy, wasn't much older. He cleaned, cooked Mengele's breakfast, laundered his uniform, even repaired his shoes.

When Mengele left the Gypsy camp, nosy little Karl would grab Dina by the hand and drag her out to the barracks. There they'd find fire-eaters, tap-dancers, and the rest of the Stojkas too – four of the five siblings and their mother. Their father, a travelling horse salesman, had died in Dachau, and little Ossi had perished in Birkenau. Mengele had become enamoured of the Stojkas and promised them they'd live. (He kept his word to the end. It was a long time before the doctor's former *pipel* could come to terms with his emotions. Then, 40 years after the war, he began putting them onto canvas. He held 80 exhibitions in Europe and America. The camp in strong, vivid colours – in red. In Hilary Helstein's film he cries out, 'Oh my God, this was yesterday! Only fire! Nobody can take it out from me!')

Finally, it happened. In late June, the staff in the Theresienstadt camp set about compiling lists according to age and occupation. Meanwhile, word went round: some people really were being sent to work, but only the strong and fit. A cry of lamentation went up in the women's camp. What should they do – stay here with their children, or choose the work squad and save themselves? The older children and teenagers urged their mothers to go, the little ones clung onto them tightly.

Klára Nová recalled a speech by Lagerältester Willy Brachmann: 'If you remain here with your children, you'll meet the same fate as the March transport. Unfortunately, it will do you no good to be stubborn, for even at the hour of your death you will not be at their side – the children will be loaded into separate carriages. Your sacrifice will be pointless and unnecessary. I beg you, save yourselves.'

Some women had several children of different ages. Should they go with these ones to life, or these ones to death? Some were driven mad.

They called Selection 'recruitment'. In the washroom, out of 500 boys, Schwarzhüber and Mengele chose the 90 most fit to learn a job. (The survivors – from Canada, Israel and Germany – sometimes gather together. They once toured the museum with the organization Birkenau Boys. The organisation for twins is called Candles.) The adults were also split up, with 3,000 men and women being transferred to other camps – Gross-Rosen, Bergen-Belsen and Stutthof – or to Hamburg, where the people were needed to clear the rubble left from the air raids.

Dina: 'When the first transport of women left for Hamburg, Mengele ordered me to paint human organs in the men's section, and he made my mother a barrack warden. I had to undergo Selection as well. Dr Mengele, Dr König and some SS women I knew were there. I marched past them naked, it was embarrassing.'

Luckily they averted their eyes.

By the morning of 12 July 1944, the barracks stood completely empty. They were later used to store objects plundered from Jews.

Snow White was still looking after Dina, but the baby dwarfs, the 14-year-old leading lady with the amazingly beautiful voice, Pepíček, Aninka and the rest of the actors from the children's opera all perished. So did Petr Gottlieb and his family, and the rest of the audience. There were 7,000 of them.

Ela Weissberger acted in Kot's *Brundibár* and survived. When the show was staged in 2005 on Broadway, she confessed to Hilary Helstein: 'I always thought that with the children going to the gas chambers that Brundibár died with them. But if I see performances now, I feel that Brundibár will live forever.'

The gong

Tadeusz Joachimowski: 'At the end of July 1944, Bonigut came to see me and said the liquidation of the remaining Gypsies was decided, there was nothing more he could do.'

Mengele, with his flair for drama, had picked out the time and place. The afternoon of 1 August, a long freight train to Buchenwald pulled up to the ramp, which was adjacent to the Gypsy camp. The young men who'd been brought from the main camp were lined up along the length of the carriages. On the other side of the fence, the Zigeunerlager fell silent. This was the start of the show.

Joachimowski: 'There followed gut-wrenching farewell scenes. The Gypsies started hurling themselves onto the barbed wire. Then Brachmann, who was acting as Lagerältester at that time, called in all the Polish working prisoners.'

They formed a cordon and drove back the surging Gypsies. Then Mengele stepped into the arena. Dressed to the nines, in uniform and boots glistening, he charged, bellowing, into the Zigeunerlager.

'He ordered the working prisoners away from the barbed wire, so the Gypsies could say goodbye. The whole scene, from the moment of the train's arrival to the row with Mengele, had been planned and superbly acted out. It was designed to reassure the Gypsies remaining behind in the camp, and convince them they would be sent to a work camp too.'

The train left just before seven, and the gong sounded in the Gypsy camp. Jews from the Sonderkommando nailed crossed boards over the doors and windows of the barracks so no one could escape. It was August and still light out. The lorries didn't start growling until nightfall, just before nine. By then Dina, the team of doctors and the Ovitzes had left the Zigeunerlager. The camp was locked up, guards were posted, and German camp wardens from other sectors were sent in with batons.

The Belgian Jew Alfred Galewski: 'We could hear monstrous screaming, out-and-out wailing.'

The tumult and the SS-men's ear-splitting commands drew out Józef Piwka from neighbouring sector BIIf.

'The braver prisoners and I sneaked out in front of the barrack. We crept about, avoiding the searchlights. We finally made it up against the wall of the bathhouse.'

Only electrified barbed wire separated them from the Zigeunerlager. They saw the SS officers driving out the Gypsies, who were clawing at them, defending themselves.

'We could hear whips cracking, swearing in several languages, crying. Now and again came the shot of a pistol. The defenceless Gypsies were fleeing among the blocks and hiding in the barracks.'

Punches, kicks, and in the midst of it all, the King of Birkenau: Josef Mengele.

It still remained to despatch the sick and the twins. They were still hopeful, because the doctor had ordered them to write ZS on their chests. They didn't know what that meant. It meant that after the gas ('*Zyklon*') they were to be autopsied ('*Sektion*').

Joachimowski: 'The operation concluded shortly after midnight, by which time the entire Gypsy camp had been emptied.'

The Gypsy Marian Pawłowski: 'They went into the ovens, and they came out of the ovens with the fire.'

But the ovens weren't open that night – 2,897 bodies were burned in ditches next to the crematorium. Supposedly they burned for a week.

The hunter

Once upon a time, a Queen asked her looking-glass: 'Mirror, mirror on the wall, who's the fairest one of all?'

And the looking-glass replied: 'My queen, you are the fairest here so true. But Snow White is a thousand times more beautiful than you.'

The Queen was horrified and turned yellow then green with rage. And from that moment, she hated Snow White. Anger and jealousy kept growing in her heart like poisonous herbs, until finally she never had a day or night of peace. So she summoned one of her hunters and said: 'Take the girl to the forest, I wish never to see her again. You are to kill her and bring me her heart as proof.'

The hunter obeyed. He led Snow White into the forest, but when he pulled out his knife to stab it through her innocent heart, the girl burst into tears and started to beg, saying: 'Oh dear hunter, spare my life, I'll go deep into the wild forest and never come home again.'

And she was so beautiful the hunter took pity on her and said: 'Then run away, poor child!'

Wild animals will devour her all the same, he thought to himself, but his heart felt less heavy because it would have grieved him to kill her. And coming across a hare on the road, he killed it, took out its heart, and brought it to the Queen as proof.

One day...

'One day, Plagge didn't come to pick me up. Willy Brachmann told me the Gypsies had been gassed. From then on, I never heard anything more about the Gypsies.'

In flames

Josef Mengele was packing. Papers, papers, papers – data from experiments; examination forms; medical analyses of twins, Lilliputians and disabled people; drawings; charts; photographs. His life's work. And proof of what he'd done.

The camp was emptying out, it was now half its former size. Poles, Russians and Czechs were being sent to work inside the Reich. But in Upper Silesia, German industry still needed slaves. In Auschwitz, Birkenau and the sub-camps, 65,000 people were clinging to life. After 28 November, no more were gassed. Now they were taking logs and pieces of wood meant to be used for burning corpses and chopping them up into small pieces, to be used as fuel for wood gas cars. The vehicles had to be up and running for the evacuation.

The staff alarm sounded at the end of July – the Red Army had captured the camp at Majdanek. The soldiers had seen evidence of war crimes, they'd even captured a few dozen SS officers. This couldn't happen again. The Auschwitz political department was pressuring them to ensure not a single witness or scrap of paper fell into Russian hands. They planned a series of actions: killing the Jews in the Sonderkommandos, disassembling the fittings in the gas chambers and the crematoria, demolishing Crematorium IV and preparing to blow up the three other crematoria, clearing out the warehouses and shipping out the stolen goods.

From December to mid-January, a million and a half pieces of children's, women's and men's clothing were shipped out of 'Canada' – from socks and underpants to furs. Construction materials, the X-ray equipment Dr Horst Schumann had used for his experiments, valuables and anything else that could be was transported out.

They left Crematorium V undisturbed in the event their luck turned on the front. But its products – the ashes and bones – were cleared away. Prisoners ground them up, then threw some into the river Soła and scattered some in the fields. They were ordered to fill in the ditches where corpses had been cremated and cover them with sod, then plant bushes and trees on the spot. They deliberately botched the job, so only a thin layer of earth covers the ashes in the former camp.

The SS officers ordered that the prisoners' identification photos were to vanish in the flames. But Wilhelm Brasse and his friends threw them into the ovens in a tightly-packed mass. This quickly extinguished the fire, preserving 40,000 negatives' worth of faces for posterity.

Paper was even more dangerous than photographs. The staff launched into a frenzy of destruction. Pieces of paper were piled high on the camp roads, and burned in the boiler rooms for the central heating and in office stoves. Records, files, receipts, registers, transport lists of Jews…

But sometimes prisoners managed to protect the paper as well. Tadeusz Joachimowski, Ireneusz Pietrzyk and Henryk Porebski sneaked out registry books for 21,000 Gypsies and buried them. After the war was over, Joachmowski pointed out where they were located.

In mid-January, snow turned the brick barracks of Auschwitz white and covered the frozen ground of Birkenau. At night, the temperature fell far below zero. The next day was chaos in motion: lorries stuffed to bursting, SS officers in plainclothes, the air full of the stench and smoke of burning sheets of paper.

On Wednesday the 17th, just before dawn, Josef Mengele set off towards Gross-Rosen. That same day, the German military withdrew from the rubble of Warsaw, and Governor Hans Frank left Wawel Castle in Kraków with some stolen Rembrandts.

Mengele didn't sully himself by stealing anything. He took only what he thought was his: the most valuable documents from his archive. Sometime later, he hid them in the home of an acquaintance in the town of Gera, then took a big risk getting them back: Nazi-hunters were on his trail.

He left the watercolours in Birkenau.

1946. In Paris with Remus

More than 12 hours had passed since the doctor's escape. Auschwitz was lined up for its last roll call. The prisoners were counted: 67,012 – including children and a few of the emaciated and ill. These were left behind to be killed.

The rest, formed up into columns, marched out of the barbed wire and through the gates, heading westward, passing under the iron sign reading *Arbeit Macht Frei*. Whoever was able wrapped themselves in a blanket, whoever had shoes put them on. They marched, striped uniform by striped uniform. An execution squad followed each huddled group, and geese, cows and horses were driven alongside.

The road led to Loslau (today Wodzisław Śląski), 63 kilometres from Auschwitz. The frost crunched and shots rang out, Alsatians barked and the news went round: 'Auschwitz is coming!' People passed them chicory coffee, water and bread behind the backs of the SS officers.

Local Silesians staged hurried funerals in the wake of this multitude. There were 15,000 prisoners who couldn't hold out. They wouldn't rest in proper graves until after the war. (The youngest victim was Irek Rowiński, buried in the cemetery in Pszczyna. After the Warsaw Uprising, his mother Leokadia was sent to Birkenau while pregnant. On the march, she made it to the village of Poręba. That night while they were stopped, she escaped with two Jewish female prisoners. A woman gave them refuge. When Leokadia gave birth to Irek on Sunday, 21 January, she christened him herself – the priest was too afraid.

The boy lived nine days. He was buried by the village chapel in an empty pasta box.)

Finally, after three days and three nights, the columns were reformed into echelons and the stiff, pale prisoners climbed into open coal wagons. The rail line took them through Ostrawa to work in the camps of Austria and Germany.

Dina Gottliebová was sent to Ravensbrück. There the women were housed in a large tent and slept on a brick floor. Three weeks later, they were transferred again, to a sub-camp in Neustadt-Glewe, but this time, they rode an ordinary passenger train that was even heated. They saw well-tended houses through the window – a rustic German landscape.

The clock struck

Meanwhile in the east, inside the gate with the cut-out letters, the SS officers were coming down from their guard towers and abandoning their camp patrols. Warehouses with piles of suitcases were burning and Wehrmacht soldiers were looting what remained. The prisoners were gathering pickaxes and shovels, dodging chaotic gunfire and forcing their way through the barbed wire to get their hands on winter clothes and food. Some of the working prisoners tended the sick – they fired up the camp kitchen to cook them something hot.

On Friday, 26 January, just after midnight and according to plan, Crematorium V was blown sky-high. Now the killing would be left to chance.

The well-known photographer Ryszard Horowitz (born to a Jewish family in Kraków and now living in the United States), who was six at the time: 'A group of us children had been lined up and were going to be shot. Then an officer arrived on a motorcycle. I remember him getting off the bike and saying that the Russians were coming, were really close, and that all the German soldiers had to leave at once.'

Meanwhile, Lieutenant Yuri Ilyinsky was storming the Auschwitz rail junction: 'There were three or four bunkers with machine guns by the station and on the tracks. They kept us pinned to the snow for half an hour. They were doing a good job, this was no improvized position, so we couldn't even lift up our heads. Someone blew up one of the bunkers with grenades, our tanks demolished another, and then we sprang across the tracks and we got them. In the distance I could see guard towers and densely-packed barracks'.

They approached. There were smoking ruins and a thick, black cloud swirling at the edge of the camp. They went in.

'Dead bodies. For a soldier on the offensive, dead bodies are nothing special, but it was different here. These people hadn't died in battle. There was pile of emaciated corpses, already covered in snow. Further along was a group who'd been executed. Men and women – and beyond them, dead children. There was a corpse sat up against a wall with its head thrown back and snow in its open mouth. There were children behind barbed wire. That experience made the greatest impression on my soldiers and me.'

They didn't know what they'd captured. Auschwitz had probably just been a point of German defence in the Red Army's orders – part of a coal basin, which the soldiers of the First Belarusian Front were meant to take intact. They attacked Auschwitz and Birkenau simultaneously, losing 231 of their own in the skirmishes. They found more than 600 corpses – as well as survivors from 20 countries.

Anna Chomicz, a prisoner hiding in a barrack, heard an explosion near the camp gates. She worked up the courage to take a look outside. She saw Red Army soldiers with rifles, ready to shoot.

'Immediately, we hoisted a sheet up the flagpole with stripes sewn on in the shape of a red cross. I called out to the scouts, saying: *zdravstvuyte, pobediteli*' – 'greetings, victors'.

'*Uzhe vy svobodnye,*' came the response. You're free now.

27 January 1945. Saturday, at three in the afternoon. A moment of silence, a moment with no name.

The road to Loslau was not yet a 'death march', or Joseph Mengele the 'angel of death', or the camp a 'factory of death'. It was yet undecided that 'kapo' was spelled with a *k* and not a *c*. The 'criminality lying dormant in German culture' was yet to be remarked in Communist propaganda. The paradox that 'Stalinist totalitarianism gave freedom to the prisoners of the Nazi regime' was yet unemphasized. The Jewish boy in the tilted cap holding his hands in the air, the old man wearing a Star of David, the bulldozer pushing corpses into a pit, the mountains of hair and eyeglasses, the gates and railway tracks in Birkenau were all unknown. The world would discover these later, if it so wished.

The icons, signs and symbols were yet to be born. Now, for a single moment, there was joy.

The clock struck. In Ryszard Horowitz's childlike recollection, the officer got off his motorcycle, the Germans fled and the Russians immediately appeared.

'They had a film crew with them and lined us up once again, having us walk through the barbed wire towards the camera. They also stood us next to the gallows – because it was such a striking background, I suppose – and filmed us there. After that, they took me to an orphanage, to Kraków.'

In truth, the Soviet film crew arrived a few days later. The cameraman Alexander Vorontsov filmed an hour-long documentary – chronicling the liberation of an already-liberated camp, staged for film and with voiceovers. The children were once again dressed up in striped uniforms and several times they rolled up their sleeves, stared straight into the camera and showed their tattooed numbers. The Nuremberg judges watched this.

But first, the Russians screened the film in the cinemas of Kraków. Regina Horowitz, Ryszard's mother, went to see it. There her son flickered on the screen.

They were reunited the next day.

Spoon-feeding three times a day

On the gloomy, cold Monday morning of 29 January, Tadeusz Chowaniec, who later became a doctor in the town of Oświęcim, decided to head for the camp. But not to loot: he explained in his memoirs 'some violent inner power' was propelling him towards the gates. Two years before, his father had been a prisoner in Block 9. They took him away to Buchenwald. Was he alive? What did he look like? The same, perhaps, as those in Auschwitz.

The block was wide open. Inside, figures with translucent, apathetic faces made deliberately limited movements, with the white aprons of Soviet doctors everywhere around them. Chowaniec felt ashamed, finding it hard to look at the prisoners. Though the nurses managed to smile, he had doubts: 'Are they receiving effective care? Is it possible for these walking skeletons to get their lives back?'

The sick lay several to a pallet. They were tortured by diarrhoea from starvation and generally something else too, most often tuberculosis. In Birkenau, they shovelled faeces from the dirt floors. Water for cleaning, washing and cooking was carried from distant wells and fire ponds, or snow was melted. In those first days, there was no one even to bury the corpses. Luckily, volunteers rapidly joined the Russian medical team. On the initiative of Dr Józef Bellert from Warsaw, the Polish Red Cross Camp Hospital was established.

The nurses would find bread under the sleeping pallets, because the prisoners didn't believe they'd receive another piece the next day. Food was given in doses, like medicine. They were spoon-fed puréed potato soup three times a day. The word 'bath' would set them running. It was the same with injections – the women were afraid of phenol. The children didn't understand it was possible for someone to die at home – they thought you had to be killed.

The youngest children, those younger than 15, numbered about 450. There were also plenty of Jewish twins, usually from the last transports. These children had survived because prisoners managed to hide them. Many didn't know their names or nationalities. They were usually fated to end up in orphanages and children's villages in Poland, Israel and the USSR. Few ever found their families.

That same cloudy, cold Monday, Stanisław Krcz, the young boy from the railway family whose sister Genia had died, arrived at Birkenau. Or maybe he came that Tuesday? He couldn't remember. But it probably was no later than that.

Karolina Krcz, Stanisław's mother, in an account given in September 1960: 'The local population went to the camp right after liberation to get firewood or whatever useful items they had there, and my son Stanisław managed to bring a child back from the camp. Aside from our woes under the occupation, I was in pain from the loss of my daughter. So right after the liberation of Auschwitz, on our neighbours' advice, my husband decided that we'd take in a child who'd survived that hell.'

Stanisław supported the decision.

'I understood that a girl to take the place of our dearly departed Genia could save my mother from her depression.'

In the barrack, there were 60 toddlers plus one woman – a barrack warden of about 50. She was from Łódź – nothing more is known of her. She pointed a girl out to Stanisław.

'At that time, Ewa had a large head, a big belly and a giant scab on her forehead. I think she was all swollen. She had rickets, which back then we called the English disease.'

She'd arrived at the camp a few months before with her parents and likely a brother as well. It was Hungarian transport – 400,000 Jews had gone to the gas in less than two months. Ewa's mother was beaten with rifle butts on the ramp, and it seems she was forbidden to bring her daughter with her. By some miracle, a prisoner smuggled the girl into the women's camp, telling the block warden the child belonged to a famous, wealthy family. Someone probably looked after her in Birkenau, acquaintances or distant relatives, and at the end, other prisoners. Now she was all alone. Apparently she was called Stoltz. Or maybe Schulz?

Who knows whether it was the child's appearance or the story that touched Stanisław. He said succinctly: 'A barrack warden I'd never met convinced me to take Ewa and adopt her as my baby sister.'

It's three kilometres from Birkenau to Oświęcim, too far for a toddler. Stanisław was in a hurry for his mother to have something to devote her time and thinking to as soon as possible. He must have carried Ewa piggyback.

Ewa for Genia

Every detail was etched on Karolina Krcz's memory.

'My son came in holding a child and saying, "Here, mum, so you can finally stop being sad for Genia." The child was female, no more than two years old. On her feet were tall red boots and she was dressed a blue velvet dress, a red jumper and a coat with black and grey pinstripes.'

Karolina heated up some water.

'She had hair matted with filth and a sort of pus-covered scab. Her head was covered in lice. Her whole body was terribly filthy and covered in tiny ulcers. Her eyes were red and gummy. At that time, you could read the camp number A-5116 on her left arm very clearly. After her first bath, I didn't think we'd be able to keep her alive.'

They lay down in bed together.

'After sleeping through the night, I found lice crawling out of the scab on her head, and she couldn't open her eyes at all.'

Ewa wailed in *Lagersprache*, a hodgepodge of different languages. Most of it was German, since in the camp, today – and tomorrow – depended on knowing that language.

Stanisław: 'My mother was in mourning, but she threw all her energy into saving Ewa. She started bathing her in all kinds of herbs, salts and medicines. Every morning, Ewa would wake up crying, terrified because she couldn't see. We were afraid she might be this way not just due to starvation, but because something had been put in her eyes as well. It seemed impossible someone's eyes could produce so much sticky pus. We were even more terrified when the doctor confirmed our fears.'

That doctor was Bernard Komraus, a Silesian. A German work order had thrown him into Auschwitz. He was a GP in the health centre, where he'd treated Poles and Germans, as well as French, Norwegian and Dutch prisoners in the I.G. Farben chemical plant. The police and army guarded the grounds, and he kept his nearest and dearest – his wife Irena and her sister Marcella – in his surgery. His other sister, Gertruda Franke, perished in the camp. The young doctor smuggled medicine into Auschwitz through secret channels. After the liberation, he also offered his assistance.

There were many people of goodwill in Oświęcim and nearby Brzeszcze. They created small hospitals for around 150 former prisoners. Maria Bobrzecka, who owned a chemist's shop, supplied them free of charge. In Brzeszcze, women and children were treated for tuberculosis, and one of the nurses became infected and died. The sick received assistance at home and food collections were organized in Kraków. Some did what the Krcz family had done: they took a child to raise.

Stainsław: 'With Dr Komeraus's help, Ewa's eyes stopped oozing pus. She began to regain some colour and look more like other children her age. The doctor took special care of Ewa, and since he knew she was from the camp, he never accepted a fee.'

Karolina didn't give up.

'After bathing and scrubbing her every day I managed to fight off the head lice and heal the ulcers. Because right after the war it was hard to get food, especially milk, eggs and butter, I did the rounds of the neighbouring villages, where I would trade various things for them, usually successfully. Thanks to intensive feeding, day by day, Ewa got healthier, stronger and more beautiful.'

Stanisław was somewhat concerned.

'Her physical state was improving, but scars remained on her psyche. For a long time, Ewa was afraid of dogs. The tiniest puppy would send her into nervous shock. When she saw a dog she would always cry out in fear, then run away and hide. Even later on, she kept her fear of dogs, although she suppressed it. She didn't know how to play. On several occasions I brought her a toy – at most she would stare at it, then drop it and pay it no attention. In the company of other children, she was introverted and serious beyond her years, she didn't know how to be cheerful. Sometimes she would turn strangely pensive, as though her mind were elsewhere.'

Ewa's oppressive anxiety started to slowly abate, which pleased her big brother. Operation 'Ewa for Genia' had been a success. In the future, he would often talk about how he'd gone all the way to Birkenau for an orphan.

He had a memento of that day: some Gypsy portraits painted in watercolours.

'The older prisoners were surprised to see a young person like me taking it on himself to bring one of the children out of the camp. One of them simply shoved some rolled-up paintings into my hand as a present. He explained he'd taken them from an SS office or barrack. I don't remember if he said anything about who'd made them. I examined these fabulous portraits over and over again, trying my hardest to work out what the signature said.'

The letters were tiny and neat. Something like 'Dinah' or 'Dinal'.

Inventory

Not long after liberation, the ex-prisoner Eugeniusz Nosal was working on the grounds of the Bauhof – the camp construction yard. He spotted a loaded Soviet train.

'There were all kinds of machines, wooden materials, cabinets, tables, ammunition cases. On one of the wagons was a bed from a camp barrack, and shoved in next to it was the sign reading *Arbeit Macht Frei*. The driver stopped when I asked. I inquired if he had something to give the soldier guarding the wagons to ransom the sign with. Because everything was being shipped off – no one was asking permission. It was the spoils of war and had to be taken away.'

The driver pressed a quarter-litre bottle of moonshine into the guard's hand. He and Nosal pulled the sign off and hid it in the town hall.

The camp was under Russian control – it wasn't transferred to the Polish authorities until spring of 1946. It was being stripped because in the wake of the Red Army, so-called 'trophy commissions' would come and take away anything of value. That included people: specialists to help man the evacuated assembly lines. The Department of Liquidation in Kraków seized the remainder of Auschwitz's assets. It sold the wire, bars, pipes, pots, plates, rags, cutlery, and fuel.

'Inventory from Auschwitz to Rebuild the Country', declared the newspaper *Echo Krakowa*. It listed '29 wagons of bricks, steel, metal sheeting, rails, trolleys, wood and coke sent to Andrychów; 3 wagons of steel to the Kabel electrical plant in Kraków; 16 wagons of bricks and steel to the Polish State Railways in Kraków; 5 wagons of steel and tin for the Craftsmen's Guild in Kraków; 65 wagons of steel, bricks, metal sheeting and rails for Warsaw and 12 wagons of wood for the Woodworking Federation.'

The barracks in Birkenau were dismantled and the wood divvied up. The stage where a 12-year-old Czech girl had enchanted the children with Snow White and the dwarfs from the film was sent off who knows where.

But the stronger prisoners had already left Auschwitz by then, on their own or on specially provided horse carts. The *Dziennik Polski* newspaper in Kraków sponsored return journeys. The road homeward for one group of Jews from western and southern Europe passed through Odessa, followed by a ship to Marseille. Still others stayed in Soviet refugee camps.

The war was continuing, and Dina Gottliebová was painting numbers on aeroplanes in Ravensbrück. Bomber squadrons were launching from the airport near Neustadt-Glewe. In April, they flew over Berlin, their engines roaring, drawing long, yellow stripes in the air, unlike the red trails of the Soviet planes. Finally, even that had ceased.

The French Riviera and a cactus skirt

The SS-men retreated on 2 May. Zofia Posmysz, author of the novel *The Passenger*, said in an interview: 'The camp gates were closed. The crowd of women couldn't get it open, so some men arrived, Frenchmen I think, from near the camp. They forced the gates and the crowd rushed out into the open – then suddenly stopped. Finally, the first woman looked around and slowly headed back towards the barbed wire. The next ones followed her.'

Years later, Erich Fromm's book *Escape from Freedom* would remind her of the liberation.

That evening, the Americans arrived with parcels from UNRRA, and before long shipped in more supplies. The next day they said, 'We're withdrawing behind the river Elbe. The Russians are on their way here, come with us.' Some obeyed.

Dina and Jana wanted to go to Czechoslovakia instead. How might that journey have looked? Crossing the Front, most likely in a group for safety. Soldiers attacking the women. Barricading themselves in barns the soldiers would threaten to burn down. If one of them knew Russian, checking in with the local NKVD command each time they stopped for the night. 'Please protect us, because your soldiers will rape us.' Sometimes being granted bodyguards.

We only know some dogs accompanied Dina on her return journey.

'I'd always had them. After the liberation, a dachshund adopted us and we crossed Germany together. Then later I found an Alsatian, and this Alsatian always found itself something to eat on its own, because it was healthy. Finally, the Russians loaded us into lorries. I couldn't take such a big dog, somehow I managed with the dachshund. The Alsatian ran after us so long it broke my heart.'

Finally, on 17 June, Dina and Jana found themselves in the golden city of Prague. Did they make a stop in Brno? They had no key, so did they knock at their own door? Whom did they find in their flat? How were they received? Why didn't they stay?

Before the war, mother and daughter would go once a year to the synagogue in Brno for Yom Kippur – on an empty stomach, because of the fast.

Dina: 'There was a lady who brought an apple with cloves in it to the synagogue, supposedly so the aroma would distract her from hunger. But I think she took little bites from the apple.'

Now how many Jews could gather together to pray? How did it feel to return to an empty house? No one who'd seen your childhood, no uncles, aunts, girlfriends from school or boys who pulled your hair. Only the dreadful past was evidence you were alive. And were you to dwell on that past forever?

You had to be reborn, bind yesterday to today and tomorrow with strong thread. Dig up something positive, something to counter it. Defend yourself against the horrible memories with even a single one that led away from despair.

This is only speculation – Dina rarely spoke about private concerns. Not long ago, she was still giving scores of interviews – she was questioned about Theresienstadt, the portraits of the Gypsies and Snow White. But never what came after the war, never her feelings.

On the street in Prague, she ran into a fellow-prisoner named Alfréd Mílk. He asked her for a portrait, just as she'd done of the Gypsies. She painted him one.

She practised drawing. Her realistic testimonial drawings of Birkenau illustrated the book *Továrna na smrt* (*Factory of Death*), by Ota Kraus and Erich Kulka.

She ran into Miša Grünwald on a tram, along with his father, a doctor. They were living on Rybná Street. They came to visit her with a bouquet of roses.

Her friend Karl Klinger made an appearance too – he was the man she'd got engaged to in the loft over the stable in Theresienstadt. He'd died in Dachau right before the liberation. Just before his death, he'd jotted down a few words.

'I received a tattered piece of paper. "I legally declare Dina Gottliebová to be my wife."'

Was she a widow?

In 1946, she left Czechoslovakia.

'I had no family there, only mum and I had survived. Two of my mother's brothers were in London – they'd served in the RAF and were living permanently in France. We joined them when they returned to Paris.'

After the camps in the East – where you scrubbed out your period stains (so long as you were having your period) with dust and stones, where a litre of water in a bowl had to suffice for a whole bath, where you'd wash your private parts in front of other people – they went on holiday on the French Riviera.

There's a picture. Slender, mischievously smiling Dina – her hair in curls, in a white bustier with a fresh sprig of leaves attached to it, in a patterned skirt with cactuses, and sandals on her shapely feet. In the background: palm trees, elegant passers-by, a limousine – you can almost hear the clink of poker chips and the roar of the sea. Dina's hand is resting on her mother's arm. Petite Jana Gottliebová is attempting to look cheerful in a pastel-coloured suit with an elegant handbag. It's no use – that isn't a smile, it's a grimace.

In Paris, Dina once again signed up for painting classes. She went for walks with her cocker-spaniel Remus. There was no way they could starve. A film studio was making a puppet version of *Alice in Wonderland*, so she applied for a job. Right then they had a vacancy – an artist from America was searching for an assistant. He was 30-odd, energetic and quite handsome. He introduced himself: 'Art Babbitt.'

He'd worked with Walt Disney, training his team and creating many cartoon characters. By 1942, America considered him 'The Greatest Animator Ever'. He'd drawn *Snow White*.

The film Dina had watched seven times before they took her to the camp.

And the last the children had seen.

Dina, to a German journalist: 'Do you happen to believe in chance? This was destiny.'

1973. From Hollywood to Auschwitz and Back

Dina Gottliebová-Babbitt stepped through the camp gate once more. On 28 June 1973, she made her way to Auschwitz I. She saw the sign reading *Arbeit Macht Frei* for the first time with her own eyes. She didn't know that almost thirty years earlier, a cart driver had bought that hunk of scrap from a Russian in exchange for some moonshine.

She was arriving from a different world. Over there, the Vietnam War was underway and flower children were protesting, the clouds of Watergate were hanging over Richard Nixon, Pink Floyd had released *Dark Side of the Moon*, the towers of the World Trade Center – the tallest buildings on earth – were rising into the sky, and in Manhattan, Motorola was boasting a prototype of today's mobile phone. The Western Bloc was burgeoning: Denmark, Ireland and the United Kingdom had joined the European Community. Relations between Israel and its Arab neighbours looked bad as usual (Egypt and Syria were gearing up for the Yom Kippur War), meanwhile Willy Brandt had become the first German Chancellor to travel to Jerusalem.

This news didn't make the headlines of Polish newspapers, which were reserved for the Communist Party. In Poland, fans of Western hit music would chat at night by the radio with their tape recorders running. The presenters knew this full well, so did their best not to interrupt the music. The whole country – from cleaning ladies to the First Secretary of the

Communist Party – was humming *Małgośka* by Maryla Rodowicz. On television, the first episode of *I'm Betting on Tolek Banan* was airing. In Chorzów stadium – the nation's largest – Poland beat England 2–0, a success the Party machine was milking for every drop of patriotic value. The Fiat 126p – the 'Polski Fiat' – was going into production, the IL-62 *Nicolaus Copernicus* made the first transatlantic flight from Warsaw to New York, and the workers and Party Leader Edward Gierek were making the slogan 'Poland the tenth world power' into reality. The country was allied with the Soviet Union, so Leonid Brezhnev made a fraternal visit. (Two years later, Gierek would welcome him to the new Warsaw Central Station and escort him to the country's first VIP lounge. They'd exit through the first automatic doors in Poland, an object of fascination for Warsaw locals. To and fro, back and forth.)

Dina lived on the other side of the Iron Curtain, on Los Tilos Road in Hollywood. In the spring, a letter arrived from the Auschwitz-Birkenau State Museum: 'Only after thorough investigation have we been able to verify your authorship and obtain the above address, which we are uncertain is still current. If this letter reaches you, we request that you send a biographical note with as many specific details as possible regarding the circumstances and conditions under which the portraits of the Gypsy prisoners were painted.'

Dina was delighted.

'I couldn't believe the paintings had survived. And it seemed like a miracle that I would hold them in my hands again.'

She had everything planned. In June, she would be in Europe, in Paris, so she'd take the opportunity to make a quick trip to Poland. 'Can I count on an official invitation?' she asked the museum, because perhaps the Communists wouldn't give her a visa without support.

And now she was walking along the camp road, hoping to get her watercolours out of there. She'd brought a solidly-built briefcase, so that nothing would happen to them in transit. She looked for the building housing the main office.

The tidy, boxy, one-storey barracks were spaced out perfectly evenly like children's blocks. There was plumbing and electricity, everything was spotless. What kind of impression did this convey? It looked like it wasn't so bad at all here. People probably counted the buildings and concluded there was no way the Germans could have killed so many there, because there was hardly any space for all those dead people, no question about it, though who can say how tightly they crammed people in. Less than 20,000, well, certainly no more than a 100,000.

Why had the Poles chosen here to build their museum? Why not Birkenau? The railway tracks, the cattle-cars, the SS officer's economical gestures on the ramp to the left or the right, the gas chambers, the crematoria, the barracks, the latrines. Genocide.

Did they talk about Jews here at all?

The body goes in here... zzzip

A small number of foreign tours would come by coach from Kraków. A few took taxis and parked by the camp itself, which is probably how Dina arrived. The town of Oświęcim would flash past the window, and the camp might as well have been on the moon – the tourists had no idea where they were.

But Oświęcim was a model town of the socialist future. Workers toiled in the huge chemical plants in nearby Dwory, and the new Chemików estate housed three-quarters of the town's population. The plants financed healthcare, sport, holidays, summer camps and classes in the community centre – as they did everywhere. But an indoor ice-skating rink and an indoor Olympic-sized pool had been constructed as well. You wouldn't find that in any other town like this one. That was because no other local Party bosses got such regular visits from the Grand Pooh-Bahs, whom they could approach directly about making investments.

The Party and the government were drafting a vision of tomorrow, but also remembering yesterday. The past was cordoned off, locked into a couple tiny places, because, after all, everything here was contaminated. Auschwitz-Birkenau, 40 sub-camps, I.G. Farben…. The museum only got enough space so that everywhere else, day-to-day socialist life – with its queues for toilet roll and coffee – could proceed.

Viewed from above, the concept was evident. In the east of the town was the future – housing estates and factories – and in the west, the past – the museum. Between these two symbols, right in the middle, stood a monument to the Red Army.

The authorities conceived of the past in their own way: it was meant to serve them. There were proposals, which some prisoners supported, to demolish the camp, plough it under, put up a monument and have done with it. The Party started looking into the matter. Why let such a piece of land go to waste?

In 1948, Jerzy Putrament – the 'literary commissary' as the émigré poet Marian Hemar called him – travelled to Auschwitz. Putrament, a former vice-president of the fascist All-Polish Youth Union and anti-Semite, had performed a *volte face*, exchanging his nationalism for the *Internationale*. After the war he was the power behind the throne of the Polish Writers'

Union and ran a number of literary journals. In *The Captive Mind*, Czesław Miłosz called Putrament 'Gamma':

> Gamma became a Stalinist. I think he felt uneasy writing his passionless poetry. He was not made for literature. Whenever he settled down before a sheet of paper he sensed a void in himself. He was incapable of experiencing the intense joys of a writer, either those of the creative process or those of work accomplished. The period between his nationalism and his Stalinism was for him a limbo, a period of senseless trials and disillusionment.

Upon his return from Auschwitz, in the pages of the weekly magazine *Rebirth*, Putrament sneered at the young people who had survived Auschwitz and were now leading tours round the camp.

> One walks up to a building and declaims: 'Here, ladies and gentlemen, is the only surviving crematorium. The body goes in here... zzzip.'
>
> He crosses to the lavatory adjacent. 'Here, ladies and gentlemen, is a gas chamber with a capacity of up to seven hundred people. Zyklon-B gas, at a temperature of twenty-seven degrees... Here was the opening in the door through which the SS officer...'

These stocky, sunburnt tour guides had worked out a crude repertoire and stammered it out for the undiscriminating public. The horrifying subject matter verged on the grotesque.

The result: a lack of seriousness, and parts were like something out of the Grand Guignol. If Auschwitz had been in America, there would have been someone called Cook selling excursions with added attractions – undressing for the gas,

SS truncheons, a number on your forearm for an extra fee. Everyone would get a handful of ashes as a souvenir.

As for these tour guides: why keep these young boys in the camp? They should be pulling the past up by the roots. 'Let them go out and build.'

Poles protested, especially former prisoners.

The camp didn't get demolished, or ploughed under, or turned into socialist factories – which is good, beacause they would never have turned a profit. The authorities paid a pittance for this cabinet of curiosities, or relics or reliquary, call it what you will. And the museum often proved useful. There, comrades from the Eastern Bloc could raise the cry: 'Never again!'

Where else did the word 'peace' carry such weight?

Preserve

At the beginning it was a big mess. In spring, just after the liberation, the farmers driven out of the Auschwitz-Birkenau Zone of Interest returned for their property. They sowed the fields fertilized with human ashes, they rebuilt, pulling wheelbarrows of bricks from the camp. There was such poverty that the children in the orphanage in Bielsko-Biała were going barefoot, so their carer took them to Auschwitz, where from the piles of shoes in the camp, each child took a pair for themselves. Next to the train station, a shopkeeper wrapped marmalade jars in scribble-covered paper – camp documents about transports.

There was a lot of discussion locally about the hustlers who made a fortune off Jewish prisoners during the war, and streams of diamonds and precious metals flowing out through the barbed wire. Word got round and attracted looters, and what once was Birkenau transformed into the Klondike.

Fresh molehills popped up everywhere. *Tygodnik Powszechny* revealed that 'the looting operation has set up an entire gold mine in the camp. Rows of "poor-man's mineshafts" can be seen, where individual looters have carried out their searches, and somewhat further along are the large technical systems of whole mining enterprises. No expense has been spared. Pipelines have been built, bringing water to search through the ashes.' When they couldn't dig any deeper, Soviet pilots stationed in nearby Balice bombarded the valleys of death in exchange for booze, uncovering further layers of earth.

The farmers were chucked out and the grave robbers driven away.

People from across Europe – widows and widowers, families and children in mourning – made pilgrimages to Birkenau. In 1946: 100,000. A year later: 170,000. No matter there was no way to get there and nowhere to spend the night. They beheld a shocking scene: a forest of chimneys as far as the eye could see, roofs caving in and listing walls. Looting, mother nature and the passage of time had taken their toll. A city of 300 barracks had disappeared.

Then the decision was taken: let's gather what remains of the wood, build a makeshift camp sector and tend to the ruins of the crematoria.

Birkenau would be a preserve.

This was no accident. Auschwitz I paid better dividends for Communist agitprop. That was where Polish political prisoners and intellectuals had met their end – lawyers, teachers, doctors and Father Maksymilian Kolbe, who volunteered to die in a starvation cell in place of another prisoner. Auschwitz stirred emotions in every family – it was a fresh wound.

The grandees of Warsaw, under Moscow's heel, wanted to make the most of this. Their plan was so audacious it boggled the mind. The goal: to appropriate an international symbol of wartime suffering, inscribe it into the history of Polish martyrdom and brandish genocide as proof of identity, since, after all, the rigged elections that formalized the Communists' power had not yet been held.

The Soviet prosecutors on the war crimes investigation commission started with a deception. They calculated four million people had been killed in Auschwitz-Birkenau, then they bundled up the captured files and went home. The grounds, and the memories, were handed over to the Poles, who never challenged the number of victims because this mountain of corpses diverted the Free World's attention from the Gulag. And when Western historians declared that 'only' a million had died in the camp, the investigation was not reopened because the larger the mass grave, the better it was politically. The ashes and bones were (and still remain) political tools.

Sheep among the camomile

The mess was disgraceful. This sight, so shocking for the families of the dead, needed to be brought under control. In 1947, Tadeusz Wąsowicz and his team arrived at the former camp. Not long before, they'd been queuing up for swede soup and shrinking from the gaze of the SS-men. Now they were to tend to the camp. It was not an easy task – the prisoners preferred to forget. Returning to Auschwitz of their own free will, living there, eating, sleeping and loving there, was inconceivable.

The men, most of them pre-war Boy Scouts imprisoned in the camp for conspiracy, worked enthusiastically seven days a week, morning until night, for next to nothing. They were driven by the conviction that it was their duty. They treated the camp as documentary evidence, and privately considered it sacred ground. Every task was urgent, they all did what they could and didn't complain. But they too had to survive the post-war shortages. Potatoes grew in the quarantine sector, sheep grazed on the camomile, there was a chicken run in the guardroom of Auschwitz I, and horses once again stood in the stables.

There were hundreds of small things to do on the site – the ceremonial opening in June was approaching. In the distance, grand political strategies were being shaped.

The West was planning to end the occupation of Germany and create a German state. Stalin was opposed, angling for a Germany under his control. To halt the expansion of the USSR, the Americans thought up the Marshall Plan, which offered financial aid for Europe – including Poland. Stalin once again said no, and the Polish Communists supported him. Somehow, they had to put this decision into words and explain it to their countrymen.

The Communist Prime Minister Józef Cyrankiewicz, a former camp resistance fighter, chose the setting: Auschwitz, at the packed ceremonial opening of the museum.

He spoke. 'The tragedy of Auschwitz, a monstrous factory of death, should not dissolve into private, individual perspectives. We must be able to re-forge it into the will to struggle for a better world.'

Obliging journalists picked up the theme. They explained that Britain and America lacked such a desire and were constantly threatening the peace, that they'd already forgotten 'what beast slumbered between the Rhine and the Elbe', and were even 'trying to placate it' with financial support.

Stalin desired a better world, so for the Eastern bloc, Auschwitz would forever be 'a warning against a nation whose every action is in opposition to human dignity'.

In his speech, the Prime Minister called the former prisoners 'soldiers in mankind's holiest cause – the struggle for freedom'. They were martyrs 'for our freedom and yours', children of the Polish Mother, sons of the Christ of Nations. It was nationalist-style Polish Messianism embellished with Bolshevik platitudes.

But what of those who went straight from the cattle cars to the gas chambers? They had only asphyxiated. They had not died in the service of an idea, they did not lend themselves to mythmaking. On the contrary, they posed a problem.

Throughout the war, support for the prisoners in Auschwitz had come from Kraków, but there, on a Saturday in August 1945, a group of hooligans showered stones on a synagogue. Someone seized one of the little troublemakers, who cried, 'Help, the Jews want to murder me!' The women running stalls at the flea market told macabre stories about children being killed to make matzo. A witch-hunt began. 'You miserable sods, if Hitler couldn't finish you off then we'll finish you all off. You're on Polish land and you're still murdering Polish children,' remarked one police officer. A year later, 42 Jews were killed and 40 injured in the Kielce pogrom. By 1947, a thousand Jewish Holocaust survivors had been murdered in post-war Poland.

Many Poles had no particular sympathy for their plight – either under Hitler or their new rulers. They thought it was the Jews who were packing patriotic Poles off to prison. The more they had on their own consciences, the more fervently they nattered about a Jewish-Communist conspiracy. After all, it was true many Jews worked in the Ministry of Public

Security (although even more wished to break free from the Communists' chains and go to America or Palestine). For the authorities, putting emphasis on Jewish suffering would be shooting themselves in the foot. Better to stick to the version that said three million Poles had died in the camp, encourage the people to take revenge and terrify them with the image of the Teutonic enemy. That way it was harder for Soviets crimes – the Katyń Massacre of 20,000 Polish military officers, the NKVD killings and the annexation of Eastern Poland – to break through the din.

The museum had no problem with Jewish people, just with the word 'Jew'. It was the Nazis who'd divided people into races. Besides, at that time, each country counted its victims by nationality.

By that standard, who had died in the camp? This was the list: Americans, Austrians, Britons, Belgians, Bulgarians, one Chinese, Croats, Czechs, Dutchmen, one Egyptian, Frenchmen, Germans, Greeks, Gypsies, Hungarians, Italians, Lithuanians, Latvians, Norwegians, one Persian, Poles, Russians, Romanians, Slovaks, Spaniards, Swiss, Turks, Yugoslavs, and Palestinian Jews.

And they're arming murderers in West Germany

The museum's first exhibition in 1947 didn't minimize the torment of European Jews (thanks to the efforts of the Central Committee of Polish Jews – which was then still in existence). It merely suggested the Poles had it just as bad. Religious garb from all faiths, prosthetic limbs, shoes and hair were on display in Block 4. At the end of the corridor stood a cross, lit from below. For some, it was a symbol of suffering, for others – of Roman Catholic usurpation.

Tadeusz Wąsowicz died, and Stalinism drove his team out of the museum. The new museum director spent more time at the county council than Auschwitz. Prime Minister Cyrankiewicz re-forged a few episodes from his time in the resistance into an image of himself as an Auschwitz fighter. For decades he stood frozen in the pose of St. George: revere me, I battled the Nazi dragon in hell.

He was aided by Communist research and propaganda, proponents of which had spent years working on the subject. They rubbed out the figure of Captain Witold Pilecki and drew in Cyrankiewicz. Pilecki had gone to Auschwitz of his own free will in 1940, where he'd founded the Union of Military Organizations (known by its Polish acronym ZOW) and authored the first report on genocide in the camp. A laundry work squad smuggled it out to the Warsaw headquarters of the Secret Polish Army. Then the report made its way through Sweden to the West. Cyrankiewicz didn't belong to the ZOW. That doesn't mean he disgraced himself in the camp, quite the contrary. He'd apparently been an idealist once.

He was a ladies' man from Kraków, an eternal student, intelligent and eloquent. He'd joined the Polish Socialist Party before the war. When Dino Grandi, the Foreign Minister of Fascist Italy, came to the Jagiellonian University, Cyrankiewicz gave him a bouquet of red roses after his speech. 'Please lay them on the graves of socialists murdered by the Fascist regime.' Furious, Grandi took out his wallet and handed Cyrankiewicz a wad of notes, to buy roses for the graves of Fascists murdered in Poland. It was a marvellous scandal, perfect for the local press.

Cyrankiewicz also showed bravery under the Occupation. In early 1941, he saved the life of Jan Karski, the legendary courier of the Union for Armed Struggle (ZWZ), who brought information about the camps to the west. At that time, Karski was imprisoned in Nowy Sącz and being tortured by the Gestapo. 'I could no longer withstand the torture, so I attempted to cut my veins open with a razor I had hidden in the sole of my shoe,' he recalled. Incapacitated, he ended up in hospital, where underground activists sent by Cyrankiewicz helped him escape.

Finally, Cyrankiewicz himself was sent to Auschwitz. He worked in the camp hospital registry and was a leader of the Combat Organization under the nom-de-guerre 'Rot'. This underground cell was made up of 140 imprisoned socialists. Rot didn't just fight for his own survival in the camp, he arranged medicine and food for the ill and sent reports to the outside. After the death march, American soldiers liberated him from Mauthausen. The majority of the Polish Socialist Party's leaders chose to go to the West. Cyrankiewicz returned to Poland.

Piotr Lipiński cited an incident recalled by the political scientist Professor Michał Śliwy: 'Cyrankiewicz admitted to me he'd endured so much during the occupation that after the war he just wanted a normal life. Eating, drinking and having fun with girls.' The Communists gave him that chance.

He didn't protest when Stalinist judges gave Captain Pilecki a show trial and condemned him to death. The sentence was carried out on 15 May 1948 with a shot to the back of the head. But for 20-odd years to come, Cyrankiewicz ate, drank and philandered.

He became hated for the words he directed at the workers of Poznań during the 1956 uprising: 'Any provocateur or lunatic daring to raise his hand against the people's government may rest assured the people's government will chop that hand off, for the sake of the working class, for the sake of the working peasants and the intelligentsia, for the sake of the struggle to raise our people's standard of living, for the sake of bringing greater democracy to our lives, for the sake of our homeland.' Such eloquence – Cyrankiewicz was considered a master of the Polish language.

In retirement, the West embraced him as a member of the presidium of the World Peace Council in Helsinki.

Under Stalin, the Auschwitz exhibitions also focused on harmonious co-existence, though of a particular nature. Headings such as: 'The Fight for Peace' and 'Imperialism Unmasked', captions screaming 'Forty million unemployed in Marshall Plan countries', one poster with a tortured prisoner in a striped uniform with the caption: 'And in West Germany the Anglo-Saxon imperialists are arming murderers once again'.

Then came the Thaw, and former prisoners made their way to Auschwitz once more. The 10th anniversary of the liberation was approaching and many delegations from across Europe were coming to Auschwitz. The political hay being made in the former camp suddenly seemed over the top.

Kazimierz Smoleń, a camp writer who studied law in Lublin after the war described it thus: 'Some of my friends and I were summoned to the cultural department of the Party Central Committee. I didn't know why they wanted me to go, because I had nothing to do with the Party. At the meeting, I learned there was going to be an exhibition in Auschwitz and we were all being transferred there to work on it. We lived in primitive conditions, in three barracks outside the barbed wire of the main camp.'

Smoleń took over the museum, but the new exhibition of 1955 had little effect on the image of Auschwitz. During the May Day parade in Warsaw, ranks of former prisoners marched past the reviewing stand in striped uniforms, and, through megaphones, announcers emphasized that Communists from many countries were murdered in the camp.

It was a new generation, but the same story of the past.

It's me: A-5116

'My name is Ewa Krcz. That isn't my actual surname, it belongs to my adoptive parents. I don't know my own surname. I don't know my own birthday. I don't know my parents. The only certain thing I still have from my time in the camp is a number showing I was brought on a Hungarian transport. I'd like to learn something about myself, about my family, and locate someone. But despite searching, I've had no success,' said Ewa, from the TV screen.

The orphans of Auschwitz were researching their past. Their first stop was usually the museum. Curator Tadeusz Szymański understood how significant a name and a history could be for a person. He would scour camp books and Red Cross records, read memoirs, send letters abroad and persuade journalists to work with him.

It was thanks to him that Zinaida Vorobeva was able to embrace her son Genka after more than 20 years. A weepy but uplifting Soviet film was made about them titled *Remember Your Name*. Zina was sent to the camp with her son in 1943. Before they were split up, the mother commanded her child to remember his name, while she memorized his number. When they finally met, Zinaida lived in Minsk, while Eugeniusz – an officer in the Polish merchant marine – was just taking command of his first ship. From then on, he'd have two mothers and two homes.

Perhaps the same good fortune was in store for Ewa?

The whole Krcz family requested the museum's assistance. Stanisław had his own house by then, and was working on the railway in Katowice. He told Tadeusz Szymański the story of going to the camp to find an orphan, the prisoners' surprise and finally about the watercolours. They belonged to Ewa now. She also had a self-portrait by the imprisoned painter Marian Ruzamski, which she'd received from an acquaintance.

In December 1963, the Auschwitz commission on collections and acquisitions met at the National Museum in Kraków. They examined the paintings. 'In discussing their artistic value, Assistant Professor Dr Helena Blum emphasized the great artistic skill of the artist of the Gypsy portraits, the expressive characterisation of the subjects and the psychological atmosphere.' The painter Jerzy Brandhuber 'considered the portraits well-made and handled realistically.' Next, the painter Tadeusz Kinowski 'emphasized the high quality of their composition and colour.' Finally, the commission 'considered the acquisition of the paintings to be desirable' and offered the owner 40,000 złotys.

(The average salary was 1,763 złotys. A stick of the cheapest butter cost 15, a stick of margarine: 6, a loaf of bread: 4, a quarter-litre of cream: 5.80, a Danusia chocolate bar: 4.50, a bar of dark chocolate: 19, one dollar on the black market: 80.)

The Auschwitz Museum opened two investigations: who painted the Gypsy portraits, and who was Ewa?

A-5116. The girl's faded tattoo was a camp code. It contained information about the prisoner's deportation date, which sector she was sent to, hospitals stays, punishments and so on. Unfortunately, Szymański didn't know how to decipher it, because the transport's documents had been burned in the bonfires before the liberation. But he didn't give up – instead he hired the documentary filmmaker Andrzej Piekutowski.

Piekutowski was collecting accounts from camp orphans and people who'd adopted them. Adoptive mothers recalled watching their girls play: one girl would put her hand on the other's forehead: 'You've got a fever so you're going to the hospital block.' Another would drag her by the legs: 'No you're not! Mengele's taking you to the ovens!' These women's voices betrayed a long-ago fear. Who were these children, what had they been through, what did they think of when they said 'mummy'?

Fingerprints

In a Socialist utopian city, a Jewish girl from Hungary became a Polish girl with a navy-blue school pinafore and a photo from her first communion. She was loved – she was the youngest. They bought Ewa a piano, and although she had no passion for playing, she went to music school.

Karolina Krcz: 'Ewa knows the only wealth I can give her is music'.

Speaking to Tadeusz Szymański, she praised her daughter as talented, hard-working and serious-minded. She had just passed her school leaving exams and had been accepted to a medical course in Kraków – she was going to be a dentist! She confessed to Szymański: 'Ewa has been and continues to be a joy in my life.'

The camp children kept in touch. Karolina: 'Once Ewa found out that Lidka, Mikołaj and Hanka had found their parents, one day she told me straight out that she wanted to find her family'.

She had to imagine what Ewa was going through. She'd needed looking after in the camp, but had been left alone. It didn't matter if her parents were alive or dead, what mattered was their absence. They'd abandoned her. It was hard to let go of that guilt, accept it, assuage it, believe they'd tried to save her. What if she'd had a twin brother and they'd informed Mengele? They were giving their children a chance.

Forgiveness requires some fact or other, even a tiny one. A name, a photograph, a story from a neighbour or fellow-prisoner. It was necessary for a person successfully to move on. They would gather the strength to pull themselves together and stop vacillating between hate and love, between fantasy, indecision and accusations of betrayal.

Andrzej Piekutowski's black-and-white documentary gave Ewa hope. Maybe someone would see her and recognize her, for there was nothing worse than being forgotten. But there was no response to *Children from the Ramp*. Then Szymański telephoned his friends in Hungary. Soon the Budapest press launched an appeal: 'Help this 20-year-old girl!' They had a picture of young Ewa with a bow in her hair next to a recent one of her as a student – attractive, with dark hair and dark eyes.

Dozens of families got in touch, and another documentary was made. The director László Nádasy accompanied Ewa on a trip for several days. Sometimes he got a look at the candidates to be her relatives even before she did. Hungary under the rule of János Kádár was surprisingly poor. In the film, people wept in cramped interiors.

One man: 'When I got home, my wife would already be asleep, so my daughter would start shaking her. "Get up, daddy's home!" I would bring her chocolate and play with her. She loved me so much!'

Another man: 'She was well-behaved and obedient as a little angel. I thought even there in Auschwitz she would charm people. She was so sweet I can't forget her.'

A woman: 'I'm her aunt, I can see a strong resemblance. She always held her hands that way!'

The next woman: 'That's Jutka, she looks just like her mother. I met her mother on the stairs after an air raid. "Please give me Jutka, just for now. No one will find out she's a Jewish child, and when it's over it will all work out somehow." Her mother said, "Please don't ask me that, I'd rather give my life." I'm glad our Jutka is so clever. Maybe she'll find more relatives.'

Yet another: 'She's so sad, so poor and forlorn. But she doesn't know anything yet. She'll discover where she's from, that will bring her comfort and she'll have no problems in life.'

Ewa visited eight families. Hungarian Jewish survivors touched her chin and her hair, brushed her fringe off her forehead and stroked her. They cried:

'The same ears!'

'She has eyebrows like mine!'

'You could hold a gun to my head and I'd say she's ours.'

Still they would make sure:

'Have you got webbed toes?'

'Do you wrinkle your nose?'

Ewa did her best to maintain her distance, but it was clear she was aching inside.

Finally, each one gave fingerprints to compare (there were no DNA tests yet).

The documentary *Éva A-5116* won a prize at the Kraków film festival in 1964. But after examining the fingerprints, the Hungarian Red Cross wrote to the candidates to inform them: 'Dear Sir/Madam, you cannot be the father/mother of Ewa Krcz.'

Snow White opens her eyes

It was her second time in Auschwitz. Dina was 50, her daughters were growing up, and she was alone.

After the war she, her husband and her mother flew to the Disney Dream Factory. They lived in Los Angeles, in an elegant house with a pool opposite the Hollywood Bowl – the amphitheatre had been built in 1919, and the letters of the Hollywood sign scattered in the Santa Monica hills formed the the backdrop for the band shell. Dina watched the Beatles perform from her own terrace – she had a perfect view of the stage.

She'd been promised a fairy-tale life. Her prince came riding through the forest and saw a glass coffin on the peak of a mountain, with beautiful Snow White inside – for she hadn't changed, not in the slightest. In death, or perhaps in sleep, she had remained white as snow, with cheeks as red as blood, and hair as black as ebony. Innocent. The young man loved Snow White so much that the dwarves let him take her. His servants carried the coffin on their shoulders – suddenly one of them stumbled, and the bite of poisoned apple fell from the princess's mouth. Snow White opened her eyes, lifted the glass lid and was alive once more.

'My God, where am I?' she cried.

And the prince replied:

'You are with me.'

Many enchanted heroes fall asleep only to be born again. The psychiatrist Bruno Bettelheim titled his book on fairy tales *The Uses of Enchantment*. He was a Viennese Jew, a prisoner in Dachau and Buchenwald, who researched autistic children in the United States after the war. They reminded him of the

'Muslims' in the camp – fleeing from the world's hostility into apathy. Bettelheim made the case that fairy-tales help children mature, and that the long sleep that appears so often in fairy-tales symbolized the difficulty of attaining adulthood. Snow White discovered herself – she came to understand others and brought new meaning to her life. Inside the glass coffin, she was still a child – she left it ready to marry.

Her wicked stepmother was also invited to the wedding. In her finest garb, she stood before the mirror.

'Mirror, mirror on the wall, who's the fairest one of all?'

The mirror answered:

'My queen, you are the fairest here so true. But Snow White is a thousand times more beautiful than you.'

The stepmother was unsure whether to go to the wedding. But she couldn't stop herself from going. When she recognized the young woman as Snow White, she was stricken with horror – and suddenly became so ugly no one could look at her, and even she never wished to look at herself in the mirror ever again. With a scream, she fled the castle to hide in the thick forest. No one ever saw her again, and no one knew what became of her.

That was the sanitized version, the one for children to read. The Brothers Grimm gave the story a crueller ending. At Snow White's wedding the vain, jealous stepmother had to put on a pair of red-hot shoes and dance until she dropped dead.

Did her dancing stepmother's screams cheer Snow White so much she could forget her past and smile happily at her husband each morning? Or perhaps the hunter's knife kept returning in her memories, so the young wife would awaken with bags under her eyes, cry for no reason and not hear what others said to her?

Seven hundred dwarfs

At first things were going quite well for Mr and Mrs Babbitt. They had two daughters, Karin and Michele. Art no longer worked for Disney. They'd fallen out a few years earlier over money.

The animators had worked like dogs during the making of *Snow White*, and though the film was an unbelievable success, the studio didn't pay overtime. The team expected a bonus, but instead of being rewarded, some of them were sacked. The studio was in an uproar and Babbitt supported the protests, though he himself earned a big salary. He was a Disney legend, a huge star – he'd created Goofy.

Goofy was a black dog with a light-coloured snout, long ears and dark eyes. In his orange jumper, white gloves and green hat, he looked a little like a person. He was an eternal optimist, none too clever, but kind-hearted, a sort of credulous feather-brain.

Art Babbitt owed his position to Goofy, and thanks to him was in charge of feature film animation in the studio. He drew some characters and scenes himself – for instance, the wicked stepmother in *Snow White*, Gepetto in *Pinocchio*, the dance of the mushrooms in *Fantasia* and, finally, the stork in *Dumbo*.

The stork gave Mrs Jumbo the elephant a son, who became the laughingstock of the circus when he grew extraordinarily large ears. But Dumbo, lonely and derided, met an ally, a mouse named Tim. With a little magic and a lot of bravery, Dumbo triumphed. He was the only flying elephant in the world!

Disney got rid of Babbitt, the ringleader of the disgruntled animators, before the film was even finished. That didn't please the staff. Three days later, 29 May 1941, a strike broke out in the studio. Art joined the trade union members of the Screen Cartoonists' Guild – he was their leader and negotiator.

Journalists were happy to photograph the protest, and many pictures have survived – all cheerful and sunny. Art Babbitt, in a fashionable suit, a white shirt and a tie, holds up a sign reading 'Disney Studio On Strike'. Women animators stand next to him, all dolled up tennis-style (in shorts, socks and flats), underneath the slogan: 'Snow White and 700 Dwarfs!'

The strike in Hollywood lasted five weeks. Supposedly, Walt Disney took Nelson Rockefeller's advice and went off to South America. That made negotiations easier. Still, there were cuts. Before the revolt, the studio had employed 1,200 people – and afterwards only 694.

Meanwhile, in the Protectorate of Bohemia and Moravia, Dina was risking of unstitching her star to go see *Snow White* at the cinema.

The war allowed Americans to live at a distance from such incomprehensible nightmares. After all, a different continent meant different problems. If the Holocaust seemed unreal in Europe, it was even more so in America. American audiences of the 1930s watched synagogues burning in newsreels. On screen, a fanatical crowd would throw Jewish books onto a fire, lighting up the city squares of Germany. During the war, information from occupied Europe reached the United States, Switzerland and the United Kingdom. The BBC and other Allied broadcasters revealed what was happening in Auschwitz. Escaped prisoners wrote reports. These, passed from hand to hand, reached Allied governments, the World Congress of Jews, the International Red Cross and the Vatican.

On 7 December 1941, a few months after the strike at Disney studios, the war hit home. The Japanese launched a surprise attack on Pearl Harbour naval base in Hawaii. Art was one of the hundreds of thousands mobilized. He served as a marine sergeant in the Pacific. He never came to Europe in uniform and he liberated no concentration camps. He probably didn't know much about them.

Information of that nature was pushed into the back pages of the newspaper. In America, part of the Jewish community feared strong pressure on the government might enocurage anti-Semitism. But a few people and organizations held mass rallies in Madison Square Garden. They begged the president to act and appealed to the military: bomb the gas chambers, crematoria and railways around Auschwitz. They were told it was out of the question. The Third Reich had to be defeated on the front, and the camps would be freed along the way.

The slogan 'Rescue through Victory' didn't do the West much credit. So after the liberation, they kept fairly quiet about the camps over in Europe.

When Dina met Art, he was drawing for Warner Bros., and later for United Productions of America. (UPA had been founded by defiant animators Disney had fired.) Art also worked for Hanna-Barbera, Quartet Films and many other studios. He was learning a lot. In 1937, he married, and soon after, divorced Marjorie Belcher, the woman who'd been the basis for the animators' drawings of Snow White.

His next relationship was with a princess who had survived much hardship. But in spite of fate, Dina and Art divorced after 14 years. Dina never revealed any details. But some of her dreams were fulfilled too – she was earning a living drawing and was working in film studios. She also worked on the cult heroes Wile E. Coyote, Speedy Gonzales, Daffy Duck and Tweety Bird.

My Tsihany, my Tsihany

The Merstein family of German Sinti – the circus artists and musicians who'd even had their horses taken away by Hitler in the 1930s – performed in Poland until the Germans invaded and deported them to Drohobych in the east. Some of the family understood what was on the cards. They fled. They went with the circus from East to West, through Krosno in the southeast, and hid everything Gypsy about themselves. They pretended to be Mexicans.

The killing of Gypsies began in 1943. The Merstein family split up as they fled. According to Józef Merstein: 'They'd had seven wagons in Poznań before the war, but when the Russians came in, granddad was on his own near Częstochowa. He wandered through the woods for weeks, whistling in an agreed-on way: he was looking for others. He met Polish, Hungarian and German Gypsies. This entire brotherhood of theirs escaped the transports and ghettos'.

The survivors left secret signs on the roads so they could find their families and clans – rags on a tree or stacks of pebbles. Not all the Mersteins survived. Some died in the Piotrków ghetto or in air raids, and grandmother froze to death in Niepołomice forest.

Each caravan had a tally. Historians made calculations as well. Some worked out that a third of European Gypsies had perished, others said it was half – between 30,000 and 60,000. No one made a specific estimate.

'The Mersteins had barely come out of hiding before the Russians nabbed them. Two uncles got sent to Siberia for being Germans. Others managed to stay – they shouted to the NKVD officers, "*My Tsihany, my Tsihany*" – we're Gypsies, we're Gypsies. They put on a show for them, singing and dancing.'

Then they purchased some new wagons and discussed what to do next. Some went back to Germany to reclaim their property, but granddad Józef wanted nothing to do with Germany. He formed a family troupe. Their audiences were military garrisons, Party secretaries, Russian officials, construction workers from the Palace of Culture or bricklaying teams from Warsaw. In the winter, they performed Strauss, excerpts from Kálmán's operettas and the popular Russian song 'Kalinka', and then in the spring, they travelled with the circus. Granddad, dressed in his best suit, went around the towns buying second-hand violins from music professors.

'The government didn't care for the Gypsy life, so the Mersteins pretended to be Hungarians. I remember, school would end and I'd go straight to the caravan.' The Polish Roma shared their lot in the caravans. And a happy lot it was, as long as no one brought up the war, which would might provoke feuds by the campfires.

'You ate a dog.'

'You betrayed your brother.'

'You sold a woman to the Germans.'

You could bathe without clothes on, kiss below the belt, make love whenever you wanted. You could take shoes from dead bodies and then put them on. You could even cheat another Gypsy. As long as no one saw, as long as no one snitched – there was no sin. So it had been and so it remained.

Feluś Baro Šero

But in Birkenau, in the ghettoes, and in the forests of Western Ukraine, everyone saw everything. Whole groups were under threat of defilement. There was mistrust, mutual contempt and revulsion.

At that time, the chief, or Šero Rom, was Feluś. The highest defender of Gypsy customs, he gave orders, took decisions, imposed punishments, settled disputes and mediated. He was also called *Baro Šero* – 'big head'. Roman Kwiatkowski, born in 1960 and raised in the caravan: 'I remember Feluś well. He was this calm, short chap with glasses. Because of the glasses we sometimes called him *Kororo*, Four-Eyes. Feluś was irreproachable – to this day, people tell stories of his verdicts.'

After the war, Feluś ordered long-ago offences to be set aside and life to be allowed to continue. That was the first time he saved the Gypsies.

Decimated, they needed to rebuild. Recalling their failings would only weaken them. Evoking the spirits of the dead would attract evil. They had to continue their day-do-day lives heroically and virtuously, not dwelling on the past.

There is a Gypsy woman in Opole named Phabuj. (Phabuj's caravan aided the partisans until it was captured: 'We brought them ammunition.') She was a patient of Dr Mengele's. She disagrees.

'That lot he experimented on never came back. They're gone for good.'

Among Gypsies, it's still forbidden to talk about the experiments on women – the taboo demands silence. There were no cemeteries for commemoration. A nomad mourns the dead and then sets out on the road. The past recedes. Auschwitz has been described by Jews, Poles, Russians. There are no Gypsy records of Auschwitz.

But why dwell on it when day by day, life was becoming more difficult? All of Communist Europe believed their nomadic lifestyle was bad. The independent caravans were an affront to the system. To curb them, in 1960, the Party Central Committee in Poland ordered the 'passportization' of the Gypsies, using methods including 'the element of force'.

Rachy from Kalisz: 'The Gypsies didn't know what the government was up to with these papers, whether they wouldn't be used against them. Gypsies don't trust outsiders; they'd eat their hat before they believed them. So they came up with an idea: the more names they gave, the better.'

Women from government offices would show up the forest clearings to fill out surveys:

'Name?'

'Józef Dębowski.' (Though his name was Jan Doliński.)

'How old are you?'

'15, ma'am.' (He was 20.)

'Where is your father?'

'He's dead.' (He was standing alongside.)

'Where did he die?'

'He ran off with his girl.'

'And when were you born?'

'During the potato harvest.'

'What year?'

'They say we had a crisp autumn then.'

This fibbing did the officials' heads in. They'd grab hold of some child:

'Whose daughter is this? Has she got a birth certificate?'

'What use have we got for papers, ma'am?' (Though she had her daughter's birth certificate in her clothes.)

'When was she born?'

'When the apple trees were blooming.'

Now she had two birth certificates. The next year, in a new forest, she'd be issued with a third.

Meanwhile, the Kraków lawyer Janusz Helfer was making friends with Gypsies in the region. He would help them with government correspondence, and they'd allow him to photograph them. Once he showed the Gypsies the prints, but they didn't like them much. 'I suddenly saw one Gyspy holding them to the fire, then using them to light cigarettes for himself and his comrades. Then they asked if I happened to have more of these photos. That annoyed me slightly. Another time, I brought pictures for the whole caravan and handed them out. I came back the next day and saw the caravan had left, I suppose because the police had arrived, and all my pictures were lying in the straw.'

In 1964, it was over – the caravans were stopped by force.

In spring after the first thunderstorms

Rachy: 'We transitioned to a settled life in Śrem. The local authority didn't have anywhere for us to live, so the caravan spent the whole summer in a field under police guard. Then they gave the Gypsies some run-down buildings and we got a tiny room by the river Warta at 9 Nadbrzeżna Street. There were seven of us living there. People weren't used to walls. They left the windows open because of the damp. Bathing and washing took place in the river. To get a flat, my father had to go to work in a concrete plant and we kids had to go to school. I went to primary school no. 2, then to trade school.'

Then Feluś saved the Gyspies a second time – from the Reds.

Roman Kwiatkowski: 'On pain of extreme dishonour he forbade us from joining the Party, the police reserve or any *gadjo* organization. I remember what an uproar there was when my aunt Wanda joined the Women's League. Feluś told us not to work state jobs, so some people, like my dad, did freelance work whitewashing boilers and mobile soda fountains. Others were traders. In town they'd buy wool for suits or silk for dresses from Poles they knew and sell them around the little villages. Today that's entrepreneurship, but back then it was a criminal offence.'

Communism on the one side and *Romanipen* on the other: after being settled, they sought a golden mean.

Rachy: 'It was like this. You've got five families in Śrem who want to travel, four in Pleszew, eight in Jarocin. That's a caravan right there. So in spring after the first thunderstorms, the chief takes the train up to see the district chief. He says, "I need 20 cattle cars." He gives him some money. The Gypsies secretly show up at the loading ramp and the whole lot of them – with wagons, bundles, horses – load into the train at night.'

They went as far as possible, near to the Russian border, so the authorities would have a harder time sending them back.

'The caravan didn't always get caught. The kids kept watch. "The *gadjos* are coming!" – and at that signal, everybody would hide. Sometimes they were a couple metres away, and nothing. We'd sleep outdoors in case they came after us, even in late autumn. We used to make the campfires with alder wood – alder doesn't give off smoke, just a low flame – and heat the ground for two hours. Then we'd put wet branches over the hot embers. Then we'd lay straw on top, to soak up the vapour, then a tarpaulin and bedding. You'd sleep like a baby!'

The Mersteins travelled in an illegal caravan too. Near Krzeszowice, outside Kraków, they would meet up with Kelderash, Lovari and, of course, Polish Roma. Now these frying pan salesmen, illiterate blacksmiths and village musicians didn't seem primitive anymore. Together, they'd buy a barrel of vodka, slaughter some chickens and throw a feast.

Józef: 'My grandfather played first violin. He was a chief, *Puru Sinto*. He had a gold-plated staff. He wanted to leave it to someone in the family after he died. No one would accept it. Everyone was planning to leave for Germany, because there was no life for them here. We put grandfather's staff in his coffin. People gossiped that it was solid gold. For three weeks, there were soldiers guarding the cemetery in Mysłowice.'

The great stoppage was already over by the summer of 1968. But the stubborn Gypsies were still travelling. They spotted military manoeuvres in the forest. Tanks were heading south, towards Czechoslovakia, so they fled north in a panic. They thought it was another war and they'd be taken to Auschwitz.

But it was more than 600,000 soldiers of the Warsaw Pact, being sent to fight the Prague Spring.

Foam

Nazi-hunters were trailing Dr Mengele. They knew he'd left Europe long ago and sailed to South America onboard the *North King*. His wife Irene had left him, but his family stayed loyal to their Beppo. They supported Josef from afar, and local Nazi comrades took care of passports, safe-houses and money. He went from Argentina to Paraguay, from there to Brazil, from city to city...

Ever since the portrait sitting, Dina had known the doctor's secret: a dark spot on his left ear, an identifying mark. She didn't feel safe anywhere – even in California, she kept looking over her shoulder. Once, she panicked at the bus station on Hollywood Boulevard, because she saw someone who looked like him.

'I thought, my God, he's looking for me. I was the one person in the world who could identify him without a doubt. He must have known that.'

What if he sent his people to force Dina into silence? Or appeared himself? Dina had an unlisted number and few people knew her address. The poisoned apple was still in her throat – for her, the war had not ended. Mengele covered his tracks, time and again he slipped away from the hunters and remained elusive. Wasn't that proof he'd retained his power? The system he'd served was looking after itself too.

You only had to watch the trials. The Allies had solemnly given their word: we'll bring the villains to justice. And what had happened?

The Nazi doctors were tried in Nuremberg. Death sentences were handed down. Exceptionally, all were carried out, unlike the rest of the trials put before the American tribunal. Nine members of the Third Reich medical service were given long sentences in 1947.

For experiments with epidemic jaundice, typhus, phlegmon, polygal and phenol, sea-water, freezing, high altitude, malaria, mustard gas, sulphanilamide, sterilization and euthanasia.

Because their patients had died of hunger, cold and thirst.

Because their patients had been drowned, suffocated, had limbs amputated and their bodies chopped up to test their endurance.

Dr Karl Genzken – life.

Dr Siegfried Handloser – life.

Dr Gerhard Rose – life.

Dr Fritz Fischer – life.

Dr Oskar Schröder – life.

Dr Hermann Becker-Freysing – 20 years.

Dr Herta Oberheuser – 20 years.

Dr Wilhelm Beiglböck – 15 years.

Dr Helmut Poppendick – 10 years.

Day after day, the American journalist Vivien Spitz diligently reported on the doctors' trial, including the events of 27 June:

Prosecutor Hardy: 'Now, Witness, for what reasons were you arrested by the Gestapo on 29 May 1944?'

Witness Karl Hoellenrainer: 'Because I am a Gypsy of mixed blood.'

Prosecutor: 'Do you think you would be able to recognize that doctor if you saw him today?'

Hoellenrainer looked around. He suddenly leapt over the German defendants' table, brandishing a small knife in his right hand. Vivien Spitz: 'he appeared to be almost flying through the air towards the prisoners' dock [...], reaching for Dr Beiglböck'.

The guards overpowered the attacker. When the room was brought to order, Judge Beals spoke:

'Witness, you were summoned before this Tribunal as a witness to give evidence.'

Hoellenrainer: 'Yes.'

'This is a court of justice.'

'Yes.'

'And by your conduct in attempting to assault the defendant Beiglböck in the dock, you have committed a contempt of this court.'

'Your Honours, please excuse my conduct. I am very excited. That man is a murderer. He ruined me for my entire life.'

'Your statements afford no extenuation of your conduct. You have committed a contempt in the presence of the court, and it is the judgement of this Tribunal that you be confined in the Nuernberg Prison for the period of 90 days as punishment for the contempt which you have exhibited towards this Tribunal.'

'Would the Tribunal please forgive me? I am married and I have a little son. And this man is a murderer. He gave me salt water and he performed a liver puncture on me. Please do not confine me to prison.'

'The contempt before this court must be punished.'

'Why 90 days?' wrote Vivien Spitz. 'Why not one or two days – just to make a point?'

When his sentence was over, Dr Steinbauer's defence counsel stepped in.

'You and your wife, too, have stated that you participated in malaria, phlegmon, typhoid and sea-water experiments?' he asked Hoellenrainer.

'No, only this one experiment, no malaria.'

'Do you admit you lied to the young doctor who talked to you?'

'No, I didn't lie to the doctor. I just told him the exact truth. My wife and I weren't allowed to marry. My wife had a child from me and it was cremated in Birkenau. My sister was cremated and both her children.'

'Listen, Herr Hoellenrainer, don't be evasive as Gypsies usually are. Give me a clear answer as a witness under oath.'

Hoellenrainer talked about the experiments with sea-water, when in the hospital block they were given nothing else to drink and no food, and how after a couple days, prisoners were foaming at the mouth from thirst.

The defence counsel: 'And that thirst was very unpleasant?'

'Yes.'

'How can you explain that these people foamed at the mouth?'

'They had fits and foamed at the mouth, they had fits of raving madness.'

'I am asking you how there can be foam on a mouth which is completely dried out?'

'I don't know.'

'You don't know. So some became mad?'

'Yes.'

'You Gypsies stick together, don't you?'

'Yes, of course.'

'Then you must be able to tell me who became mad?'

'I don't remember.'

'You must know. If a friend of mine – I was a soldier twice – and if a friend of mine had gone mad then I would have noticed it.'

'It was a tall man who was in the first row. He was the first one to start. He became raving mad and had fits and thrashed around with his hands and feet. He was a tall slim Gypsy.'

Dr Wilhelm Beiglböck got 15 years, which was later commuted to 10. By 1955, every one of the doctors was living their lives peacefully and in freedom.

After the war, the German judiciary appointed committees of professors to consider the sins committed by men of science, including doctors. But even the worst were innocent in their eyes, because they thought of them as professional colleagues.

What about the SS officers from Auschwitz-Birkenau? No public prosecutor's office in Germany wanted to charge them. Only after Adolf Eichmann's trial did they decide that it was indecent to delay any longer. So 18 years after the war, guards and camp administrators were put on trial. They differed in age, education and origin. What did the educated Dr Lucas, the level-headed merchant Mulka and the little snot

Stark have in common? Just one thing: they were unmoved by mass killing.

The grand trial was meant to demonstrate German complicity in murdering the Jews of Europe. Round the world, survivors who could testify were sought. Like Karl Hoellenrainer, they didn't perform well. They were too unspecific, they couldn't reconstruct the awful events precisely enough. Finally, in 1965, 22 sentences were handed down. The public was furious that criminals had been found innocent. It is the individual person who is judged, explained the lawyers. Guilt requires proof, democracy demands it.

The wheels of justice were sparing murderers. But there was nothing to prevent the victims from suffering persecution.

My Rex knows everything

At this time, an only child named Lizzie is growing up in south Tel Aviv. She was born in 1953, the same year as Dina's daughter. There's only one thing she wants: to get as far away as possible. From her poor neighbourhood, which is actually a survivors' camp. From her mother, who doesn't allow her to cross the street because Israelis live there. From Roza, Dorka and Guta, her neighbours who crowd around Zaychik's beauty parlour. They don't speak Hebrew, they keep casting their memories back to Poland, Romania, Czechoslovakia, Hungary. They cook strange food, following late grandmothers' recipes. They live in the ghetto – the ghetto is in their soul.

'Until the age of seven, I had a private language – a blend of Polish, Yiddish, German and Hungarian. I didn't learn Hebrew until I was in year one. My parents survived in Poland. I didn't know my father, he died of tuberculosis. My mother thought if anyone from the family had survived the war they would have come to Palestine. Zionism wasn't her choice. It was the same with our neighbours. They felt the Jews couldn't live in Europe any longer. They were looking for somewhere far from the Germans where they could be together.'

After school, Lizzie often stopped by the beauty parlour. She loved smelling the acetone, applying nail varnish, and the stories people told there in various languages. Everyone had their own story. She learned them all by heart.

One woman who got her hair done at Zaychik's was Tania, who would only talk about her wartime experiences to her dog Rex – in Polish. Her son didn't care to listen. He only developed an interest once his mother was dying. With her last breath she took hold of his hand: 'Yosele, ask Rex. My Rex knows everything.'

Zaychik covered up the number on his forearm with a sticking plaster. Once, his assistant Lea saw him sweeping up hair after work. 'Suddenly he started shivering, his head shook from side to side, he was blinking as though he'd got sand in his eyes, and he held the broom handle so tightly that blood flowed from his hands and they turned white like a dead man's.'

From then on, Lea swept up the customers' hair. But once, she lost her nerve too. When a German turned up in the neighbourhood, she quickly closed the door of the parlour. 'I've never been as frightened as I was then. Even in the bomb shelter I hadn't felt such horrible fear. I was even scared of my own thoughts.'

Lizzie: 'The people in my neighbourhood had dark-coloured eyes, so even in winter they wore dark glasses to hide them. I also got sunglasses from my mum, as well as an encyclopaedia, naturally. When mum bought shampoo, she'd pour out two-thirds and refill the bottle with sulphur, which turned me into a blonde. Everyone bleached their children's hair. They were afraid the Germans would make it all the way to Israel. This way, they'd be able to tell right away no Jews lived in our neighbourhood.'

(After she turned 40, Lizzie started losing her hair. The doctor said there was nothing wrong with her. 'He asked who'd done this to me. I said, the Germans, I guess.')

Lizzie's mother went to synagogue during the holidays, because it was the done thing. Her friends did too. They put bits of paper with recipes into the prayer books. They'd pray quickly in Hebrew: two cups of flour, half a cup of sugar, three tablespoons of cocoa... It was cooking club in the women's section. Lizzie knows many of these recipe-prayers by heart.

Her mother went to church in Tel Aviv too, and the priest even considered her devout. Once they had the following conversation:

'Mummy, are we Jews or Catholics?'

'Jews.'

'So why do you go to church?'

'Because the Jewish God doesn't listen to us anymore, I think we have more success with the goyish God.'

But at church she would curse Him in Polish. What kind of God was He? He'd killed six million people. She had no one to pray to.

Lizzie: 'Home was utterly mad growing up. I knew something was wrong with my mum, but what? Much later, I came to understand. The adults of my childhood had wanted to live out the Jewishness they'd lost, but it was impossible to revive it in Israel. Every immigrant has to give something up, but people from the diaspora didn't want to change their traditions or their character. They were attached to Yiddish, and meanwhile, until the start of the 1960s, Hebrew was used exclusively in schools and theatres in Israel. My mum said a country that banned speaking Yiddish was killing its Jews a second time, and she lost her sense of security. She couldn't be an Israeli, because she had no common language with Israelis.'

Scum

At that time, a new Jew was being born. A citizen of a young country and ready to fight for it, because there were only enemies all round. Brave and strong, unlike the Jews of Europe, who had gone to the gas chambers under Hitler like lambs to the slaughter rather than taking up arms like the warriors of the Warsaw Ghetto. Anyway, they had no one to blame but themselves, since they'd chosen the diaspora. If before the outbreak of war, they'd heeded the Zionists' warnings and moved to Palestine, they would have escaped their misfortune.

Israel was taking in the surviving Jews – others were not so eager. At first, the arrivals from Europe made up a quarter of the population – later, as much as a third. Prime Minister David Ben-Gurion said out loud what many thought silently: 'These people, if they hadn't been what they were – cruel, brutal and selfish – would not have survived. What they lived through tore all the best elements out of their souls.'

Ben-Gurion, the architect of the State of Israel, came from Płońsk, near Warsaw – at that time in Russian-ruled Poland. He was born in 1886 and lived on Kodzia Street. In the town today, he has a monument, a memorial plaque in Polish and Hebrew and a museum exhibit. Płońsk considers Ben-Gurion a local hero. Ben-Gurion recalled his hometown in *The Book of Płońsk Jews*. He described the house where he grew up, the street and his neighbours, the Zionist organization

Poale Zion and his friends. Over a dozen pages, he never uses the words 'Poland' or 'Poles'. Ben-Gurion knew Russian, but he never learned Polish. He lived in Płońsk for over 20 years and didn't think he would ever need Polish. He emigrated to Palestine in 1906. He reportedly said, 'anyone who doesn't believe in miracles isn't a realist'. He was a radical idealist. On one side of the barricade, he placed the six million gassed to death – and on the other, one million pioneers.

'Collaborators', 'scum', 'Nazi helpers'. That's what those who'd escaped the ovens where called. Some were put on trial because they'd acted as *kapos* in the camps. Until the trial of Eichmann – the murderer behind a desk captured by the Mossad – these survivors were charged with genocide. None were proven to have caused the death of a fellow-prisoner. Thanks to reasonable judges, none were put in prison. But they felt painfully inferior. They hadn't irrigated the fields of Palestine, planted olive groves and vineyards or founded kibbutzim. They were pilloried for still being alive. They were enclosed in a conspiracy of silence. They preferred not to talk either.

Men had the hardest time of it.

Lizzie: 'Closed in on themselves, withdrawn, weak. They would meet only at synagogue, while every day our mothers would come to school and bring us juice, vitamins and sandwiches. They cultivated us by buying books. They were the ones who decided our futures. They became friends. They watched us play and that gave them strength. My mum decided I'd been born for the future, so I received no information about the past.'

Adolf Eichmann's trial began in 1961. (45 years later, the international media reported American intelligence had known where Eichmann was hiding long before Israel located him.

However, according to classified documents in the US, the Americans weren't interested in unmasking him. They were afraid in court he would inform on former collaborators in high positions in West Germany.)

As the head of the Jewish affairs department, Eichmann was responsible for transporting Europe's Jews to the camps. He was obsessed with the trains running on time. He calculated the Reich's railways cost four *pfennigs* per person per kilometre travelled. Even in 1944, when German generals on the Eastern Front were begging for each train of ammunition and food, Eichmann made sure his trains had priority. He said he liked Jews. He had a dog, he was a vegetarian.

Dozens of victims testified at the trial of the coordinator of the Final Solution. Until then, Israel had never heard survivors' voices. Now many Israelis understood why their neighbours who'd come from Europe would scream at night in an incomprehensible language. The trial was broadcast live on the radio, and even in America people crowded around their receivers. It was a media holiday, maybe the first ever – a courtroom thriller. Hannah Arendt wrote that the American broadcast, financed by the Glickman corporation, was constantly interrupted by real estate adverts. The defiant philosopher, author of *The Origins of Totalitarianism*, reported on the trial as a correspondent for *The New Yorker*. The huge spectacle, in her opinion, served political, educational and propaganda purposes. It was meant to be proof of Israel's strength. 'Jewish blood will never be defenceless again'.

(After Eichmann's trial, the tragedy of the European Jews was put into the Israeli school curriculum. Idith Zertal, a researcher of contemporary Jewish history and a spiritual follower of Arendt's, had studied it. Years later she declared:

'Despite omnipresent, bombastic memorialisation of the Holocaust, the people of my generation, born and raised being told "you won't remember", were not only "children of the dream", as Bruno Bettelheim called us, and children of the kibbutz, but also children ill-born, the generation of a hidden, suppressed, unspeakable misery, and products of a messianic and noble beginning. Meanwhile, we were torn up inside because of our tragic past, which refused to fade into oblivion'.)

Incest

Meanwhile, Lizze was leaving Zaychik's beauty parlour with lacquer on her short-clipped nails. She was eight years old and reluctantly heading home.

'Children are afraid of weak parents. The first year of primary school was when the distancing process began. We were ashamed of them. We wouldn't listen. We forced them to speak Hebrew, pull open the blinds, change the furniture, live like the people outside our estate. Being in the Scouts gave us real hope for the future, leaving our parents, moving forward.'

It became more difficult to understand one another.

'The only foreigners my mother knew were Yemeni Jews. They were a family with ten children who lived next door. Every Friday they would drum on empty olive tins, sing and dance. Once she went over to theirs. 'Which one is your eldest son?' When he stood up, she asked him, 'Why don't you marry my daughter?' The boy answered, 'I don't want to, she's ugly and white.' The whole estate heard about it, and I was 16 years old! I was furious. 'Why did you do that?' Mum said: 'Because with him you'd have a large, happy family. Not having a family is the worst fate, and everyone in this neighbourhood has lost their families.'

She thought survivors' children shouldn't marry one another, because that was like incest. It was dangerous.

But the young people weren't afraid of anything. There were 41 of them on the estate. In the military, they all joined special units and left home for good.

'My friend broke our rule and stopped by the estate on leave. He was in uniform, armed. When he walked in, his mother was ironing in the kitchen. She looked up, saw a soldier in the doorway and fainted. The iron fell on her, it burned her arm. They took her to hospital.'

'Why Poland?'

Did Dina tour the museum? Again there are no accounts, the witnesses are no longer alive. Let's say she mustered up the courage like other prisoners did... What, after all those years, did she see in Auschwitz-Birkenau?

She saw the same as a group of American scholarship students also arriving at Auschwitz right then: the summer of 1973. One of them was 24-year-old Jeffrey Goldfarb, an early-career researcher. He was writing a book on Polish independent theatre. In Warsaw, he met the sociologist Elżbieta Matynia, who had been involved in that movement for years. She knew the avant-garde theatre troupes Theatre of the Eighth Day, STU Theatre and the Plastic Theatre of the Catholic University of Lublin. She introduced her New York friend into the scene, and he met artists thrilled to welcome a visitor from the Free World. Jeffrey travelled to Gdańsk, Wrocław and Kraków. In Lublin, he made friends with the renowned stage director and designer Leszek Mądzik. He shared the fate of these rebellious alternative artists, including being arrested – briefly, but significantly.

'After that I saw the relationship between art and freedom differently.'

For Brooklyn-born Jeffrey, Poland was not just a spot on the map. His grandparents – Victor and Brana Frimet – came from near Lwów , where his family had lived for generations. Yet in 1920, with no regrets, they abandoned their homeland. Poles spat on them in shops, and in the army, Victor was beaten up for being Jewish.

'I remember asking my grandfather, amazed: "You fought for our enemies?" After my grandmother died he sold his house to some Poles. We discovered he spoke Polish! He'd never mentioned it to my mother. When I was grown up, *Fiddler on the Roof* was on Broadway – it was a big hit. But we couldn't drag my grandfather to the theatre. He kept saying he didn't want to even be reminded of those awful times. He had no fond memories, even though he was a young man back then.'

All the Frimets' European relatives were killed in the war, and their close and distant acquaintances who by some miracle had managed to escape with their lives decided to leave the continent.

'In the 1950s, immigrants were constantly coming through our house. I would ask my parents what those numbers were on their arms. They explained: "Wherever you go, you'll meet anti-Semites. The Holocaust is what results from anti-Semitism, it's a part of our suffering".'

That was the history the Jewish community told their children in America. It wasn't taught in schools or written about in the papers, no one criticized the US government's conduct during the genocide, and the Holocaust hadn't broken into mass consciousness.

Jeff understood why Americans kept silent.

'They just felt helpless. How could you believe it? What could you do with it? Especially because all around the world, people were asking the same questions: why didn't the Jews of Europe rebel? They should have taken up arms and fought!'

They'd failed. It was unpleasant to say out loud.

Meanwhile, in synagogues and homes, refugees from Europe evoked painful memories: how they'd wandered streets or country roads in search of somewhere to stay or sometimes a slice of bread. How they'd hid in root cellars, and how their greatest joy had been spending the night in a cowshed, because it was warm. How Nazi collaborators lay in wait for them. How the Poles bringing them aid feared their own neighbours. For Jews, the Germans were the enemy – but Poles often were as well.

These stories built on the sentiments and memories of pre-war immigrants. Being spat on in shops, the truncheons of nationalists, segregated education (where Lwòw Polytechnic had led the way). Angry, humiliated and ashamed, the Jews were looking for someone to blame. Why had the concentration camps been built in Poland? Because the Poles were anti-Semites, they said, even worse than the Germans. They were responsible for the Holocaust. After all, the fact that some Jews survived and others didn't was down to the actions of individual Poles.

Jeffrey: 'I realize the distance between an anti-Semite and someone who commits genocide. But you can't have the second without the first.'

'Why Poland?' asked Mrs Goldfarb, upset when her son informed her where he was going.

Encyclopaedia entries

Jeffrey's mother's question stayed with him at Auschwitz. He expected he would feel rage, terror or amazement. He felt true emotion walking through the gates.

'I was right by the entrance to the museum – because right there, they had written the nationalities of the prisoners, but the Jews were not mentioned. Later I looked around the national exhibits and the Polish one was especially disturbing. There were lots of photos of the victims with their names. Not one sounded Jewish! The exhibit commemorating the fate of the Jews had been closed in 1968 "for renovations", but the tour guide didn't even bother to mention it. We walked past it silently. It was hard to even tell any Jews had been in the camp at all.'

After Auschwitz, Jeff, angry and hurt, visited Kazimierz – the Jewish district in Kraków.

'It was a slum, empty and decaying, some synagogues being used as warehouses and the others closed to visitors. [...] We did manage to see the ancient Jewish cemetery [...] where an elderly man noticed us looking around. He introduced himself as the caretaker of the grounds. We spoke in our only common language, Polish, he with a strong Yiddish accent. Yet, he insisted that he was a Polish Catholic for some reason difficult to discern.'

Finally, he went to Zakopane, in the Tatra Mountains. An American friend of Polish descent went to buy presents for her friends in America. She complained that *she was not able to Jew down* the salesperson.

'I overheard the conversation and objected [...]. What surprised me was [...] her subsequent defence of it as being meaningless: just an expression, having nothing to do with Jews. Everyone she knows uses it, she explained.'

He would have to talk it over with his friends, because they were open-minded people, artists. They sought inspiration in the West, they admitted taking part in the student revolt of 1968, they criticized state anti-Semitism. It was they who told Jeffrey about the last few year's chain of anti-Jewish events.

It had started in 1967. The eighth volume of the *PWN Great General Encyclopaedia* came out, with the entry 'Nazi Concentration Camps' and the information that 99 per cent of the victims of the gas chambers were Jewish.

The Interior Ministry, led by Mieczysław Moczar, responded immediately. This was an attack on Polish martyrdom! Officials sent an accusatory letter to the Central Committee and the Ministry of Justice. 'The contents of this entry align with the propagandistic arguments of Zionist centres', and the figures given 'are based on the calculations a Jewish Anglo-American commission'. Nearly a hundred people in the publishing house lost their jobs. Young Poles heard the word 'Zionism', but didn't understand what it meant. They thought it was some Jewish clique. Soon a supplement to the encyclopaedia was released with a new, politically correct version of the entry.

Soon afterward, the Six Day War broke out. The Kremlin and the entire Eastern Bloc supported the Arabs, and Poland severed diplomatic relations with Israel. What did Poles of Jewish descent think? The poet Antoni Słonimski: 'If I have to be patriotic about a country, then fine. But why Egypt?'

Anyway, there were hardly any Jews left. The 'Enemies of People's Poland' were emigrating. There were 15,000 people who received one-way tickets: scientists, writers, engineers, soldiers, members of the Party *nomenklatura*. But first they had to renounce their citizenship.

Jeffrey knew the slogan 'Students to their studies, writers to their pens, and Zionists to Zion'. *The New York Times* and *The Washington Post* had described the anti-Semitic witch-hunt. But it was one thing to read, and another to see it firsthand in Oświęcim, Kraków and Zakopane.

The young sociologist told some acquaintances in confidence about his experiences on the trip. And what did he hear from many of them? That it's no accident so many Jews were living in Poland before the war. You could see they had it good. That under the occupation, Poles had risked their lives to hide Jews in their basements. And more, about a country without pogroms, about centuries-long tolerance, about the Polish-Lithuanian Commonwealth....

'Here was the Poland my grandparents fled from,' he wrote. 'It then became clear to me that if I were to spend the next year in this country, [...] I had to do so as American and not as Jew.'

Are you German, Mr Rose?

On the other side of the Iron Curtain, a new generation of Sinti were coming of age. Romani Rose, born in 1946, was living in a home for artists and art dealers in Heidelberg. At first, the Roses were nursing their wounds after the war – they'd been through a lot.

'My uncle Vinzent, his wife and his daughter fled into the General Government to avoid deportation. The Gestapo arrested them in Schwerin. Little Natalie was crying loudly, and my uncle asked the policemen to let his wife bring something for the child. They gave permission. Then, in our language, he told them to run. And they got away. My aunt left Natalie with some people, it seemed like she was safe. And Uncle Vinzent ended up in Auschwitz. When he stood on the ramp one day in front of the Arbeitskommando, he saw his two-year-old daughter with a woman he didn't know. They went to the gas.'

His grandfather was murdered in Auschwitz, his grandmother in Ravensbrück, his aunt in Bergen-Belsen.

'I can give you a long list. In our family, 13 people died in the camps.'

Oscar Rose managed to hide and escaped deportation. He obtained false papers for the *Kraft durch Freude* organization ('Strength Through Joy': they promoted a healthy Nazism in the wilds of nature). The KdF put on shows for the soldiers.

'My father passed himself off as Italian. He and a group of close friends would travel from city to city, register with the authorities and promise variety shows. They got a roof over their head and ration cards. When the day of the performance came, they'd be gone. They sent parcels with food rations to the camps. Dad managed to help my uncle escape when he was transferred to the sub-camp in Neckarelz.'

After the war, Rose kept up the old customs.

'As a child, I was terribly proud of speaking two languages. I would show off to my friends, they liked it too. But they stopped inviting me to their birthday parties. It wasn't their fault – it was the grown-ups. Still, I can't complain. I had one privilege that set me apart – my parents ran a cinema. So at first I would watch adventure films with my friends and then later, when I was a teenager, romantic films with girls.'

But they didn't know whom they were flirting with.

'I was careful to hide it.'

Young Rose sold paintings after school.

'Customers would ask, "Mr Rose, you speak such good German, but you're not German yourself?" I would answer, "But I am, I was born in Heidelberg". Then they'd say, "But your parents weren't German?" I'd say my parents were born in Upper Silesia. "Then for sure your grandparents weren't German". And I'd say, "My grandfather was Jewish". Then the customers would shake their heads sympathetically: "It's awful what the Nazis did to them".'

If you know a dozen Gypsies, you know them all

That was the problem: who was Romani Rose exactly?

'German? German identity was still too closely related to Nazism. I could accept being Jewish – they'd been through the same thing. But when I spoke to a Jewish man in America who'd lived through the war, a wall came up between us. Because I spoke German! I explained my first language was Romani, that I was born in Germany, that I couldn't emigrate to America or Israel, that the Holocaust had harmed my family as well. I was suffering in this split identity.'

The crimes against the Gypsies weren't recognized as genocide either at the Nuremberg Trials or at any post-war conference. They were a footnote in the war-crime statistics.

'That set us apart from the Jews. In order to return to the international community, the Germans had had to own up to the destruction of the Jewish population. The Adenauer government – the new government of a new, democratic country of laws – had done so under pressure. For a long time, it had been explained to people that everything said about the Jews back then – about conspiracies, commercial speculation and criminality – was a lie.'

Nazi propaganda had accused the Gypsies of the same things – their whole ethnicity was considered criminal. But after the war, no one repudiated this and no one stood up for them.

1949: in Baden-Württemberg state, the police gazette declared: 'The true Gypsy is inclined to begging, theft and deceit. He wants to live without working, at others' expense.'

1950: another police gazette, this time in Frankfurt, said: 'The Gypsy's behaviour is always instinctual. The more the Gypsies differ from other people, the more they are alike the world over. Anyone who knows a dozen knows them all.'

Under Hitler, many Gypsies had their documents confiscated. Although they'd considered themselves German for generations, now they had to prove it. Whoever could not obtain papers became stateless, losing any chance of compensation for their persecution.

1950: the finance minister of Baden-Württemberg gave instructions on how to proceed with compensation claims from Gypsies and mixed-race Gypsies. He announced they were not persecuted for racial reasons, but rather by dint of their criminal and antisocial activities. Therefore, every Gypsy claim had to be cleared by three criminal police departments: in Stuttgart, Karlsruhe and the main department in Munich.

This was the notorious Munich police department: the same one that had handed 19,000 files over to Dr Ritter, the yield from the 1926 anti-Gypsy law (which said to expel the foreign ones, imprison the local ones in workhouses and put their children in correction centres). The staff of the office was even unchanged: Hans Eller, Georg Geyer, August Wutz and the head of the Gypsy department, Joseph Eichberger. These very people had organized the deportations.

1952: Mayor Eusserthal in the Rhineland, who also took part in deportations under the Nazis, wrote to the district council: 'I will not tolerate the settlement of Gypsies in the area of my village and I will use all means at my disposal to attempt to stop it.'

He threw them into the middle of the woods. Most local officials were pushing Gypsies into deprived areas on the edges of towns, where they lived in cramped conditions without water or electricity. They were refused compensation.

Camouflage

During this time, Robert Ritter was a doctor in a public institution in Frankfurt, and also in charge of a clinic for children with mental illnesses. The public prosecutor had tracked him down, but there was nothing to be done. The case was closed for lack of evidence.

Eva Justin was working at Ritter's side in the Frankfurt children's health centre. She'd been included in the denazification process. She had much on her conscience: she'd done research on Gypsies in Dachau and their children in an orphanage. She'd concluded they were criminally inclined and asocial. These characteristics were innate, stronger than their upbringing. When Justin finished her Ph.D., the children were transported Auschwitz and slaughtered.

But after the war, Ritter's protégée had filled out the questionnaires so cunningly that she was considered 'politically blameless'. In the 1960s she even returned to her passion, once again studying Gypsies.

The old Gypsy laws were still in force. Ritter's anthropological charts could be found in Tübingen University. Sophie Ehrhardt was basing her academic career on them, writing about Gypsy skulls and Gypsy fingerprints. Hermann

Arnold, an expert in racial hygiene and a colleague of Justin's, took a different approach to the Nazi data, adapting it to be useful to the police. He also conducted research, hoping to discover the 'Gypsy gene'. His passion was analysing criminal behaviour, and he published a book on the subject in 1958. His academic source turned out to be a nationalistic pocket dictionary of criminology from 1936. He'd copied whole sections from the entries for 'race' and 'Gypsies'.

Across Germany, anti-Gypsy laws remained on the books. In Saarland state, a Police Order to Combat the Gypsy Plague was introduced in 1948 – and remained in force until 1970. In Hesse state, the Combating the Gypsy Menace Act 1929 wasn't repealed until 1957. In Baden-Württemberg state, an Interior Ministry directive titled 'The Prohibition of Collective Travel by Gypsies in Hordes', first issued in 1905, was in effect until 1976.

In the 1970s, Giessen University promoted the theory that there was no Gypsy Holocaust. The Gypsies had been accidental victims of poor hygienic conditions – it was bacteria that killed them. Some right-wing students founded the 'Gypsiology Project' at Giessen with their professor, a supporter of the neo-Nazi National Democratic Party of Germany. Its leader, Adolf von Thadden, was known as the new Führer.

In 1956, the brothers Oscar and Vincent Rose founded the Union of People of Non-Jewish Faith Persecuted for Reasons of Race. The first Gypsy organization in post-war Germany did not have the words 'Gypsy' or 'Sinti' in its name.

Romani Rose: 'It was camouflage. People were afraid to acknowledge who they really were. They'd hidden their origins so as to free themselves from poverty. Government officials didn't conceal their disappointment that they hadn't succeeded in breaking our will to live during the Third Reich.

Although 11 years had passed since the war, the thinking about Sinti people hadn't changed at all. Our parents' generation lacked self-confidence.'

Their children's generation would turn out to be stronger.

Don't believe anyone over thirty

Rose: 'We grew up with a sense of injustice. Neither the state or society allowed us to live with honour. Our ancestors had died, but how could we transform that into good? How could we reach out to people when our victims had been stripped of their honour? We came to share our parents' humiliation. That caused us more pain than the impoverished conditions to which many of us had been condemned. We'd been raised in democracy, and we wanted the right to it too.'

In the election campaign, Willy Brandt exhorted: 'Let's dare for more democracy'.

Young people were supporting him with a drive no one had expected, because the country was doing well. They had decent pensions, social security, a Volkswagen Beetle for almost everyone, mass tourism, pop culture, the conquest of space, television. Thanks to the contraceptive pill, people could have sex without fear. On top of all that, there were plenty of university places.

In November 1967, two young socialists disrupted Hamburg University's 500th anniversary celebrations. They marched before the professors in full academic dress holding a placard: 'A thousand years of mustiness under their gowns'.

'Mustiness' became a slogan of the revolt. There were a few others.

'There's no true life in falsehood'.

'Don't believe anyone over 30'.

'A whole government in the grip of fantasy'.

Chancellor Konrad Adenaur had hired Nazis, and answered naysayers by saying: 'Gentlemen, you can't dump out the dirty water when you haven't yet got any that's clean'. Whenever he founded a government department, a generation of war criminals, draft dodgers and ex-Nazis would move into power.

The German writer and journalist Uwe von Seltmann, grandson of a Nazi: 'Men were killed in every family, more than ten million Germans were displaced, there was rape in the East, Cologne and Nuremberg were destroyed. Germans compared their own suffering to what they'd caused others. They felt they were victims too. They swept the past under the carpet and worked like dogs. They fought to carry on, and out of that came the economic miracle. The British and Americans wanted them on side against Stalin, so the Communists were a common enemy. That's why denazification ended so quickly.'

Back then, German schoolchildren knew more about the conquests of Alexander the Great and Napoleon than the Nuremberg laws. They were subjected to an authoritarian upbringing – until they finally started asking questions.

Uwe von Seltmann: 'But they didn't always listen to the answers. Their questions were accusations.'

On 7 November 1968 in Berlin, the journalist Beate Klarsfeld (age 29) sneaked into the Christian Democratic Union party conference. She wanted to draw attention to then-Chancellor Kurt Kiesinger's past in the Nazi Party and the Ministry of Propaganda. She burst onto the rostrum and cried out, 'Resign, Nazi!' Then she slapped Kiesinger in the face.

She was arrested.

A few years earlier in Paris, Beate had been working as a children's carer. She met Serge Klarsfeld, a journalist and her future husband. Serge revealed his family history to her. His father had been deported to Auschwitz and died there. He met this fate because he was Jewish. This modern history was entirely new to Beate. She didn't feel guilty, but she thought she had a duty to fulfil.

Together, they documented Kiesinger's case, got his files from the archives and informed the German newspapers. Beate asked the journalists who was the better example for young people: Kiesinger the high-ranking Nazi, or Brandt from the resistance movement. She kept saying the disgraced must resign. The reaction was always the same. There was nothing to be done, the Chancellor had been elected democratically. So then the Klarsfelds resorted to drastic action.

Beate Klarsfeld said, in an interview: 'I stood before the summary court. They asked me: "You used force. What is your relationship to the 1968 movement? Do you consider your activities part of it?" I replied, "Without this movement, Nazis who held high positions, especially in the judiciary, would not be uncovered. That's why I joined. Can you help me in my fight against former Nazi leaders? They were aware of what was going on in the camps and now they stand at the head of government."'

The verdict: a year in prison, the most severe possible sentence. It was quickly commuted to parole, and the slap in the face went into the history books.

In 1969, Willy Brandt became Chancellor of a socialist-liberal coalition. A year later, he fell to his knees before the memorial to the victims of the Warsaw Ghetto.

And Romani Rose received an invitation to meet with a human rights organization, as well as a poster saying 'The Holocaust was also the extermination of half a million Gypsies'.

'I went there and publicly acknowledged who I was. That's how my work began.'

1971: a star-studded conference of Gypsies from the West, near London. They establish that from then on they wished to be called Roma. That was what they called themselves: 'Rom' in their language meant 'man'. The word 'Gypsy' – foreign, imposed – implied a sense of contempt. The first Roma world conference adopted a Romani anthem and flag. The nomads' symbol was blue on top and green on bottom, and on that background, a red Hindu chakra – or perhaps the wheel of a wooden wagon. It looked like it was spinning.

A year later in Heidelberg, the Roma Anton Lehmann was shot to death by a policeman. It provoked a wave of protests – the first open expression of violence. The Union of German Sinti was founded, no longer with any camouflage in the name.

Romani Rose co-organized the protests.

'We joined the civic movement. It finally worked!'

Mrs Babbitt is so naïve

It ought to have been easy for the former prisoners to reach an agreement. Their shared experience meant they could understand one another straight away. Dina met people in Auschwitz who had survived the same misery. Kazimierz Smoleń was still the director, but he wasn't the one who came out to meet their guest. 'I never met Mrs Babbitt.'

But someone invited Dina in, maybe Tadeusz Szymański or Irena Strzelecka.

And there they were: she touched the watercolours.

'I burst into tears. They'd been a part of me, they'd helped me survive. The museum had put them in little cheap frames with glass covers, the paper was yellowing. They never explained to me who exactly they'd bought them from. I was only meant to testify that I'd painted the pictures.'

There were seven of them. Ewa Krcz had handed over six, and the seventh belonged to a former prisoner who'd asked to remain anonymous.

Dina gave her testimony and Irena Strzelecka recorded the account on tape. Curator Szymański knew German and Czech, so he probably accompanied them. It was he who discovered who'd painted the watercolours. He'd got hold of the book *Továrna na smrt*, published years before in Prague, and he'd noticed the signature under the pictures: 'Dinah'. Ota Kraus – the former prisoner and the book's co-author – helped him establish the artist's place of residence.

They agreed Strzelecka would send a transcript of the testimony to the United States, then Dina would initial it and send it back to Auschwitz. It closes: 'I am happy having survived the camp and I am happy to be alive. I would be grateful if I could obtain photographs of the Gypsy portraits, originals of which are in possession of the Museum.'

This request for prints corresponds to Kazimierz Smoleń's polite proposal in the first letter sent to Los Tilos Road: 'If you are interested, the museum can send you black-and-white photographs of the portraits. Yours respectfully'.

There are two facts remembered from the visit.

First, the briefcase for the watercolours: it was apparently borrowed, because Dina had no money. It's a subject that comes up again and again in interviews, and returns in conversations with the museum as well. Why bring a briefcase for a few paintings? Artwork is transported in stiff, cardboard portfolios. How much does one of those cost? Without exaggerating, she could have bought one in Kraków for a few pennies. She's a woman of class, from America via Paris, and she can't afford a silly portfolio?

Second, the sentence: 'If anyone has the right to the paintings it's only Dr Mengele, although he probably won't come forward for them.'

Who said that to Dina?

Suspicion falls on Director Smoleń. (The prisoners talk roughly to one another, no one cares if they're 'sir' or 'madam' or just 'my friend'.) But Smoleń repeats:

'I never saw Mrs Babbitt with my own eyes. If she thought she'd pack the portraits in a briefcase and take them abroad, then she was being naïve. First she would have had to obtain the approval of the Minister of Culture, then the opinion of the National Museum – these are collections, after all. Right after the liberation, for a few pennies prisoners bought camp cupboards, broken stools, even furniture from Höss's house. They took their possessions out of there. If she'd come then, she'd have got the pictures for free, because plenty was given away. But that ended long ago.'

Two sets of photographs and the testimony are sent to the US by post. A letter from December 1973:

Dear Mrs Babbitt,

The Auschwitz State Museum attaches great importance to maintaining contact with those former prisoners who made works of art in the Auschwitz camp, including the Gypsy portraits executed by you.

Your visit to Auschwitz gave the museum a series of valuable pieces of information. As per your request expressed at the time, the Museum once again respectfully asks that you send:

1. Two photographs of yourself (one current and one from shortly after the war).
2. Any photographs of artistic works completed after the war, as well as exhibition catalogues.
3. The personal information and camp numbers of your mother, father and brother Petr, whose suitcase survives in our collections […].

You may keep the attached copy of the typescript for yourself. We ask you to sign the following three final pages […].

During your stay at Auschwitz, you asked about the possibility of organizing an Auschwitz exhibition in the United States which could include your portraits of the Gypsies. Such an exhibition would have to be initiated by a gallery or organization, e.g. an association of former concentration camp prisoners or the Union of Poles. […] Thus far no one from the United States has come forward with such an initiative.

We respectfully thank you for your ongoing interest in our work, for your visit to Auschwitz and for submitting valuable information.

We are sending certificates based on surviving camp documents regarding your loved ones […].

With friendly regards.

No response.

Transference

In May 1974, Kazimierz Smoleń signed yet another letter. Had his package reached the United States? No response had come in the post. 'Our contact with you has clarified the origins of valuable mementos, and once we've received the further information we requested we will be able to complete the documentation for the watercolours.' 'Prompt and comprehensive' information could be submitted 'in Czech, German or even English'.

Silence. More letters were sent, registered, with delivery receipts and without. No answer. Dina never signed her Auschwitz testimony.

Recently, Professor Dora Apel from the Art Department of Wayne State University in Detroit discovered something interesting. Although Dina broke official contact with the museum, for seven years she corresponded privately with the curator Tadeusz Szymański, until 12 October 1980, when he appears to have written that in his opinion Dina didn't have a right to the portraits, and that she wanted to reclaim them to remove something disgraceful from the camp.

Tadeusz Symański died in 2002. It's not known how many letters he exchanged with Dina, how close they were, what other subjects they brought up, or who first used the word 'disgraceful'. Both had survived Auschwitz.

Kazimierz Smoleń, who was a friend of Szymański's from their camp work detail: 'The watercolours show how prisoners protected themselves from death. Dina Babbitt painted them not even to survive, but to live. In no way was it a calculation: "I'll paint, then he won't kill me". He might have killed her anyway. She painted the Gypsies simply because it was a necessity. What else could she have done? Mengele says: "Paint me this," and she replies: "I won't. You're an SS-man?" That didn't happen in Auschwitz. If the people imprisoned here had all been heroes, today we'd hear nothing about the camp. No one would even lay a flower here – the Germans would have shot everyone. Doing what you were ordered without harming your friends – that was the whole code of a slave.'

Smoleń thinks Szymański was talking to Dina in that spirit. He certainly wasn't casting blame.

But perhaps she blamed herself? She wondered why she was such an incredibly lucky woman when millions had died. Had she stolen someone's life away? Nothing can repay the dead, day after day you live under their stern gaze.

The Holocaust witness Primo Levi knew that for a survivor, only their own death would free them from the feeling of guilt. He struggled with it himself, and he discussed the reasons, both rational and irrational, at length. For instance, human solidarity was abandoned. 'The presence beside you of a fellow prisoner who is weaker, more unprepared, older, or too young, pestering you by asking for help or by simply "being there," which is already asking for help, is a constant feature of life in the camps. The request for solidarity, for a kind word, a piece of advice, even just a sympathetic ear, was permanent and universal, but it was rarely satisfied.'

Incessant memories, continual blemishes on your conscious. 'Once it was over, it would dawn on you that you'd done nothing, or too little, to resist the system that had swallowed us up.'

To Dina, Mengele was the face of the system. She'd collaborated with evil.

She spoke to an Israeli journalist about the doctor: 'The whole world was searching for him, but I decided not to testify if he was caught. Not because I felt gratitude – after all, he didn't care if I lived or died and did nothing to save me either. But he allowed me to keep working for a while and to keep going.'

The Polish reporter Marek Miller met Dina in Brno several years ago. He asked what would happen if she met Mengele on the street. She considered.

'The first thing that comes to mind is I would spit in his face and walk away. But I don't think I would – I have nothing to say to Mengele.'

Most likely she was considering what she owed anyone.

'I found it difficult to accept the fact it was an SS officer who'd saved me. Later I explained to myself it wasn't so much that he saved me as that he spared me. I found that easier.'

She didn't mean Mengele, but rather Doctor König.

'Him I would thank on the street.'

Was it easier to take being granted life by a milksop in an ill-fitting uniform than what the Angel of Death offered? Had she dismissed Mengele from her memories to silence her own fears?

Again, these are suppositions, because we know nothing about Dina.

She entertained Marek Miller with a joke about her American therapist.

'She told him he looked like Dr Mengele. And he gave her this erudite explanation, saying this was a psychological mechanism called transference. In the United States at that time, every couple months there was some explosive piece of news to do with Mengele. The media was saying he'd been sighted here or there, and were showing pictures. During the next session the therapist admitted, "My wife saw a picture of Dr Mengele in the paper, and she said I do look like him."'

How could Dina have stood the trip to Poland? Did she reach out to touch the suitcase of her brother Petr, whom she couldn't save from the gas?

In psychiatrist Katarzyna Prot's book *Life After the Holocaust*, Otto talks about his return to Auschwitz: 'In 1977, I went to Auschwitz for the first time since the war. Afterwards my friends told me, "You went pale and didn't move for two minutes, like a stone statue." What did I see? The railway tracks the train ran along. I saw the whole scene when we reached Auschwitz, which is to say Birkenau. When we were unloaded from the carriages, I saw Dr Mengele during Selection – the uniform, the badges. And I pointed to a spot on the ground, saying "Our barrack was here".

'I'd never seen our barrack from above before.'

1999. On the Banks of Zayante Creek

At over 70, Dina was doing well, there was much she remembered at this age.

A white horse, for instance.

The Americans were wearing clean, pressed uniforms, but they were drunk. The Soviets followed right on after: Mongols from the East, filthy, they'd still been fighting not long before. Her friend Leša teased her: 'Those are your brothers.' They used to banter with one another. The Soviet officers invited Leša, Dina and her mother to have some wine, they wanted to celebrate.

But first, the women crossed the barbed wire.

'I found a bicycle and rode straight on. I felt unbelievably free. On one side was the forest, the tree trunks were black from bullets and they had no branches at all, they'd probably been burned. I suddenly saw a horse, trotting slowly. I threw down the bike.'

The horse was too tall for her to get onto. Then up rode an Italian who'd been working in the camp, Doni Antonio Turzi. He laced his fingers together and she climbed on.

'Except I was thin and the horse had a broad back, so I ended up losing my balance and almost fell on my face.'

Doni helped Dina to her feet, told her to hold onto his bicycle and a bundle he had with him, then chased after the horse.

'I stood there holding this bike in amazement. He didn't think I'd steal it. This was after three and a half years of the camp.'

The horse didn't have a harness, just reins, and Doni led him beautifully.

The day of liberation, every prisoner in Neustadt-Glewe knew someone was coming, they just didn't know if it was the Americans or the Russians. They were expecting an air raid, until a German woman came and told them there were no guards left in the camp. Dina ordered her mother: 'Sit on the bed and don't move.'

She ran outside alone.

'Some Frenchman had cut the barbed wire and the girls were struggling through it.'

She dashed to the German barracks.

'I looked to see if maybe I could find a piece of bread or some margarine, I wanted to take it to mum. But there was nothing left, not even sheets on the bed. The girls had taken everything – I was always the last one.'

Suddenly she saw some black, men's underwear, the kind footballers wear. She had just lost her underpants – someone had pinched all the underclothes they washed every night.

'I put them on straight away. They didn't have elastic, they were tied on with a drawstring. That turned out to be very useful when a Russian tried to rape me.'

His was called Pavlik. He dragged Dina to a ravine in the forest.

'I didn't know Russian, I was desperate. I told myself, "think of mum," but it didn't help. He badly wanted to do it, but finally he left me alone. He lay down on the ground and lifted up my leg to show I'd won. That general of his had sent us to bring food, and on the way Pavlik had thought, why not enjoy himself? In the end we reached a place where there were soldiers. The first thing they said to me was I was incredibly thin and needed to eat. Gladly, I said, if you give me something. Pavlik brought preserves, sausage and sardines.'

Another time in Dina's memory, there appeared a scene from before the war. Her mother was learning to pronounce the Czech letter ř; she wanted to show how Czech she was, but she was having a hard time of it. Her grandmother and aunt Mely couldn't pronounce the ř at all – most often they spoke German. Mely's daughter Lička was in the house too, and the maid as well. Nothing but women.

Lička's father, a Czechophile and legionnaire, would come to visit. He was so short Jana called him Shpunt, even though his surname was Fischer. And Lička was like an adopted sister...

But most often, memory led Dina to the Zigeunerlager: Céline in her blue headscarf mourning her child, a woman tying a crawling infant to her by the leg so she wouldn't lose it, fire-eaters blowing plumes of flame and raising the spirits of the SS officers.

Dina thought constantly of the watercolours. They were probably deteriorating, hidden in some storeroom, unneeded. But it was only thanks to them her mum had lived to be 82, and she herself had children and grandchildren. She complained to her daughters that she couldn't sleep. It was because of the paintings. When she recovered them, the insomnia would go away.

Did she miss these portraits of strangers?

According to the author Wiesław Myśliwski – whom she certainly didn't read – that was possible, because events of the past didn't repose in the memory like holy vestments in a chest. They continue happening, with memory providing more fulfilment than it did testimony. Perhaps things must also ripen in memory. 'Perhaps things are defined not so much by their authenticity as our yearning for them, our regret, our finding ourselves in them, for from day to day we are nothing short of lost in things […]. Perhaps through memory we also wish to assure things of our existence in the here-and-now, which is the only possible eternity.'

The watercolours or NATO

The Cold War was over and the post-Communists were following in the footsteps of the West: human rights, democratic elections and market competition. Dina had no doubt: totalitarian Poland had imprisoned and detained the portraits, a free one would return them.

After years of silence, she sent letters to the museum. But the administration was deaf to her demands. Things kept going in circles. The watercolours – acquired legally and in good faith as anonymous works – had to remain in Auschwitz. They were part of the camp's heritage, documentation of Dr Mengele's criminal activities. The artist was only entitled to property rights: copyright and royalties.

It was inconceivable. Had the system really changed in Poland?

Dina didn't give up and set about making appointments with journalists. She told them of Mengele's obsessions, the white bread for Céline, the runaway's heart, finally of the soulless Poles, who had no understanding of morality or property.

The journalists were indignant. In newspapers and online they declared the Auschwitz-Birkenau museum was withholding stolen art. When the victim asked what right they had to do so, the management spoke of the public good being superior to private property. It was a Stalinist stereotype: the state mattered, not the individual. Over there, they probably still believed in Jewish greed and depraved bourgeois individualism.

All you had to do was look at what was happening in Poland: scandal after scandal. During the recent commemoration of the fiftieth anniversary of the liberation of Auschwitz, President Lech Wałęsa didn't once utter the word 'Holocaust'. There was no set time in the programme to pray for the murdered Jews. So during the lunch break some of those attending the commemoration went to Birkenau and gathered by the crematoriums, including Elie Wiesel (the Auschwitz prisoner and Nobel Prize winner spoke in Yiddish), Shevah Weiss (the president of the Knesset gave his speech in Hebrew) and Jean Kahn from the European Congress of Jews (he reprimanded Wałęsa in English). Then came the Kaddish. The president of Germany, Roman Herzog, was there to listen.

The Poles were giving the world no opportunity to change its opinion.

The coverage quickly intensified and the media rattled sabres. Poland – like it or not – was now a part of the Western world. Property was to be respected under capitalism. If the post-Communists dreamed of joining NATO, then they should give back the watercolours first.

Dina had allies. The West had recognized the survivors' dignity long before. They were no longer accused of cowardice, no longer felt uneasy pangs of conscience, no longer cut off friendly conversations. Wartime memoirs were in demand. The Holocaust survivors and authors Tadeusz Borowski, Primo Levi, Elie Wiesel and Imre Kertész had not exhausted the subject. Publishers were ordering new autobiographies and studios fresh screenplays, while documentary filmmakers were questioning witnesses.

This was the fashion. Pop culture had stood on the side of the persecuted ever since the American TV channel NBC had broadcast the miniseries *Holocaust*, starring Meryl Streep, over four January evenings in 1978. The episodes (almost eight hours altogether) tell the fate of the Weiss family, assimilated German Jews. The story, which began under the Weimar Republic, could have come out of a history book: the Nuremberg Laws, *Kristallnacht*, Babi Yar, the Warsaw Ghetto Uprising, Buchenwald, Theresienstadt and Auschwitz.

Critics panned the series, and they still do. It was crude and implausible, full of historical errors and insulting to survivors. To make things worse, the station interrupted it with advertisements. Was it ethical to make a fortune from a tragedy? Nonetheless, in 1979, *Holocaust* was nominated for three Golden Globes and won two, as well as eight Emmys, the so-called 'Oscars of Television'. It beat out the BBC miniseries *I, Claudius* in its category. All of Western Europe was glued to their televisions. (The East had to make do with *Claudius*).

The film director Agnieszka Holland said in an interview: 'It gave you the feeling this was the first time the Americans and Germans had heard about the tragedy of the Jews.'

The series marked the start of the golden age of Holocaust cinema. It inspired, enraged and provoked debates about racism and anti-Semitism, the rights of artists and the oversimplification of history, as well as about culture and politics.

This kind of cinema plays on the emotions of viewers, who know they will survive. A Holocaust canon for the masses was formed. Kinga Krzemińska, a scholar of the subject, wrote about *Schindler's List*: 'Schindler's Jews are pushed into the gas chambers and, instead of Zyklon-B, water pours down on them. This is the emotional climax of the film, because if Spielberg was able to change Zyklon-B into water, then nothing is impossible for him.'

Jeffrey Goldfarb: 'A lousy TV series, practically a soap opera, provided 120 million Americans more information about the Holocaust over a few days than had reached them in decades. It brought concrete political results, but the production values were second-rate.'

Goldfarb had lectured for years at the New School for Social Research. A group of intellectuals founded the university in 1919, in opposition to violations of academic freedom (Columbia University was forcing academics to conduct research for the army). When Hitler came to power, the institution became a haven for 170 European academics escaping Fascism. Hannah Arendt, Erich Fromm, Claude Lévi-Strauss, Jacques Maritain, Roman Jakobson and others lectured at the University in Exile.

A new era brought different challenges. Scores were settled over at least 20 years in the US, Europe, South America and Africa – hence the need to commemorate a difficult past.

Amy Sodaro, a doctoral candidate at the New School, is interested in memorialisation: in plain language, how memorials of atrocities and museums present the things we remember. She's examined several locations, including the Holocaust Museum in Washington. She was puzzled why the American government put up money for it, since the Holocaust was committed in Europe.

'The reasons were purely political. Jimmy Carter, the Democratic candidate for president, was losing the support of Jewish voters. So he floated the idea of commemorating the Holocaust. A special commission was called, which for over 10 years gathered materials and testimonies, visited Auschwitz and Yad Vashem, and discussed how to do it.'

The American public were sceptical. Why was the government insisting on placing the museum near the National Mall, a park of national monuments within sight of the Capitol and the White House? The location was too prestigious. People kept saying, 'of course we fought in World War II, but the Holocaust wasn't our experience.'

Jeffrey Goldfarb: 'The NBC miniseries marked the moment in the United States when the Holocaust stopped being exclusively part of Jewish memory.'

Amy Sodaro: 'The exhibition begins and ends with the information that the Americans liberated concentration camps in Germany. Lots of space is given to the history of the post-war Jewish emigration to the United States. This Americanizes the Holocaust.'

The Holocaust took place in another time and another place. Imagination is meant to take visitors, especially young people, to that time and those places. Ralph Appelbaum, the main designer of the museum, explained: 'If we followed these people under all that pressure as they moved from their normal lives into ghettos, out of ghettoes onto trains, from trains to camps, within the pathways of the camps, until finally to the end [...] if visitors could take that same journey, they would understand the story because they will have experienced the story.'

(He undoubtedly believed that was true.)

The exhibition's script draws on the conventions of cinema. The birth of Hitler's state is Evil, the Americans' struggle and the liberation is Good. And on the way, there are gruesome projected images, one after the other, illustrating phenomena contrary to American values.

Amy: 'The exhibition arouses powerful emotions which are meant to educate, to reinforce national identity. The message is clear. American pluralism and freedom of speech is our defence against the threat of another genocide. After visiting the museum, the audience, morally transformed, recruited as witnesses to history, is supposed to shout at the top of their lungs: let's defend democracy.'

(When the museum opened in 1993, a bloody war was underway in Bosnia and Herzegovina.)

The building on the National Mall is one of the most-visited museums in the United States. Dina declared to the art critic Dora Apel that her daughters and granddaughters would never see the watercolours, because they would never visit Poland. It wouldn't be so far for her family to get to Washington.

The certificate

Jana Gottliebová was working as a clerk in Mr Hon's shop on Nová Street, which sold carpets. Dina had learned what socialism was, and burst into the house, excited. 'We're proletarians!' Her mother interrupted: 'What do you mean, proletarians? We're the poor middle class.'

After the Munich agreement, the new Second Czechoslovak Republic introduced anti-Semitic race laws and locked Gypsies up in camps (one was built in Hodonín, another in Lety). Dina was expelled from school.

That didn't mean she'd been left on her own: for years, Jewish youth had been forming organizations. She chose the Techelet Lavan, further to the left than Maccabi HaTzair. She signed up for the Hachshara – a summer training camp where she learned Hebrew and farming techniques. For Zionists who wanted to go to Palestine, it was preparation for life on the kibbutz.

But there was no space left for Dina. She turned to the local Jewish community for help finding work. She got an address and went to the village indicated (what was it called?) and looked for the Spáčil family. But everyone there was called Spáčil! She finally got where she needed to be, but the landlady didn't want her. She gave Dina's pink-varnished fingernails a reproachful look.

'I said I'd work a week for free and she would take that time to make up her mind. I milked seven cows and tended six calves and pigs. I didn't like the pigs so much, because I had to clean their sties. And then there was work in the fields.'

Two months of slogging and finally a space opened up for in the Hachshara. The landlady despaired, but Dina went to join the young people. She studied, and met Lotka and Frycanek Kestenbaum, Jindra Leckner and others.

Suddenly, the opportunity presented itself to leave for Palestine – an illegal emigration. Dina packed, squeezing her riding boots into her suitcase. She knew she needed a certificate, but she didn't manage to get her hands on one, because at the last minute the father of a rich girl from Ostrava had snatched it out from under her nose.

'That girl went and I didn't. I was glad because of mum, but I didn't go back to Brno. Our whole group went with the Hachshara to Prague.'

Remembering, weighing up – what would have been if.

If she had succeeded back then, she'd be Israeli through and through. After the war, she'd have looked down her nose at survivors. Or what if she'd gone to Israel after the camp? Then she'd have lived to see respect as well, because although youth judges, maturity forgives.

Lizzie Doron, who escaped her ghetto-neighbourhood in Tel Aviv and today is a well-known writer, says: 'I believed I could cast off the past like dead weight, and my peers believed the same. That ended without warning on 6 October 1973.'

Right then, Israel was celebrating Yom Kippur. Suddenly, sirens howled in the cities. Soldiers on leave rushed out of synagogues and family homes. When the enemy attacked, the borders were being defended by young, untrained boys. There was confusion, conflicting decisions, a hasty mobilisation. Troops and equipment went to the front, but Egypt and Syria were pushing ever deeper into the Sinai and the Golan Heights, which Israel had taken in the Six-Day War.

At that time, Michael Sobelman – today an official at the Israeli embassy in Warsaw and a translator of Hebrew literature – was fighting in the occupied Egyptian village of Sharm el-Sheikh. Leonard Cohen – the Jewish bard – came to the base to give a concert to boost morale. At night, the soldiers listened to radio broadcasts from Cairo in Hebrew, featuring Israeli POWs who'd surrendered to enemy forces.

Michael: 'When I heard their voices, I understood it was possible to lay down your weapon and go like a lamb to the slaughter.'

Lizzie Doron: 'Among 41 of my peers, seven died. We'd suddenly become weak, humiliated and terrified. That war built a bridge between us and our parents' generation. The trauma on the front brought us closer to them. It was the biggest psychological change I had ever experienced. After the war, we went back to our neighbourhood. My relationship with my mother grew more mature. In fact, it was the first time we really talked.'

Israel overcame the aggressors, but paid for it with the deaths of more than 2,500 young people.

A few years later, Michael Sobelman was speaking to a man in Haifa who'd survived the German occupation of Poland.

The man said: 'I only felt Israeli after the Yom Kippur War, when it turned out Israelis could lose too. My experience of the Holocaust, an experience of defeat which until then no one had wanted to hear, was no longer foreign here.'

Lizzie married a son of pioneers whose family had arrived in Palestine in 1882. 'That made me an Israeli. But not until 10 years after the war, when we already had a family, did it get through to us that Israelis were made up of different groups of people. Immigrants from Russia were coming and asking about the Holocaust. We started to hear how it had been, what our parents had survived. After that, we saw them differently.'

The Yom Kippur War altered the political jigsaw. The radical Menachem Begin – the first Israeli leader to appeal to survivors directly – stood at the head of a new bloc of right-wing parties, called Likud (Unity). Four years later he was prime minister, because Likud had defeated the governing Labour Party.

Things also changed at Yad Vashem.

The institute had been founded in 1953 by an act of the Knesset. The idea was older, dating to September of 1942, when the Holocaust was still ongoing and it was uncertain if a Jewish state would be founded. Mordechai Shenhavi, from the kibbutz Mishmar HaEmek, proposed the idea.

Michael Sobelman: 'Shenhavi dreamt of a mausoleum. For years, he took the idea from door to door. He even got to Ben-Gurion, who didn't take him seriously either. But after the war the French got the idea to build a Holocaust museum in Paris. Then the prime minister panicked that someone might beat him to it, because building monuments to the victims and hunting down the perpetrators was a job first and foremost for Israel.'

The institute's work proceeded sluggishly, until Israel Gutman took over the directorship after the Yom Kippur War.

A historian, a lecturer at Hebrew University in Jerusalem, one of the last living veterans of the Warsaw Ghetto Uprising and a witness at Eichmann's trial, he focused on gathering testimonies. He hired people who'd survived the war in Europe, and the museum transformed into a research institute.

Soon Israeli television broadcast the pop-culture miniseries *Holocaust*, which landed, with its message, on ground prepared by the war.

Michael Sobelman: 'It was more powerful than Claude Lanzmann's *Shoah*. It was shown on Channel 1, in prime time. It was a colossal embarrassment that the Americans had done it and not us.' In the United States, the series had uplifted the Holocaust and led to the birth of a pioneering museum. Michael: 'Yad Vashem, small and a bit primitive, looked like the Jewish pavilion in Auschwitz. Eventually the complex was deemed "outdated" and the exhibit not sufficiently aggressive in its articulation.'

The new management focused on multimedia installations. Visitors got to feel as though they were part of the events. Nazi marches echoed through the windows of a German Jewish flat, and a newspaper from the 1930s lay on the table. The Warsaw Ghetto: Leszno Street. Supposedly original cobblestones with tram lines, lamp posts, benches. On monitors, the recollections of survivors. And so on, room after room, until the trail of death led the visitors outside.

Rebirth: a view of Jerusalem.

Michael: 'Not all Israelis are religious, as time has gone on the Holocaust has become our religion. It unites everyone. The form of Yad Vashem parallels that.'

Dina wondered what could have been, and reflected.

Under different circumstances, it would be Yad Vashem fighting for the watercolours. And they could have got them.

They had transported the author and artist Bruno Schulz's murals from Drohobych in Ukraine to Jerusalem in secret. Because it didn't matter that he wrote in Polish, he died as a Jew. In 1942 – the year of his death – the Gestapo officer Felix Landau had ordered him to paint a few scenes from *Snow White* on a wall in his children's room.

I am Jewish, and you smell

Five-year-old Dina was drawing dachshunds – on paper, on Bristol board, on empty sugar bags. But now from the balcony, she could see Lička, who was in year one. And look! Children ran around her. They shouted merrily: 'You're a smelly Jew, you're a smelly Jew!' Dina wanted to laugh as well, and she shouted out those very words.

Her mum signed her up for a German primary school. Once she heard the children saying: 'You're a smelly Jew, you're a smelly Jew!'

'Grandma said, "Next time tell them, I am a Jew, and *you* smell."'

In the park on the hill, Lička and Dina would chase one another around a monument made of Swedish granite. They would shout: 'I am a Jew, and you smell!' Alongside stood their friend, a German girl.

That is the only animosity her memory offers up.

Her memories of Czechoslovakia aren't bad. In winter they celebrated Chanukkah, but on Christmas a small tree stood in the corner – for tradition's sake, though there were no Christians in her family. Uncle Fischer – 'Shpunt' – advised Jana to transfer her daughter to a Czech school. Dina went there from year four. She encountered no harassment, and her teacher – Mr Schoř – took notice of her talent. It was thanks to him she studied graphic art and sculpture.

Now Leša lived in Czechoslovakia, and was still a friend from Auschwitz. Dina would sometimes visit her, and Leša's daughter would come to Los Angeles. When Czechs or Czech Jews invited Dina to commemorations in Terezín, Prague or Brno, she didn't refuse.

It was only Poland she steered clear of. But this time she had to go, for the watercolours. The visit would definitely not be pleasant. For years, Jewish organizations had been sounding warnings that Christians were appropriating Auschwitz. There was television footage to confirm it.

Pilgrims, journalists and onlookers stood on a mound overgrown with grass, which had once been a gravel heap. Children ran about. Coaches were arriving constantly with sightseeing tours from the Netherlands and Germany. They would slow down, because this was a must-see when visiting the camp. Everyone could take pictures in front of crosses. The crosses were made of wood, metal or plywood, some small ones and some several metres high.

Crosses in a Jewish cemetery!

The American press were incensed, they made no bones about it. But how could anyone understand it?

It had started with the Discalced Carmelites. The sisters were housed in a building called the Old Theatre, where during the war, the Nazis had stored Zyklon-B. They were caring for the cross under which the Pope had led Mass at Birkenau in 1979.

The sisters' presence just outside the walls of the camp became an international issue in 1985. That's when the Catholic organization Aid to the Church in Need placed an advertisement in a Belgian newspaper calling for support for the convent, which 'was becoming a spiritual fortress', 'a guarantee of the conversion of our stray brothers' and an expression of the desire to 'blot out the insults so often encountered by the Vicar of Christ'.

Konstanty Gebert was following the events – under Communism, he had been a co-founder of the independent Jewish Flying University and the Polish Council of Christians and Jews, as well as a journalist in the underground press under the pseudonym Dawid Warszawski.

'The Carmelites in their "spiritual fortress" were supposed to pray for the souls of murdered Jews. They didn't say it was with the intention of proselytization; still, it was an ecumenism of ignorance. The various Jewish groups shared a common conviction – Auschwitz was built by people raised in Christianity, so under the sign of the cross. First they murder a million people here, and now they're triumphantly planting the murderers' symbol at the execution site?'

Edgar Bronfman took action. The multi-billionaire and heir to the Seagram alcohol consortium was at that time head and sponsor of the World Jewish Congress (a federation of dozens of Jewish organizations from different countries).

It went as far as holding talks in Geneva. The Jews explained to the Catholics that they don't build synagogues in cemeteries and don't hold religious services there. Christians believe true life doesn't begin until after death. A cemetery is a place where rituals abound. In Judaism it's different – today is what matters, and no one knows what comes after death. The dead are gone and there's nothing they can do, and in cemeteries, the living are not permitted to do what the dead no longer can. That's why – the Jews said – we don't want there to be Christian prayers and symbols in Auschwitz. It would be yet another appropriation. First you took our Torah for yourselves, only to teach us afterwards what it 'really' means. Now you want to put crosses up in our cemetery over our dead, and it's a double insult.

Konstanty Gebert: 'For the first time in history, the Church behaved as though it understood the point of the Jews' arguments and recognized they were put forward in good faith.'

In 1987, an agreement was reached. The Christian side promised the Jewish side that in two years, the sisters would be out of the Old Theatre. But the Carmelites remained. In silence, contemplation, with no contact with the outside world – Carmelite nuns even disavow their parents.

Meanwhile – beyond the convent walls – steel mills, shipyards and ports were going on strike. Lech Wałęsa was speaking on TV, the Round Table was being set up in Warsaw, the Communists suffered a devastating defeat in the partially-free elections. There was delirium, enthusiasm and hope.

The rabbi plays the kettledrums

Several Jews came to Auschwitz from America, furious with the Catholic Church, saying it had been evasive in Geneva and tried to hoodwink them. The small group was led by the American rabbi Avraham Weiss, whom they called 'Avi'.

Weiss, in private a moderate idealist, acted like a political performance artist. He went on hunger strike for Soviet Jews whom the authorities refused to allow to emigrate to Israel. He protested the imprisonment of the underground human rights activist Natan Sharansky in the Perm 35 labour camp, on accusations of spying. During the Geneva Summit between

Reagan and Gorbachev, Rabbi Weiss managed to get into the local Aeroflot office. He pulled out his credit card and loudly demanded a one-way ticket for Sharansky from Mordovia to the West.

In 1986, Kurt Waldheim took office as the president of Austria. When he was revealed to have a Nazi past, Rabbi Weiss declared personal war on him. He swore he'd stand holding a placard wherever the Austrian president went to meet leaders of other countries. He protested twice against Waldheim's talks with the Pope. When he followed him to Turkey, at Weiss's side was Beata Klarsfeld – the German who'd slapped Kiesinger in the face. Reportedly, the Turkish police beat them up, and after being overpowered, they even got roughed up in the police car.

They experienced beatings, nights spent in ditches and criticism, including from their own side, saying Weiss didn't represent anyone, he crudely played on emotions, he was after cheap publicity. In a word, he did the Jewish cause more harm than good.

The rabbi responded in an interview: 'Every orchestra needs a drummer and a flautist.'

In Auschwitz, he banged on pots, then put on a prayer shawl and jumped over the Carmelites' fence with his students following after him.

Afterwards he explained to journalists: 'We started praying on the steps. This was at five in the afternoon – we wanted to spend Shabbat peacefully protesting. But the builders who were working on extending the convent poured a bucket of dirty water mixed with urine on our heads.'

The nuns and the local priest did nothing as they watched the protestors being driven away. Someone shouted: 'Jews to the gas, Heil Hitler!' The police didn't respond.

The Rabbi summed it up: 'You treated the Jews the same as your Church did 50 years ago.'

The Primate of Poland, Józef Glemp, not understanding the significance of Jews being beaten in Auschwitz today, responded: 'Not long ago a squad of seven Jews from New York made an attack on the convent in Auschwitz. It did not reach the stage of killing the nuns or destroying the convent before the attackers were subdued.'

So dialogue transformed into open conflict.

In Poland, breaking into the grounds of such a strict convent was practically sacrilege. People couldn't understand what the nuns had done to provoke such ire. Praying in a cemetery? The town of Oświęcim had a Jewish cemetery on Dąbrowski Street, but the convent bordered the camp, and people of many faiths perished there. The newly-free press printed astonishing reports of ongoing Jewish protests in Auschwitz and the locals' angry opposition.

Father Stanisław Górny, the parish priest at Oświęcim's St. Maksymilian the Martyr Church, couldn't tolerate this chaos any longer. At the end of July 1989, with the agreement of the Carmelites (but without the bishop's approval), he moved the cross to the gravel mound, a few metres from the convent walls.

It was meant to provoke – for what harm did prayer do?

This is how crosses and chapels were put up in Communist Poland: quietly, at night, in secret, as a fait accompli. If people considered them sacred and inviolable under Communism, it was even more so now. The priest's action gave national-religious immunity to the convent, the cross and the gravel mound where the Nazis had shot 152 Poles.

Manfred Deselaers, a priest from West Germany, was living in Oświęcim at this time. When he finished school in 1972, he didn't want to do military service. He chose alternative service and went to Israel with the Action Reconciliation Service for Peace. He cared for disabled children and talked to people who'd survived the camps. Later in Germany, he immersed himself in theology. He was fascinated by John Paul II. He wanted to become acquainted with the Pope's homeland, so he set off for Kraków on a student pilgrimage. He visited Auschwitz. He wrote an angry letter to his father: why didn't you tell me? His father had been afraid to. Terrorists and Communists were preying on radical young people. But Manfred planned to do something concrete for peace, and definitely in Poland.

He felt bad in Oświęcim from the start, because he was a priest and a German. He kept quiet, wrote his doctoral thesis and observed. He knew what the camp was like under Communism: no references to religion, only politics, friendship with the Soviet Union and gratitude to the Red Army. Meanwhile Karol Wojtyła, when he was still bishop of this place, had stressed this point – we must pray here.

Father Manfred: 'At the fall of Communism, from the Polish point of view it seemed natural to turn the camp into a place of prayer. Jewish people protested. This awakened unpleasant associations among the Poles. Fascism was anti-Christian, Communism was anti-Christian, and now freedom had arrived and they were stopping us from putting up a cross and praying?'

The dispute quietened down and months passed. The Autumn of Nations was winning victories across the continent. The British historian Timothy Garton Ash joked about the democratic transitions in Central and Eastern Europe: 'In Poland it took 10 years, in Hungary 10 months, in East Germany 10 weeks; perhaps in Czechoslovakia it will take 10 days!' Meanwhile, the nuns were still living in the convent.

Relief

In March of 1993, the World Jewish Congress informed the bishops and the government that, because of the Carmelites, it would boycott the commemoration ceremony of the 50th anniversary of the Warsaw Ghetto Uprising. In April, the Pope wrote a letter to the nuns. Politely but definitively, he told them to leave. ('At present it is the will of the Church you are to move to another location in Oświęcim.')

Before they left, they leased the Old Theatre building and the gravel mound with the cross to the Association of War Victims for 30 years. Whether that was legal was a question the courts struggled with for years to come. (The museum didn't take control of the land until 2004. Until then, they had no influence over what was going on there.) The Association promised its members it would obtain compensation on their behalf for those who'd been harmed by the Third Reich. The chairman was Mieczysław Janosz, a hero of 'Operation Iron'. (At the end of the 1960s, the secret police had sent the brothers Kazimierz, Jan and Mieczysław Janosz to the West. They'd robbed shops and warehouses in Germany and France, and split the profits with the government.)

Meanwhile Konstanty Gebert was in charge of the Jewish monthly *Midrasz*.

'Discussions about the papal cross were continuing quietly. The Jewish side explained that a cross on the gravel mound wasn't so irksome, but its height was. It towered over the camp, it was nearly eight metres tall. The cell where Maksymilian Kolbe died had become a Catholic shrine, but you could visit Auschwitz without seeing that place. It functioned a little out of the way, so it went without protest. If the cross were shorter and weren't visible from the grounds of the camp, it would be possible to ease the conflict. The Catholic side wanted a cross but didn't insist on whether it was big or small.'

The government's plenipotentiary for contact with the Jewish diaspora announced the discreet agreement. He let slip to a journalist from the French paper *La Croix* that a memorial to murdered Poles with an engraved cross would stand on the gravel mound, and the papal cross would go back to the Carmelites.

One hundred and thirty MPs rushed to the cross's aid, and a committee to defend it was even founded in Oświęcim. At times, volunteers protested in front of Parliament in Warsaw, and every day, they prayed near the former convent.

Kazimierz Świtoń stepped onto the gravel mound on 14 June 1998, the feast of Corpus Christi. He announced to the journalists he was ready to die for the cross. He went on hunger strike and refused to accept fluids. He lived in an orange tent where he had a basin, water and a toilet.

Janosz, the Cold War mercenary, supported him: 'By defending the cross, we defend all of Poland, all of faith.'

Before this, Świtoń had been, in chronological order: the owner of a television repair shop, a free trade union activist and a prisoner under martial law. In 1991, he became an MP and on the floor of parliament called President Wałęsa a foreign agent. He founded the Movement of Citizens Mistreated by the Authorities. Finally, he published a list of 100 'known Jews leading Poland to ruin'.

From the gravel mound he cried out the slogan: let's build a valley of crosses here. Just bring light-coloured ones so they'll be visible from far away.

Factory delegations appeared, as well as hastily set-up societies, committees and associations. There were lay people and clerics, Lefebvrists excommunicated by the Pope, young skinheads in combat boots, stooped-over men who'd missed out on the fruits of the democratic transition, and the 'mohair berets' – a legion of prayerful old women regarded as being troublesome. The country was on the march towards the European Union and NATO. There was no sense bothering with old ladies who'd be dead soon anyway.

There were Polish, Marian and Papal flags. There were rosaries. There were masses, singing and the Stations of the Cross. There were sermons comparing the site to Westerplatte – where the Nazis had launched their invasion of Poland in 1939.

This unleashed an international uproar. Israel was protesting, letters were coming from the American House of Representatives, Rabbi Weiss threatened to come, American unions threatened to boycott Polish airlines at Newark airport. Jan Karski, the wartime underground courier (who'd lived in the West since 1942), published a bitter declaration: 'I never expected that, toward the end of my life, a part of which was devoted to a futile struggle to save "our older brothers" perishing in the Holocaust, I would live to see my countrymen raising blasphemously the sign of the cross against those through whom our God was revealed.'

The Primate's mouth got away with him again. He was standing in defence of Świtoń and his side: 'This coalition arose not out of fantasy, but because of constant and growing harassment from the Jewish side. The cross should stand, because thousands of Christians died here, including Jewish Christians. This ground is Polish.'

Finally, weeks later, the episcopate changed tack and announced the papal cross would stay, but the unofficial ones had to be taken away. But who was supposed to make the change? The Church called on the government, but the government was hiding its head in the sand.

Things had got lively on the gravel mound. Świtoń had been living there for almost a year. He was signing autographs and calling press conferences. If he didn't like a question, he would call the journalists Jewish bumpkins and turn them out, because there were skinheads about and skinheads don't mix with lackeys. They didn't want to put up any new crosses with the reporters there. The crosses lay on the grass – they were well made, from pine, and plainly visible.

It was media catnip. Correspondents from the West sensed it too, and they'd pigeonhole whoever they could. A veteran from Warsaw happened along. He prayed: 'Jesus, don't allow the destruction of this land we Poles have inherited. Don't allow Poland to be split up into counties and Euro-regions.'

When Dina passed the gravel mound on 15 May 1999, 291 symbols of suffering stood by the walls of Auschwitz.

Don't do this to my mother!

More than a decade earlier, Dina had walked through the gates of the camp, abandoned and defenceless. Now she had her daughter, a lawyer and a TV crew from the American NBC network by her side. The well-known journalist Katie Couric was filming a report on the portraits for the *Today Show*. They marched boldly up to the block where the watercolours were on display. They didn't knock on the door of the administrative offices.

After all, Dina was at home.

The video isn't on the NBC website or in the Auschwitz archive. But Krystyna Oleksy, deputy director of the museum, remembers bits and pieces.

'My colleague noticed a group of foreigners hanging out near Block 25 with cameras. That was the day before Mrs Gottliebová's expected visit. I wondered if it was the camera crew that was supposed to be accompanying her, and sure enough it was. Our whole meeting, from the moment she walked into the block, took place on camera. Mrs Gottliebová wanted to hold the watercolours in her hands, but they were permanently attached to the walls. The journalist was asking why we wouldn't give them back. Mrs Gottliebová's daughter would shout hysterically every now and again, which didn't make the conversation easier. Finally, she grabbed me by the arm: "Don't do this to my mother!" Of course they made a lot of that in the segment. We'd already said goodbye when Mrs Gottliebová unexpectedly said she'd like to have a coffee with me, alone, without her daughter.'

They sat in the office with their coffee cups.

'She knew German, and fluently; I speak it too, but she communicated with me in English through an interpreter. I didn't ask why. The conversation was calm. I explained what the watercolours meant for the Roma. Finally, Mrs Gottliebová said, "I thought you were my enemy, but I see you aren't," as though she accepted that I had a point. She behaved like a lady.'

The whole team went from Auschwitz I to Birkenau. Krystyna Oleksy thought it was odd Karin sat on the grass and posed for pictures. Alone, Dina wandered the sector of the Theresienstadt Jews – one last time, to say goodbye.

Soon everyone loaded up into their cars and disappeared.

Katie Couric wanted to know what the Polish authorities thought about returning the watercolours. She went into Potocki Palace in Warsaw, which houses the Ministry of Culture. She was in for a disappointment: Minister Andrzej

Zakrzewski had no intention of appearing on camera. He spoke to Dina and her daughter. Karin was in hysterics, and Zakrzewski handed her some tissues and suggested she went outside to cry.

Was the situation under control? Two months later, it turned out it wasn't.

The museum announced: 'American members of Congress have begun a vigorous campaign for Poland to return the paintings of a former prisoner.' In Congress, Shelley Berkley, a Democrat from Nevada, made an appeal to the Polish government and the Museum.

The Americans suggested replacing the originals with copies. Dina agreed.

Stefan Wilkanowicz, vice-president of the International Auschwitz Council, responded first. He wrote a letter to the director saying it was a dangerous idea. 'We must take special care to ensure authenticity.'

An Auschwitz of replicas: prayer shawls made in China, artificial hair, reproduction shoes and suitcases. That vision terrified the museum administration.

Paintings like death certificates

A few days later came the official position. 'The Museum fully understands Mrs Gottliebová's emotional relationship to these works, composed under conditions that doubtless have had influence on her life. Yet in carrying out our statutory obligations, we express the profound conviction that the watercolours should remain in Auschwitz. [...] Both the death certificates, prisoner registrations, and so on produced in large quantities by the scrupulous Nazi bureaucracy, and works of art composed on the grounds of the camp – whether made by prisoners on orders of the SS or illegally – are unique documents that speak most strongly in the place in which they were made.'

There followed a section about the thousands of objects left or created in the camp: 'We may pose a theoretical question: what would happen if further former prisoners or their heirs began arriving here to demand – justly in their view – the return of works of art, pictures, suitcases, maps drawn in the camp or other objects that belong to their relatives, such as the *Arbeit Macht Frei* gate, which the master of artistic metalwork Jan Liwacz made in the camp forge? How should the residents of Brzezinka behave, when to this day they may recognize the windows and doors of their pre-war houses in the barracks of the camp, and posts taken from their fences which retain initials and dates of construction? The Museum entirely understands individual rights, but it was created to serve all – as a place of memory and the only research centre of its kind – and therefore, fully respecting the rights of people who created some of the documents found here, we take the position that every loss from the collections of a place of memory will cause irreparable harm.'

Then there was a further argument over the definition of the images. 'The Museum was not founded as an art gallery. Yet the Museum's statutory obligation is to collect all evidence of war crimes, as well as objects connected to the history of the Auschwitz concentration camp, including artistic works. In this context, the portraits of the Gypsies are, regardless of any interpretation, documents.'

Finally: 'It must also be emphasized that our institution is not an "ordinary" museum. The Auschwitz-Birkenau State Museum is the only institution of its kind. Every square inch of this place is soaked in the blood of the victims of Nazism: Jews,

Poles, Gypsies, Russians and other people murdered here. The main goal of this place is to make itself available to hundreds of thousands of pilgrims and researchers, as well as documenting in the broadest possible fashion the crimes committed here. [...] In the case of the watercolours it is a question of the few traces of evidence left from the Roma Holocaust. Both Roma who survived the Holocaust and representatives of European Roma organisations share the position of the Museum that the portraits should remain in Oświęcim.'

Dust on his fingers

Marian Pawłowski – thin, swarthy and toothless – was posing for a picture in a hat and his best jacket. He was gazing at a field and resting his hand on the rubble of a brick oven. You couldn't see what he was looking at. The lens was fixed on his eyes.

The shutter clicked.

Meanwhile, he moved his hand over the oven, which left traces of plaster on it. Pawłowski wasn't looking at the field anymore, just the dust on his fingers. He was focused and sensitive.

Every year on All Saints' Day, he would wander among the barbed wire. Before retreating, the Nazis had burned the Zigeunerlager, and there was nothing to visit. Only the chimneys were left, and the gate was usually locked. Now he entered it for the first time since he'd been deported from Sułkowice, south of Kraków.

'Tell me, uncle, what was it like here?' ('Uncle' was a term of respect.)

'I was about 20 back then. The Germans just kept on saying, "transport, transport". We didn't know they were sending us to Auschwitz. But by Czechowice we knew. Mum and dad didn't frighten us any. Dad said: 'Whoever's gonna die is gonna die, but maybe you lot will get out. Then other people arrived, Gypsies from Hungary, Romania, Germany… God knows where they found those people. They went to the ovens, and came out with the fire. Lots of sobbing and crying here.'

He smelled the grass.

'When you've experienced something firsthand, it sticks in your mind. I remember there was no grass before. Ugly, this was all mud. Now it's clean and tidy at least. There wasn't much heat from the stove. And the Gypsies, when they went off to work they'd come back looking like they'd fallen in the mud. One would hold the other up under his arms. And they didn't want to dry their clothes on the stove.'

'What did the children do?'

'The kids stayed on their bunks.'

'Did they beat you?'

'If you deserved it.'

'Did you deserve it?'

'Once, when I was having a fag during work. I got 25 lashes. And I got 15 right there, by the barrack, for nicking bread. I'd got it off a civvie. I couldn't eat it fast enough. A German noticed I had a chunk. I didn't grass on him, that civvie I mean, I just said I'd found it behind a brick.'

'Did they beat the women?'

'A German would pick out one of the birds to ladle out soup. If she ever gave her family more, there'd be a big row: not enough here, too much there. Then they'd beat her. Another bird would start up crying cos they were beating this woman. Then they'd all be crying, the kids too.'

'What was the food?'

'Swedes.'

'And to drink?'

'Not much to drink.'

He fell silent and looked around. An empty field, if not for the chimneys. Now the Zigeunerlager existed only in his mind. But he knew where the kitchen was, the hospital, the bath house. He didn't say anything, but you could see he was afraid. Part of his life was sinking into oblivion. He was struggling. He checked where the railway tracks ran to the crematorium and where the ditches were. Success: he found the place where the barrack he slept in used to be.

He walked toward the gate, he moved with difficulty. He muttered: 'If you fell, you fell. If you lived, you lived. That was it.'

Roma romenge, gadje gadjenge – it was an old saying meaning something like, we'll go our way, you go yours. Two worlds: in one, *romanipen* was what mattered; in the other, it was work, property, accumulation and growth. After the war, Marian Pawłowski had bought a wagon with flowers painted on it and roamed the roadways of the Małopolska region. He'd lived like his forefathers, not expecting anything, the camp hadn't torn down any of the walls separating his world from the rest. Old men on their deathbeds taught their children: 'Stick to your own kind, because they're the only ones who'll hide you, the only ones who'll help when you're in trouble.'

But their children started crossing the lines.

The Roma were planning their own pavilion in Auschwitz – Block 13 had been vacated of East German antifascists. The Gypsies were absent in the camp, uncertain traces remained, usually in other prisoners' memories and in the books dug out of the ground by the clerk Tadeusz Joachimowski. It was time to change that. At the young people's request, old men in brimmed hats were telling journalists rambling stories about the Zigeunerlager, even though it was torture for them.

Torch it! Poland is not yet lost

Pogroms – the first in Communist Poland – contributed to the breakthrough.

The musician Józef Merstein: 'The Roma have a head for business, that was how it all happened. Under Communism, you could get passports under the table. I was at my family's in Dortmund, they'd sorted me out a furnished flat and a job as a postman. I came and my relatives looked after me. You had to help out a poor guy from Poland. Everyone gave me a hundred marks. When I went back, I had to get a porter for all the packages. It wasn't bad at home either. The blokes in power wanted to have fun, so I played along. I was always moving. I bought chickens at markets in Vienna, women's dresses and baby food for my daughter in the foreign exchange shops, I took a taxi to Zakopane to pick up a rug. I was spending 50 bucks on fruit. In the shops there were just jars and waiting lists. Meat, buckwheat, rice and flour were rationed. My neighbours kept writing denunciations: he just wanders about with a guitar, how's he got money for ducks?'

The Roma swapped Fiats for Škodas and Škodas for Volkswagens. They bought televisions and washing machines. They got the hang of walls and stopped opening all the windows in late autumn. Cars, carpets, antiques – that's what they dealt in. The carnival of Solidarity had no effect on them.

Freedom came to Oświęcim too, but its cost turned out to be shocking for the town. The chemical plants – which for years and years had given out benefits like holidays on the

Baltic coast and sacks of potatoes in winter – could no longer paper over the gaps in Socialist economics. Some people were going as far as the Silesian mines for work. It turned out the workers' better tomorrow had been yesterday. And someone had to pay.

Roman Kwiatkowski, a resident of Oświęcim: 'It was in 1981, in October. I'm coming back from a date and I drive down alongside the castle. I see something's burning. Flames are coming up from the direction of my house. I drive into a crowd. They're smashing up a house. Someone shouts: that Gypsy is here!'

He fled in fear. What about dad, what about mum? He sped through the narrow streets.

'I've got my lights on and I'm trying to speed up. I shout: get off the road, I'm not stopping! They stood stock still. Holy Mother of God, I was so afraid. They could have killed me, lynched me. I closed my eyes and then opened them again. I don't remember where I went. The windscreen had been smashed with a rock, the windscreen wipers were torn off, but I was alive. I got to 8 Stolarska Street. The crowd was pushing through the gate and shouting: torch it! Gypsy children to the stake! They were singing miners' songs and "Poland is Not Yet Lost". The police were laying into them – if not for the police, all the Roma in Oświęcim would have burned. 140 people.'

The next day at the police station the Roma heard neither the police, the local authorities or the Party wanted them in the town. They had to leave. If they stayed, the authorities would wash their hands of them. They were given one-way tickets, just like the Jews had got in 1968: 'The bearer is not a citizen of the Polish People's Republic'.

'I got to Lund in Sweden on 13 December. In Poland, they had just declared martial law.'

The grapevine

At that time the *romani lila*, or the Roma grapevine, was carrying electrifying news from Germany all over Western Europe.

The Roma were making it known that they'd perished in the camps too. They were fighting for compensation. The government were trying to wiggle out of it, they didn't acknowledge the extermination. They said whoever felt wronged should go to court. But judges were refusing compensation, because just like the average German, they thought the deportations were preventative. The Gypsies' criminal tendencies were the deciding factor, certainly not their race.

The Roma response: a protest in Bergen-Belsen.

'I'm surprised, Bergen-Belsen is a concentration camp, well exactly, says the Taxi Driver, well exactly, sir, that's where they obliterated the Gypsies' – that's from *The Death of a Czech Dog* by Janusz Rudnicki. 'No bloody bigwig paid any attention to their protests, even though they were so spectacular. That's why they protested for so long, until they felt at home protesting, literally. The camp in Bergen-Belsen became their new home for a long time, until the police turfed them out.'

Luckily the reality was a little different. Romani Rose, who organized the demonstrations, said, 'Simone Veil, the president of the European Parliament, was there with us. She'd survived Auschwitz, but she lost her mother there and later they sent her to Bergen-Belsen. She said we were fighting for human rights, that Jews and Roma were equal in the Holocaust, and their ashes mingled together here. We had Simon Wiesenthal, Isaac Bashevis Singer, Yehudi Menuhin and Ignatz Bubis from the Central Council of Jews in Germany on our side.'

For the first time in history the Sinti and Roma were voiciferously reminding Europe of their existence. A year later, on Christmas Eve 1980, came a real shock: a hunger strike in Dachau.

Romani Rose: 'Twelve men were on hunger strike, including three former prisoners. I myself encouraged them. Mature people, over 60 years old, were doing it for their children and grandchildren. Of course, a debate broke out over whether we had the right. The Bavarian state government, which had authority over Dachau at the time, threatened to send the police and not let us into the camp. We explained it was a gigantic cemetery. No one had the right to it except those who suffered and died there and their families.'

So the authorities started talking to them. The head of the museum helped them, and Catholic priests allowed them to move their mattresses into a church. The hunger strike lasted a week, and echoed around the world. The *New York Times* made a lot of noise.

The German elites had something to consider.

Rose: 'If the Jewish Holocaust was a crime, what was the Roma Holocaust? Since we've condemned Nazi legislation, isn't agreeing to its continuation in any form giving recognition to a travesty of justice?'

In 1982, Chancellor Helmut Schmidt officially recognized the persecution of Sinti and Roma as racism, and their deaths during the Nazi years as a Holocaust. Soon Helmut Kohl – at that time leader of the opposition – declared the same during a debate in the Bundestag. In the German states, foundations were set up and supported by the government. They investigated claims and paid compensation for the war to German Sinti and Roma.

Meanwhile, after the return of democracy, Roman Kwiatkowski returned to Oświęcim and built a house. It was the first house in town with a Western-style white façade – and his thinking was Western too. 'In Germany, I'd met several Sinti from good families – evangelical Christians. They got in touch with me. They said: you have to pray for the murderers, so God will forgive them. I asked: why not pray at the death wall in Auschwitz and in the Zigeunerlager? I convinced their pastors and 5,000 Roma from all over Europe were meant to come pray at the camp. They were already on the way, and then Mława happened, and, terrified, they went back home.'

A pogrom.

In June 1991, a Roma teenager caused a road accident, knocking down two young people in Mława, a town 120 kilometres north of Warsaw. The boy died and the girl was permanently disabled. Two days later, a drunken mob ransacked Roma houses. Contrary to the rumour that set it all off, the perpetrator's father hadn't paid off the prosecutors and the police. He took his son to the station himself. Officials hung posters all over Mława saying the perpetrator had been arrested, but it didn't help. A curfew was introduced and reinforcements were brought in.

At this time, unemployment had reached 35 per cent in Mława, and it was even higher among young people. An average 122 applicants were battling for each vacancy. But the Gypsies were living in 'mansions', they were coming in droves from Germany decked out in gold. The aggression didn't affect the poor Roma in shacks, the attackers were destroying houses.

A toast

Roman: 'After that business in Mława, things got unpleasant.'

At such times in the past, the Gypsies would hide and wait it out. Now was different. The first Association of

Roma in Poland had been founded in Oświęcim: that meant representation in facing the authorities. The chief and the Roma elders had given their blessing. (Today there are dozens of such organizations.)

The association sought out allies. On 2 August, the anniversary of the liquidation of the Zigeunerlager, who would stand in an overgrown field with an abandoned group of Polish Roma? The editor-in-chief of the newspaper *Gazeta Wyborcza*, Adam Michnik, decided he would. He spoke a few heartfelt words. After the pogrom, he wanted to show they were not alone. His gesture of solidarity bore fruit. From then on, every year, MPs and foreign politicians would come to Birkenau for the anniversary.

And then came something that had never happened before in the 500-year history of the Polish Roma. In the town of Nowy Dwór Mazowiecki, the Labour Minister Jacek Kuroń – a legend of the anti-Communist opposition and the hope of the poor – met with Roma elders and Henryk Kozłowski, the Šero Rom. Behind them, against the wall, stood women in colourful dresses and headscarves.

'What are we drinking? Vodka or cognac?' the Šero Rom asked Kuroń.

'Cognac,' answered Kuroń. He raised a toast: 'To your health, your majesty.'

There were cold-cuts, fruit and alcohol. Kuroń told a Gypsy woman her fortune. But there were serious moments too.

Henryk Kozłowski: 'Now let Mława speak.'

Ludomir Waćkowski stood up.

'I'm 62 years old, I'm a simple bloke. I've never hurt anyone, but they've hurt me, because they've destroyed everything I had, everything my kids and friends had too. Now we've got nothing and we're old. We want compensation.'

After the Autumn of Nations, the Polish Roma lived better than their counterparts in other countries, who had plagues raining down on them: poverty, unemployment, crime, lack of education and segregation. 'Pool access forbidden to Gypsies', 'No service to Gypsies'. But what united all the Roma after Communism was the constant threat of violence, and memories of violence bridge differences of generation, political system and country.

The Holocaust was the height of their persecution and the Roma political elite were building their identity on it.

They were mobilizing a community with no history. It didn't exist – had no one studied it? Perhaps it had been completely forgotten? Or had it been hidden from fact-finders for the sake of security? Europeans had taken advantage of information about the Gypsies to discriminate against them more effectively.

The German Sinti and Roma created a special centre in Heidelberg to document the extermination of the Gypsies. There was still no name for this massacre. Sometimes people called it 'the forgotten Holocaust', but that offended some Jews. So as not to compete, they invented the Roma words *Porajmos* – 'devouring' – or *Samudaripen* – 'genocide'.

Would either term be accepted? Many Roma didn't like the idea of a national history with the Holocaust as its cornerstone. Some preferred for their culture to continue in the old way. Looking back, towards the dead, was an offence, a betrayal of Roma identity. Others wanted to learn about a different past: their origins, paths of migration, and their success and ability to endure.

Yet the tone was set by the young generation of political leaders in Poland, Germany, Austria, the Netherlands, Hungary, the Czech Republic, Ukraine and the former Yugoslavia.

To them, gatherings in the Zigeunerlager wouldn't summon any ghosts. At the Auschwitz Museum, they declared: we don't have our own country. Let us show all of our persecution in Block 13. We suffered before the war too, and where can we talk about that?

And the Museum made an exception.

Behind glass, to say goodbye

Auschwitz Museum Director Piotr Cywiński, a historian and member of Warsaw's Club of Catholic Intellectuals: 'Exhibitions are normally mounted with the support of governments or ministries. So many groups, institutions or people didn't believe the Roma would manage it. The number of documents was miniscule: the photos of the castrated boys, a few letters, some testimonies. And Dina Gottliebová's watercolours.'

It was an empty past. No diabolical liquidation plan existed. The authorities of the Third Reich had given out inconsistent directives. There was no way of retracing the chain of command. There were no rich archives with information about killing the Roma. After the war, Hitler's allies and collaborators from the occupied countries preferred not to return to the subject. European Roma chose silence, not wanting to complicate their difficult relations with the majority.

Everything to do with this mass killing was on them.

The renovation of Block 13 and the exhibit demanded serious money. The project alone cost 900,000 deutschmarks. Romani Rose, the president of the Central Council of German Sinti and Roma, was covering the cost. He promised to share the materials with the Council's headquarters in Heidelberg. He invited a well-known German curator to collaborate.

In January 1998, Wieland Schmied came to Auschwitz. At first he could only make out two guard towers – everything else was obscured in fog. The place seemed impossible to comprehend. He thought over how to design the exhibition so that it didn't victimize the victims once again. Finally, he made up his mind – he wouldn't provoke strong emotions or even embarrassment.

'If I want to work myself up into a feeling of mourning, I need to sit at the ruins of the crematorium in Birkenau. And I do that. The exhibit has a different goal. The ideal is to make a sort of collage from these documents such that captions are unnecessary.'

Block 13 was the collision of two realities: on the one hand, ordinary people with their intimate lives, on the other – the perpetrators. So they built a room within a room. Visitors first saw the world of the Roma before the Nuremberg Laws. They observed the everyday lives of civil servants, officers, musicians, restaurant owners – before they'd come to harm. They saw the attack on private lives begin when the laws came into force. This was shown using pointed, knife-shaped walls bearing photographs of the perpetrators and documents. The knives stuck further and further in, until privacy was destroyed. The room-within-a-room fractured, and you stepped into the reality of the camp. The visitors were no longer in the exhibition, but in Auschwitz. They were walking on the floor of the real block and seeing the inhuman military architecture through the actual windows.

Now they knew a Holocaust could be carried out in chaos. High-ranking officials of the Third Reich weren't the only ones responsible: priests, local officials, community policemen and doctors in health centres all joined in. This sort of spontaneous genocide was always possible.

Piotr Cywiński: 'The exhibition is among the best. The watercolours are to say goodbye: they're behind glass, especially lit and guarded. They are there to emphasize Roma identity – for European Roma, they are a holy relic.'

The Roma fiercely defended the portraits from Dina Gottliebová-Babbitt.

Parcelling out and satisfying vanity

There was no ignoring Congress. Shelley Berkley's appeal caused a diplomatic furore. Civil servants on both sides of the ocean wrote back and forth, solicited opinions and engaged legal expertise.

Letters poured in for Dina as well.

The first was from Roman Kwiatkowski: 'May I be so bold as to ask you to read my letter and consider the suggestions contained in it. Little evidence has remained of our Holocaust. For myself and others, your portraits are important above all. We Roma are in your debt. [...] Understanding your motivations, Mrs Babbitt, I warmly ask in my own name, as well as in the name of the Roma nation, to make these historic pieces available to us, so they might remain where they will give testimony to our descendants. Please do not deprive them of what is most valuable – memory and history. I am sure, Mrs Babbitt, that your own experiences, your knowledge of others' experiences and your sensitivity will allow you to fulfil this request, which is difficult but so important for our minority.'

Deputy Director Krystyna Oleksy was unsure about her latest letter. After all, Dina Gottliebová knew that no other museum, no collection, no exhibit or locked safe was more worthy of holding the watercolours than their place of origin.

She also knew what this place meant for her, for the other victims and for the modern world. Did Dina think her experiences in the camp deserved to be parcelled out, sold or used to satisfy someone else's vanity? Was that why she was mobilizing the mighty of this world, to call her intentions and her good name, which the museum was promoting, into doubt in the eyes of many? Did she really want to tell the museum's employees their efforts were pointless? Would she tell those friends of hers who had created the museum and gathered its collections that their work was in vain? Oleksy wrote down some of these questions in a private letter.

Dina responded to no one.

The Oświęcim Roma association sent kilogrammes of letters. They were addressed to: Aleksander Kwaśniewski – the President of Poland, Jerzy Buzek – the Prime Minister, Maciej Płażyński – the Speaker of the Lower House, Alicja Grześkowiak – the Speaker of the Senate, Andrzej Zakrzewski – the Minister of Culture, Bronisław Geremek – the Minister of Foreign Affairs, Władysław Bartoszewski – the President of the International Board of the Museum, Mounir Bouchenaki – UNESCO, and Daniel Fried – the US ambassador.

And they sent letters overseas, to American members of Congress. 'Ms Berkley, Mr Gilman, Mr Ackerman, Ms Baldwin, Mr Berman, Ms Brown of Florida, Ms Capps, Mr Capuano, Mr Cardin, Mr Crowley, Ms DeLauro, Mr Delahunt, Mr Deutsch, Mr Engel, Mr Filner, Mr Foley, Mr Frank of Massachusetts, Mr Frost, Mr Gonzales, Mr Gutierrez, Mr Hastings of Florida, Mr Jones of Ohio, Mr Lantos, Mr Levin, Mrs Lowey, Mr Lucas of Kentucky, Mr Luther, Mrs Maloney of New York, Mr Matsui, Mrs McCarthy of Missouri, Mr McDermott, Mr McGovern, Ms McKinney, Mr McNulty, Mr Moore, Mr Nadler, Mr Neal of Massachusetts, Mr Pallone,

Ms Pelosi, Mr Pomeroy, Ms Rivers, Ms Ros-Lehtinen, Mr Rothman, Mr Rush, Mr Sandlin, Ms Schakowsky, Mr Shows, Mr Sisisky, Mr Slaughter, Ms Stabenow, Mrs Tauscher, Mr Udall of Colorado, Mr Udall of New Mexico, Mr Waxman, Mr Weiner, Mr Weygand, Mr Wexler, Ms Woolsey and Mr Wu'.

In Germany, Romani Rose organized a similar action. The Czech Roma joined in.

News came back in the post that their brothers in the United States were supporting Dina's claim. This was announced by Ian Hancock – a linguist and professor at the University of Texas at Austin, a member of the president's United States Holocaust Memorial Council, and a representative of the Roma at the United Nations.

Talisman

Why weren't the American Roma standing firmly behind those from Europe? Because they didn't understand the fuss over these watercolours. After all, collecting mementos after a person's death conflicted with Roma customs and rituals to honour the dead.

Stanisław Stankiewicz of the Central Council of Roma in Poland responded: 'For us, the watercolours are our own kind of talisman, they're holy objects, and they shouldn't be held by someone who isn't Roma. [...] Keep in mind Mr Ian Hancock, who lives in the United States, cannot express his position in the name of European Roma, although he is a member of the International Romani Union. This is only his personal view.'

German Sinti and Polish Roma appealed jointly to Congress and the international community: 'We understand and respect the personal experience of the artist of the paintings, we know about the inhuman fate the Jews encountered. However, we expect respect for our traditions as well. No copy can take the place of the originals. For us, these portraits represent both historical and sacred value. It would be a profanation of the Roma victims of Nazism for them to find themselves in private hands.'

In a 2001 resolution, the House of Representatives called on Poland to return the watercolours. It mobilized President George W. Bush and Secretary of State Colin Powell to make 'all efforts' in the case of Dina Gottliebová-Babbitt.

The journalist Michele Kane, Dina's daughter: 'Dina wasn't the one who tried to get politicians interested in the case, I was. I called Shelley Berkley, she wrote the first congressional resolution for me. Later, my sister Karin went to Auschwitz with a film crew. It was upsetting to her to see the place where her mother, grandmother and members of her family were imprisoned and died. Several times she was moved to tears. When NBC broadcast the documentary, the reaction was universal fury at the Auschwitz-Birkenau Museum and the Polish government for the wrongs they were doing to my mother. The federal government worked most energetically of all. Shelley Berkley introduced a second resolution in Dina's name, Senator Barbara Boxer and Senator Jesse Helms did the same.'

The Polish ambassador to the US, Przemysław Grudziński, exchanged letters with Shelley Berkley. The Congresswoman didn't mince words: 'Let's be clear from the start. The pictures painted by Dina Babbit do not belong to the whole world. They belong only and exclusively to her. They were made with her own hands, and Mrs Babbitt never had the chance to possess the things that saved her and her mother's lives, and which legally belonged to her. In your letter you write: "I cannot imagine a more appropriate place to exhibit these priceless documents of genocide than the Auschwitz-Birkenau Museum". On the contrary, it does not take much imagination to assert that the best and most lawful place for these pictures is the home of Dina Babbitt.'

She goes on: 'Are we to conclude from your letter that Mrs Babbitt's suffering should continue for the purpose of maintaining the coherence of a museum collection? That takes no account of her feelings or her rights. She was imprisoned, and afterwards physically and emotionally tortured in Poland, and now the Polish government informs her that paintings which unquestionably belong to her must remain far away because of their documentary, not artistic, character. That view is unacceptable and I will not consider it.'

Michele Kane: 'Dina had no intention of keeping the paintings for herself, as the Auschwitz-Birkenau Museum and other institutions suggested. Absolutely not! She planned to exhibit the paintings in one of the Holocaust museums in the United States. She wanted the pictures to remain her property, and after her death, the property of myself and my sister.'

Behind the political scenes, the great and the good were conferring, including Israel Gutman, Elie Wiesel and the Polish statesman and Auschwitz survivor Władysław Bartoszewski.

Krystyna Oleksy: 'I'd already reserved a room for a press conference in Warsaw and I was preparing the documents. Minister Zakrzewski's reaction was reluctant. Everyone was a little afraid of this issue. The thinking was to return half of them. But no one ever said to me: "I recommend returning the watercolours." Then I would have had to do it or resign. There were pressures – for instance I got a phone call from [the

World War II Resistance hero] Jan Nowak-Jeziorański. It was unpleasant. Mr Jeziorański shouted at me to send yet another letter to Gottliebová. She, unfortunately, didn't respond. The debate was taking place exclusively on the political level and in the media.'

Why didn't Dina sue the Museum? Probably because she had no chance of winning.

They belonged to Mengele

The New York Rabbi Andrew Baker of the American Jewish Committee, one of the most eminent Jewish organizations in the United States, had the idea of dividing up the portraits and making a settlement.

Director Piotr Cywiński: 'He was wondering how many pieces to give to Mrs Babbitt. Four out of seven, two out of seven? Even one. But to give them, not return them. They weren't hers, they were Mengele's.'

In 2006 the composition of the International Auschwitz Council changed. It was the Council that decided matters having to do with exhibitions and collections. It was composed of the most outstanding Auschwitz and Holocaust historians from Yad Vashem, the United States Holocaust Memorial Museum and other institutions. When Rabbi Baker became a member, he returned to the subject of the claims. But during the decisive meeting no one supported him – now for the second time.

Romani Rose voted at that meeting.

'If the Roma had freely posed for Mrs Gottliebová in her studio in Prague, and years later the pieces had ended up in

Auschwitz, the paintings would be her property. But they were
forced into it, just as she was forced to paint. No one refused
because that would have been the end. The watercolours show
that in the factory of death the prisoners were unable to decide
their own fate. Mrs Gottliebová received no payment from the
Roma, they were painted by force. This is proof of the racist
views and practices of Dr Mengele. I'm surprised that members
of Congress, a few people from the White House and Rabbi
Baker have supported Mrs Gottliebová, instead of being guided
by reason.'

Father Manfred Deselaers voted at the meeting as well. In
the time since he'd examined the arguments over the Carmelites
and the cross during the fall of Communism, he had come to
settle in Oświęcim. He'd lectured in theology at the papal
academy in Kraków and he'd trained as a Holocaust educator
at Yad Vashem and led tours around Auschwitz. He worked in
the Oświęcim Centre for Dialogue and Prayer. He was doing
his best to bring together individual Poles and Germans, and
individual Christians and Jews.

There was no concrete decision about what to do next with
the portraits.

'Because I've never spoken to Mrs Gottliebová, I asked
myself the basic question: what was the reason for the museum's
existence? There are certain prisoners and their families who
would rather hold onto some object or other from the museum
just for themselves. They treat these items as their property or
inheritance. The council is made up of serious-minded people.
The majority acknowledge we must maintain standards and
avoid setting precedents, and show evidence of the prisoners'
suffering in the place were they experienced it. I consider that
an expression of respect for the fate they met.'

The political pressure eased.

Krystyna Oleksy: 'The watercolours are on Congress's agenda. Every now and again some congressman takes a look at what hasn't been resolved yet and goes back to the case. It's sort of tedious harassment.'

Let's defend freedom suitcase by suitcase

Meanwhile, Dina's case was no longer exceptional. Michel Leleu, a retired engineer, went with his daughter and son-in-law to visit the Memorial of the Shoah Museum in Paris. He looked at a pile of suitcases, read the signatures on the labels and discovered his father's name. It was a popular name, but it seemed to him to have been written in his mother's handwriting. Pierre Lévi had perished in Auschwitz and the suitcase from the exhibition was on loan from there.

From then on, the script was the same: his son demanded its return, the Auschwitz Museum refused, the authorities got involved and the news went round the world.

As President of the Auschwitz Council, Władysław Bartoszewski gave his view: 'Of course we can hand everything out, send it away. But if we did that, why have a French pavilion in Auschwitz, why did President Jacques Chirac and Simone Veil come to the opening? If we do that, let's liquidate the Cemetery of Defenders of Lwòw as well, and move Katyń to a forest near Warsaw.'

For Daniel Finkelstein, a commentator for the British newspaper *The Times*, this was the point: 'The only way to protect our fundamental freedoms is one old, battered, empty suitcase at a time.'

Dina, in *Süddeutsche Zeitung*: 'There are hundreds of suitcases in the Museum. They should be happy to find even a single owner. Imagine how much that object means for the family.'

The suitcase would stay in Paris for a long time yet: an agreement was reached. But there was no sign of peace in the dispute over the watercolours.

'If you found something and knew who it belonged to, you'd give it back,' Dina argued to the German journalist. 'They say, finders keepers.'

When the American politicians gave up, Dina's friends hit upon another thought. Why not display the watercolours for a while in the Holocaust Museum, so the family could see them?

Director Piotr Cywiński: 'Then the paintings would get entangled in lawsuits. I talked to Washington, they weren't interested because of the legal issues.'

Why threaten a smooth collaborative relationship? A large batch of loaned materials had just come back from Washington and Auschwitz was sending the next one – again, on loan for several years.

The Auschwitz Museum had broken with Communism and changed the sections of the exhibition which were indefensible. The multilingual plaques were removed from Birkenau, because they fabricated the number of victims. When they were put back in place, they said that around 1.5 million people had died. The current death statistics: Jews – 960,000, Poles – 75,000, Gypsies – 21,000, Soviet political prisoners – 15,000. Altogether – at least 1.1 million. Years before, such figures had infuriated many former Polish prisoners. They stuck to their four million. Some Jews had protested a million was too low. Today no one argues anymore – Polish and overseas museums keep in friendly contact, they send representatives to one another for training. Everyone has to tell the same story about the Holocaust. Memory is uniform.

Dina confided to the readers of *The New York Times*: 'I'm at a total loss. I feel just as helpless as I did when I was in the camp.'

She had a heart attack.

Valentine's Day

Dr Rafael Medoff from the respected David S. Wyman Institute for Holocaust Studies in Washington was reading the newspapers. He was moved by an elderly woman's appeal – her helplessness was causing her pain. Why oughtn't a survivor get her property back? A few years ago, Congress had recommended that the State Department intervene. What did the State Department do? Nothing, so as not to set off a dispute with Poland. But it was tragic what Dina Babbitt was going through. This had to change.

Medoff knew what made today's world go round. Celebrities were more powerful than kings. The demand for first-hand Holocaust stories was outstripping the supply. Consumers were becoming demanding. An ordinary story wasn't enough, there had to be something juicy hidden in it. Authors were earning fame, respect and money, and that was luring in others.

There had been three cases from roughly the past 15 years.

In 1995, Binjamin Wilkomirski from German-speaking Switzerland published his memoirs, *Fragments: Memories of a Wartime Childhood* – the Holocaust through the eyes of a child. He went from wintry Riga to Majdanek, then to Auschwitz. There was a chimney, lice, corpses and rats. After liberation, little Binjamin was taken out of an orphanage in the care of a Swiss family who ordered him to forget everything. When he grew up, he wanted to shout it from the rooftops.

The book won several prestigious awards and was compared to the works of Primo Levi and Anne Frank. But before long a certain Swiss reporter discovered the memoirs were a hoax. The author had never been in a camp.

Wilkomirski stuck to his guns.

Meanwhile, Herman Rosenblat won a contest in the tabloid *The New York Post* for the best Valentine's Day story. As a kid he'd been sent to Schlieben, a sub-camp of Buchenwald. He said he was saved by a nine-year-old girl, a Jew with Aryan papers. Every day she threw bread and apples through the fence for him. After the war, Herman settled in New York and became an electrician. In 1957 he went on a blind date. There he met Roma – his 'angel at the fence'. He proposed immediately and they married.

The New York Post paid for a romantic, candlelit dinner, a Broadway show and a ride in a limo for the couple. The Rosenblats went on Oprah, and said they'd already written a children's book and they were thinking about a memoir for adults and selling the film rights. A historian checked out their heart-warming tale. Roma had been hiding far from Schlieben, near Breslau.

Mr Rosenblat made a short statement. 'It was my imagination, and in my mind, I believed it. Even now, I believe it.'

In 1997, the Belgian Monique de Wael, under the pen name Misha Defonseca, published *Misha: A Mémoire of the Holocaust Years* in the United States. The Polish title was *Surviving with the Wolves*, because in our unfriendly country, it was wolves who cared for this girl wandering 'Eastward' in search of her parents, a prisoner of the unknown. Misha's unusual fate sold extraordinarily well: 200,000 copies in France alone. The memoirs were translated into 18 languages and a commercially-successful film was made based on them. A few years later, an inquisitive person discovered the author's family weren't Jewish, her father had joined the Nazis – although earlier he'd belonged to the opposition movement – and de Wael hadn't crossed Europe with a pack of wolves at all. Instead she was at primary school in Brussels at the time.

Why had she made herself out to be a survivor? Because she didn't want to be 'a traitor's daughter'.

People were lying to get something. Everything in Dina Babbitt's story was true. They only had to pick one unique detail that would stimulate people's imaginations and help Dina defend herself.

In August 2006, Rafael Medoff announced on the Wyman Institute's webpage: 'Gentlemen: Attached below please find a mass petition […] concerning the matter of Dina Babbitt's paintings.' There was a list of 450 famous names. There were comic book artists from the largest American publishers – Marvel Comics and DC, colleagues from smaller companies, the retired old guard of cult comic book artists, Pulitzer Prize winners Art Spiegelman and Michael Chabon, freelancers and even artists from Europe.

They were demanding justice.

The fundamental principle that art belongs to the artist who created it is recognized everywhere except in totalitarian countries. One would hope that Poland, having been liberated from totalitarian rule, would not revert to the mentality that regards everything as the property of the state.

We agree that the display of Mrs. Babbitt's artwork is of great educational value, and we are pleased that the Auschwitz-Birkenau State Museum recognizes its importance. But that educational purpose could just as easily be achieved by displaying high-quality reproductions of the paintings, while returning the originals to their creator and rightful owner.

Mrs. Babbitt has suffered enough. We implore you to do the right thing and give her back her paintings.

Why had these artists supported the petition en masse? Medoff gave two reasons. Dina was a friend – she'd worked in Hollywood studios for many years. And in Birkenau, on the wall of the barrack, she'd painted Disney's *Snow White*.

My heart is still in...

The Auschwitz Museum said the watercolours were a document. Joe Kubert was indignant: 'The reasons or circumstances under which art is created has little or no bearing on the art, except for historical references. Art can be created under any circumstances, anywhere, by anyone.'

He supported Medoff enthusiastically.

Kubert had started out in the 1940s and had drawn many superheroes – from Hawkman to Sergeant Rock. He was the author of a graphic novel about the Holocaust: *Yossel: April 19, 1943*. This was his alternative CV: 'If my parents had not come to America, we would have been caught in that maelstrom, sucked in and pulled down with the millions of others who were lost. There's no question in my mind that what you are about to read could have happened.'

Little Yossel (Joe in Hebrew) ends up in the Warsaw ghetto with his parents. He draws wonderfully and dreams of making comics. The SS-men recognize his talent and order him to draw their portraits; sometimes he draws scenes from comic books for them. In return he receives small privileges.

When the Nazis deport the boy's parents to a camp, Yossel joins the resistance movement. He dies in the Ghetto Uprising.

This couldn't have happened at all.

Kubert sent Warsaw's Jews to Auschwitz – but they died in Treblinka. On the cover he put a drawing of a forearm with the prisoner number 0713142. The numbers never started with zero, and such a high number was never assigned at Auschwitz. One of the heroes stated: 'I learned that Jews were not the only inmates in that place. Soviet POWs, Gypsies, Jehovah's Witnesses and homosexuals were also consigned to that purgatory.' But in 1941, when this part of the story took place, it was mainly Poles in the camps, whom Kubert didn't mention at all, because he didn't like them. He showed the ramp in Birkenau – which was built three years later – and gas chambers in trucks – which they had in Chełmno. The descriptions of the camp meals were inaccurate, and the barracks had the wrong number of beds and the wrong dimensions.

But did it matter?

The artists' protest reached the Auschwitz Museum and the Polish ambassador. They knew beforehand it was futile. Diplomatic efforts had failed, a celebrity mass culture campaign had to be different.

Kubert persuaded two comics masters to work with him. Neal Adams (Superman and Batman) and Stan Lee (Spider-Man) worked with him on the story's artwork. Rafael Medoff wrote the story about Dina.

Joe Kubert: 'The cartoon story was a graphic depiction (to be understood by all) of the unfairness, and cruelty administered to the artist.'

The Last Outrage: The Dina Babbitt Story, made for the Disney studio, was six pages long. It was in black and white – the only colours were in Dina's artwork. Soon an educational channel created an animated version of the comic and put it on their website.

It was her life story in pictures and simple film scenes. A small girl from Brno draws on paper bags, with pictures of Donald Duck, Mickey Mouse and Goofy hung up on the wall behind her. As an art student, she goes to Theresienstadt. Dr Mengele stands on the ramp with a 'calm, cruel face'. Fredy says: 'The children wait until the Germans come for them. After they are taken away, no one ever comes back.' He asks Dina for a mural, but he warns her: 'If the Germans catch you, they might kill you.'

'Freddy, it doesn't matter. I'll take my chances.'

She paints the mural of Snow White on the barrack wall, and Mengele personally demands Dina's talents. The girl asks:

'Am I to be killed?'

'If you paint, you will live.'

'My mother is a prisoner here. If you spare her, I will paint. Otherwise I will kill myself. I will kill myself because I cannot paint a soul if my mother dies.'

'And if I agree?'

'Then I will paint this world.'

'*And so it went.*'

In the following shots: the doctor's experiments, the death march, Paris and Art Babbitt.

'As good stories go, they married and moved to Hollywood. For 17 years the girl who had been forced to paint portraits of evil was now a woman who painted to make children laugh. She worked as an assistant animator for Jay Ward Productions, Warner Bros. and MGM. The nightmares had turned to dreams.

'But… a piece of her heart was still in Auschwitz.'

The visit to Poland with the big suitcase, the refusal.

In the comic book, there was the suggestion that years before, Auschwitz had received stolen goods. 'Officials of the Auschwitz State Museum [...] were contacted in 1963 by someone who had possession of six of the paintings. The museum purchased them from that person. The museum has never revealed the identity of that person... or if he was operating for himself or as an agent of another person, who was unwilling to expose him or herself. Some years later, the museum purchased a seventh of the paintings from an unknown party.'

The finale. 'And so Dina, now 84, continues to wait and hope that one day, the museum will realize the wrong it has committed and will finally give back her paintings. How long will this outrage continue? How long will the international community accept this injustice? How much more suffering must Dina Babbitt endure? Finally, who sold the paintings to the Museum in 1963 and 1973 to their profit?'

It was calmer in the film. 'Dina Babbitt hopes one that day these portraits will be returned to her. So that her heart and soul may finally be complete. But for now, she waits.'

'Find out more at www.dinababbit.com.'

Bastards, scum, pigs

E-mails were coming into the Museum.

Subject: Dina Babbitt
To whom it may concern. My name is Andrew, I am 20 years old, I live in Montreal. I recently learned

you don't want to return Dina Babbitt's work. That's disgusting. You're too greedy to give them up, you're holding them hostage. Maybe my opinion doesn't mean anything to you, and maybe you'll even delete this e-mail, but know this: what you're doing is evil. Evil will haunt you.

Subject: In defence of Mrs Dina Babbitt
Dear museum employees, please, give those seven paintings back. I understand you use copies fairly frequently, so the originals aren't necessary. Dina has suffered enough. Really, how can you argue? I find it hard to accept that a few pigs are depriving Dina Babbitt of a glimmer of hope in her life.

Subject: bastards
You scum, you perverted swine, give Babbitt her work back! You don't belong to the human race, you're too stupid and retarded for that. You should be killed like any wild animal. Give back what isn't yours.

Director Piotr Cywiński: 'Every year we get around 1,500 e-mails like this, mainly from the United States. The majority of them sound identical. They come in waves after articles in the press. They're vulgar. Sometimes they call us Hösses, Eichmanns and Mengele's successors. We answer every letter, except the extremely vulgar ones. The collections department has worked out a form letter, which sometimes changes someone's mind.'

'Dear Mr Cywiński, thank you for writing back and your clear explanation of the facts. I see how important it is for the portraits to stay in the Museum. You have changed my mind.

Please continue your important work keeping the memory of the past alive.'

Piotr Cywiński: 'In our contact with Dina Gottliebová and her daughters, we haven't managed find a balance to the arguments. The International Auschwitz Board analysed the issue: healing the wounds of a former prisoner on the one hand, and on on the other, the images – which are symbols of all the victims. The history of the watercolours will never be private, but it's a history of defeats.'

'Let's return the watercolours,' appealed Robert Sołtyk in the newspaer *Gazeta Wyborcza*. 'The paintings, which are the dearest treasure of an elderly woman who went through hell in the camp, her only memento from the war, can and should be returned to her. A free Poland should be able to afford a heartfelt gesture like this.'

But public opinion remained silent. Let them argue, it's none of our business. What was the point of one more argument? It'll all sort itself out somehow. The authorities were apologizing for the Jedwabne pogrom of 1941, Jan Tomasz Gross's books on Polish anti-Semitism were coming out, the Papal cross was standing as it had stood before.

Only there was trouble in Oświęcim.

The Red Army monument disappeared from the town square and was put in a faraway municipal cemetery. But the lay of the land hadn't changed. Communist Poland had been careful to maintain a balance: something for the living and something for the dead. In the mid-1980s, the townspeople were still living in symbiosis with the camp.

Michał Olszewski, a journalist from Kraków, recalled: 'Bakers baked cakes on the grounds of the former Auschwitz concentration camp. Children played soldiers in the Old

Theatre building. Teachers took their classes to build bonfires in Birkenau; the birch forest next to the camp, near the clearing where the Sonderkommando had burnt murdered prisoners' corpses, was renowned for mushroom-picking. Anglers came to the fire ponds placed on the former camp grounds. When the water froze, young people played ice hockey on them.'

But now foreign tours were zipping through Oświęcim, not even stopping in town to have a coffee. They would visit Auschwitz and sometimes see young people from Oświęcim scouring the birch forest on their knees, searching for hallucinogenic mushrooms.

What did the young people get from the camp? In Świtoń's time, cars would drive up onto the gravel yard, so boys with buckets made money washing windscreens – sometimes in dollars – but that didn't last. When the Maja company announced it would build a shopping centre in the warehouses across from Auschwitz, their CEO got called a *lagergeszefciarz* – one of the swindlers who operated in the camps. American congressmen, who are supposed to consider private property sacred, tried to give the Polish government an ultimatum: the supermarket or NATO membership. But everything happening in Oświęcim was entirely legal.

People wanted to have fun, so for a year there had been a dance club in the former Lederfabrik tannery. Once, it had held a sorting office for suitcases and a storeroom for hair from those who'd been gassed, but the building stood beyond the hundred-metre dead zone around the Museum. It was a kilometre from Auschwitz and four from Birkenau. Its neighbours – the International Youth Meeting Centre – protested. Guests were coming for spiritual reasons, and next door there was booze and techno.

It's Auschwitz, it's not meant to be very nice

The Zone of Interest had hurt and was hurting Oświęcim. The townspeople thought maintaining this invention of Hitler's was an attack on the constitution and the free market, and condemned the city of 40,000 people to stagnation. The supermarket had been closed down, the dance club too, and people were being called anti-Semitic so much it rattled them. At one stage, they organized a grassroots committee and demonstrated in memory of the murdered Jews and against the zone. As for the people accusing them, why didn't they come and try to live here?

Oświęcim was facing uncertain prospects. The Jagiellonian University in Kraków formed a partnership with Gloucestershire and Birmingham Universities in the UK to determine the reason for all the conflict. They found local business was right to worry. Local economic initiatives sparked international controversy. In a time when image is everything, that was disastrous. Oświęcim was falling victim to Auschwitz. The town's future had never been given sufficient discussion. The Catholic Church and the World Jewish Congress spoke up more often than entrepreneurs, the government or international institutions.

But that passed too. Resigned, the town lay dormant next to the Museum and waited for the money it was promised. Young people were fleeing and pilgrims were arriving: Scottish kilts, Buddhist prayer wheels, Japanese monks' robes, Jewish yarmulkes, cornettes, cassocks.

There was also the ordinary tour traffic and people in trainers with cameras. They would look at one another – you had to wear a pious expression. It was a mandatory formula: the Nazis' gruesome violence and the saintly, mournful victims.

'Where were their lawyers?' said one shocked American student as she choked back tears.

Every year, the inter-faith Peacemakers Order, founded by the New York Zen master Bernie Glassman, would meditate in the camp. People who were hurt by the past came there as therapy. European and American Jews, Germans, Italians and Belgians slept in crowded rooms and squatted in front of the bookshop in Birkenau, eating soup from plastic bowls. It wasn't supposed to be very nice.

The meditation took place on the ramp, and in the camp barracks at night. Besides meditating, they talked a lot. Everyone spoke exclusively about their feelings, that was the rule.

The Poles found it more difficult.

The artist Joanna Krzysztoń: 'We're not too expressive or open. One time, the emotions all this can cause exploded out. We felt like we were in the background, and one of us couldn't stand it. Hold on, we're in Poland but we have no voice? Of course what happened to the Jews is most important of all, but there was more to it than that. You expect us to explain, to apologize. What purpose would that serve? To make you more comfortable? Don't you see where you are? All this started from dividing people into "us" and "them".'

Tomasz Jeżowski, who designed furniture for collectors, was doing his best not to imagine Auschwitz.

'When I listen, the stories exist, when I speak, they can free themselves. Here I'm looking for my own identity, rather than a Polish one. I think to myself: this happened. Without any political spin… I don't judge myself or others. I like to meditate in the crematorium, in the evening it's a peaceful place. A mat, a pillow and a candle. We sit in silence – we know what this place was. Peace, relief and joy come to us. Because the souls here don't need despair, just our presence and witness.'

A young French Jew felt disappointed.

'I look at Poland and I have the feeling I'm at the centre of nothing. But they told me in Auschwitz I'd be at the centre of the world.'

Snow White and Mengele

In 2006, a journalist from the German *Süddeutsche Zeitung* noticed the screaming headlines his American colleagues were attaching to stories about Dina. 'Snow White's Nightmare', 'Snow White in Birkenau'. Maybe the next one would be Snow White and Mengele.

He got moving. It was two hours by car from San Francisco going north, toward the Pacific, then a winding, one-way road through the rainforests of Santa Cruz, to the wooden house surrounded by sequoia trees on Zayante Creek.

He stood before the door. An elderly woman opened it energetically. She had strawberry-blond hair, carefully coiffed, heavy metal earrings and bright lipstick. Her striking eyes – large and steely blue – scrutinized him.

She invited him into her studio and they talked about her health. For a year, Dina had been wondering if she ought to move. It was a 20-minute drive to the nearest town – an ambulance might not make it.

The journalist examined the pictures on the easels: a balustrade like in a Swiss chateau with vases of flowers on it. Beyond that, a green field, blue sky and fluffy clouds. Snow White was dancing on the grass with Dopey, and the rest of the dwarfs were jumping up and down.

Dina didn't tell him much about Mengele. Was she still afraid of him?

In June 1985, crowds of policemen and journalists had gathered in a graveyard near São Paulo. Dr Jose Antonio, a pathologist, held up a skull over an open grave. The Nazi hunters had no doubt whose it was. The trail had led to Brazil, where six years earlier, Josef Mengele had died. He was swimming in the ocean, had a stroke and drowned.

Television stations broadcast the scene at the graveyard. An upset Dina explained to an Israeli reporter: 'I painted Mengele's portrait, I know the shape of his skull exactly. And that wasn't the skull the pathologist was holding. Mengele's face was much wider. In my opinion it's his family, their helpers and their helpers' helpers who are purposely misleading us to buy some time.'

Later, its identity was confirmed by DNA analysis. Did she believe it?

Why did she have that painting on the easel, a barrack from Birkenau on the shores of the Pacific? Was the princess in a yellow skirt and court shoes an expression of resistance to evil, or an attempt to cheer herself up? Snow White was looking for a better home, maybe she'd become a home herself? She was white as snow, while everything in the camp was reprehensible. Did people start being kind to survivors too late for Dina to forgive herself? Who had the Gypsies been for her, the ones whose names she couldn't remember?

When Jesus was carrying the cross, Veronica gave him a kerchief – the divine countenance remained. The Gypsies went to death – it took their last breath from them. Their faces live, their bodies have vanished in smoke. Watercolour paints, a brush on a blank page, the touch of a hand – there is only one original.

Something unites Dina and the people in the portraits.

Michele Kane: 'My mother wanted to free the spirits of the Gypsies from the Holocaust museum, where they were imprisoned, and bring them to the free world.'

Auschwitz and oppression have forever been intertwined. First, they sent her there in a cattle-car and took everything from her. And when years later, she found what belonged to her, they did it again. That's what they can do there. But they shouldn't, because the camp belongs to the survivors. If someone recognizes their shoe or their jewellery box – let them take it.

The soup is coming, you'll all eat

Dina was in agony. She was suffering from cancer, and knew she would die soon.

She hadn't got off the train on her 19th birthday, it was two days earlier. She'd just read that somewhere. But the gathering place for deportation had been on Merhautova Street in Brno, that was for sure.

'At my old school. I was glad to go to Theresienstadt, because I didn't like being a Jew in Prague anymore. People looked at us strangely when we were had those stars on, but I had friends in the ghetto. In the Hamburg Barracks, they gave us great big sacks and straw to fill them with. I volunteered to care for the ill at night. Růžena Buschová was there, she was incredibly funny, we became friends. She was 21 and had a husband. She could never decide what she liked more, food or sex.'

Růženka had a beautiful soprano singing voice. She performed in a Theresienstadt theatre, but whose theatre was it? Probably Karel Švenk's, the famous cabaret artist. She performed with a tall, slim guy with ears that stuck out and a prominent Adam's apple. He would embrace Růženka from behind and she'd flutter her eyelashes.

Once, Růžena dropped in on Dina's shift. She knew someone who had chocolate custard. Dina didn't believe her.

'We would burn dry branches, sticks and brushwood in the courtyard. We toasted ourselves bread over the fire, that's what we had instead of sausages, and we had air for dessert.'

But she went upstairs with Růženka. They met Franta Klinger in the kitchen, who told them he was hiding some custard in his room. He invited them in. Dina looked around. A patient was lying on a pallet, bandaged-up as though he had an earache.

'And suddenly he started playing with my hair, I had these long curls back then. It felt strange sitting there, especially since Růženka and this Franta were already... I ran off.'

The next morning a tall man stopped her in the corridor.

'Well come on now, darling, are you mine or not?'

It was Karl Klinger, Franta's brother. The one who'd dragged a horse, a cow and two sheep from Malešice to Theresienstadt. She didn't recognize him without the bandage. And from then on, they were together.

Once, an innkeeper asked Dina whether she'd paint a picture for his daughter, who was getting married.

'I had some pastels with me, and he gave me some paper. I went out to the garden and quickly drew an enormous blue bowl of flowers on the table. It was a really great picture. And in exchange I got – listen to this – a cake with whipped cream. A whole one! For us... We were always talking about whipped cream, I don't know why. Nowadays I don't like it at all, but back then whipped cream was what we dreamt of... He gave me some other food and for a day and a half it was like we were in a fairy-tale, until we'd finally eaten everything. But I never saw custard with my own eyes, although Růženka did.'

This Růžena was incredible, she always knew how to land on her feet. In Birkenau, a bloke called Malinka from the men's camp used to bring her bread and cheese.

'She was still plump when she went to the gas. She said when I saw a fat piece of soot on my nose...'

All the women who made it through the death march were crammed into a large hangar in Ravensbrück. It was impossible to describe the hunger. A woman SS officer walked in and smacked her riding crop against her boot.

'All right, the soup is coming, you'll all eat. But the Jews aren't getting anything.'

They brought the soup. Everyone got plenty.

Dina: 'It was sort of like rice soup, there was even a little meat in it. I thought it was the best soup I'd eaten in my entire life.'

In her tenement in Prague after the war, in the room in Paris she shared with her cocker spaniel Remus, in her elegant villa with a pool next to the amphitheatre in Hollywood, in her wooden cabin under the sequoias – Dina would buy rice and meat.

'To this day I've tried my hardest to cook soup like that, but I've never managed to.'

Bibliography

Translator's note: Watercolours *makes use of source material originally written in several languages, including Polish, English, German and Hebrew. For Polish sources, I have quoted from established English translations when these were available – if there were none or if the published translations were flawed, I have translated them myself. For other materials, when it has been possible for me to locate English originals or direct translations from the original languages, I have quoted from these – otherwise, I have translated from Ostałowska's Polish.*

Alphen, Ernst van. 2004. 'Zabawa w Holokaust' [Play in the Holocaust], *Literatura na świecie*, 390-391: 217-244.

Apel, Dora. March 2002. 'The Auschwitz Memorial Museum and the Case of the Gypsy Portraits', *Other Voices* 2(2). http://www.othervoices.org/2.2/apel/ (accessed 20 February 2016).

Arendt, Hannah. 2006. *Eichmann in Jerusalem: A Report on the Banality of Evil.* New York: Penguin Classics.

Auschwitz-Birkenau State Museum, Oświęcim and Documentation and Cultural Centre of German Sinti and Roma, Heidelberg (eds.). 1993. *Memorial book. The Gypsies at Auschwitz-Birkenau – Księga pamięci. Cyganie w obozie koncentracyjnym Auschwitz-Birkenau – Gedenkbuch. Die Sinti und Roma im Konzentrationslager Auschwitz-Birkenau*, Heidelberg, Munich: KG Saur.

Bettelheim, Bruno. 2010. *The Uses of Enchantment: The Meaning and Importance of Fairy Tales.* New York: Vintage.

Borowski, Tadeusz. 1976. *This Way for the Gas, Ladies and Gentlemen.* New York: Penguin.

Borowski, Tadeusz. 1991. *Utwory wybrane* [Selected Works]. Wrocław: Ossolineum.

Czech, Danuta et al. Wacław Długoborski and Franciszek Piper (eds.). 2000. *Auschwitz 1940-1945: Key Problems from the History of the Camp, Vol. V: Epilogue.* Oświęcim: Publication Department PMAB.

Czech, Danuta et al. Franciszek Piper, Teresa Świebocka (eds.). 1993. *Auschwitz. Nazistowski obóz śmierci* [Auschwitz: The Nazi Death Camp]. Oświęcim: Publications Department PMAB.

Czech, Danuta. 1992. *Kalendarz wydarzeń w KL Auschwitz* [Calendar of Events at KL Auschwitz]. Oświęcim: Publication Department PMAB.

Dębski, Jerzy and Joanna Talewicz-Kwiatkowska. 2007. *Prześladowania i masowa zagłada Romów podczas II wojny światowej w świetle relacji i wspomnień* [Persecutions and mass murder of Roma during the Second World War in Testimonies and Recollections]. Warsaw: Wydawdnictwo DiG.

Doron, Lizzie. 2003. *Yamin Shel Sheket* [Days of Tranquility]. Jerusalem: Keter.

Ficowski, Jerzy. 1985. *Cyganie na polskich drogach* [Gypsies on Polish Roads]. Kraków: Wydawnictwo Literackie.

Friess, Steve. 2006. 'History Claims Her Artwork, but She Wants It Back', *The New York Times* (New York), 30 August 2006.

Friess, Steve. 2006. 'Return of Auschwitz Art Sought', *The New York Times* (New York), 20 September 2006.

Goldfarb, Jeffrey. 2012. 'Why Poland?' *Deliberately Considered*. 9, 18 and 27 April 2012. http://www.deliberatelyconsidered.com/2012/04/why-poland-poles-and-jews-before-the-fall-of-communism/, http://www.deliberatelyconsidered.com/2012/04/why-poland-part-2-commemorating-auschwitz/ and http://www.deliberatelyconsidered.com/2012/04/why-poland-part-3-thinking-about-jedwabne-addressing-premature-holocaust-fatigue/. Accessed 20 February 2016.

Grimm, Wilhelm. 1982. *Baśnie braci Grimm. Baśnie domowe i dziecięce zebrane przez braci Grimm* [Fairy Tales of the Brothers Grimm: Family and Children's Fairy Tales Collected by the Brothers Grimm], vol. 1–2. Trans. Emilia Bielicka i Marceli Tarnowski. With afterword and notes by Helena Kapełuś, illustrated by Elżbieta Murawska. Warsaw: Ludowa Współdzielnia Wydawnicza.

Grossman, Ron. 2006. 'Staking Claim to Holocaust History', *Los Angeles Times* (Los Angeles), 5 November, 2006.

Gustines, George Gene. 2008. 'Comic-Book Idols Rally to Aid a Holocaust Artist', *The New York Times* (New York), 8 August 2008.

Haska, Agnieszka. 2010. 'Zapętlenia pamięci i wyobraźni. Trzy opowieści o Zagładzie' [The Enganglement of Memory and Imagination: Three Stories About the Holocaust], *Zagłada Żydów. Studia i Materiały*, 2010 (6).

Helfer, Janusz. 2005. *Cyganie – Romowie. Zapomniane obrazy* [Gypsies – Conversations: Forgotten Pictures]. Warszawa: Wydawnictwo DiG.

Höss, Rudolf. 2000. *Commandant of Auschwitz: The Autobiography of Rudolf Hoess*. New Haven: Phoenix.

Huener, Jonathan. 2003. *Auschwitz, Poland, and the Politics of Commemoration, 1945–1979*. Athens: Ohio University Press.

Kalabiński, Jacek. 1991. 'Nieortodoksyjny rabin ortodoksyjny' [An Unorthodox Orthodox Rabbi], *Gazeta Wyborcza* (Warsaw), 10 December 1991.

Kapralski, Sławomir. 2009. 'Czego możemy się nauczyć, studiując zagładę Romów w czasie II wojny światowej?' [What Can We Learn by Studying the Roma Holocaust During World War II?], *Midrasz*, 143.

Karny, Miroslav. 1993. 'Obóz familijny w Brzezince (BIIb) dla Żydów z getta Theresienstadt' [The Family Camp in Birkenau (BIIb) for Jews from the Theresienstadt Ghetto], *Zeszyty Oświęcimskie*, 20: 123-215.

Klee, Ernst. 1997. *Auschwitz: Die NS-Medizin und ihre Opfer* [Auschwitz: Nazi Medicine and its Victims]. Frankfurt am Main: S. Fischer.

Klüver, Reymer von. 2007. "Auschwitz-Zeichnungen. Mengeles Malerin" [Auschwitz Drawings: Mengele's Painter], *Süddeutsche Zeitung* (Munich), 16 January 2007.

Kodurowa, Aleksandra (ed.). 1985. *Xawery Dunikowski i polscy artyści w obozie koncentracyjnym Auschwitz w latach 1940-1945. Rysunki, obrazy, rzeźby. Wystawa styczeń-kwiecień 1985, Muzeum im. Xawerego Dunikowskiego* [Xawery Dunikowski and Polish Artists in the Auschwitz Concentration Camp 1940-1945: Drawings, Paintings, Sculptures. Exhibit January-April 1985, the Xawery Dunikowski Museum]. Warsaw: Narodowy Muzeum.

Koren, Yehuda and Eilat Negev. 2013. *Giants: The Dwarfs of Auschwitz*. London: Robson Press.

Korotko, Dariusz and Marek Nycz. 1999. 'Spacer po bastionie Auschwitz' [A Walk Around the Bastion of Auschwitz], *Magazyn* (Warsaw), 13 May 1999.

Kowalczyk, August. 2010. *Refren kolczastego drutu: trylogia prawdziwa* [Barbed-Wire Refrain: A True Trilogy]. Poznań: Videograf II.

Kowarska, Agnieszka. 2005. *Polska Roma. Tradycja i nowoczesność* [Polish Roma: Tradition and Modernity]. Warszawa: Wydawnictwo DiG.

Krajewski, Andrzej. 2011. 'Józef Cyrankiewicz, czyli jak kończą idealiści' [Józef Cyrankiewicz, or How Idealists End], *Newsweek Polska* (Warsaw), 3 May 2011.

Krzemińska, Kinga. 2010. 'Kicz w kinie holokaustowym' [Kitsch in Holocaust Cinema], *Zagłada Żydów. Studia i Materiały* 2010 (6).

Kubert, Joe. 2003. *Yossel: April 19, 1943*. New York: Vertigo.

Kubica Helena. 1993. 'Dr Mengele i jego zbrodnie w obozie koncentracyjnym Oświęcim-Brzezinka' [Dr Mengele and his Crimes in the Auschwitz-Birkenau Concentration Camp], *Zeszyty Oświęcimskie*, 20.

Kubica, Helena. 2002. *Nie wolno o nich zapomnieć. Najmłodsze ofiary Auschwitz* [We Cannot Forget Them: Auschwitz's Youngest Victims]. Oświęcim: Publication Department PMAB.

Kucia Marek. 2005. *Auschwitz jako fakt społeczny. Historia, współczesność i świadomość społeczna KL Auschwitz w Polsce* [Auschwitz as a Social Fact: the History, Modernity and Social Awareness of KL Auschwitz in Poland]. Kraków: Universitas.

Kuźniak, Angelika and Lidia Ostałowska. 2007. "Europa to też ojczyzna Romów" [Europe is the Roma Homeland Too], *Gazeta Wyborcza* (Warsaw), 13 January 2007.

Lachendro Jacek. 2007. *Zburzyć i zaorać...? Idea założenia Państwowego Muzeum Auschwitz-Birkenau w świetle prasy polskiej w latach 1945–1948* [Blow it Up and Plough it Under...? The Idea of Founding the Auschwitz-Birkenau State Museum in the Polish Press from 1945 to 1948]. Oświęcim: Publications Department PMAB.

Lenburg, Jeff. 2006. *Who's Who in Animated Cartoons: An International Guide to Film and Television's Award-Winning and Legendary Animators.* New York: Applause.

Levi, Primo. 2015. *The Complete Works of Primo Levi.* Trans. Ann Goldstein. New York: Liveright.

Lipiński, Piotr. 2003. *Towarzysze Niejasnego* [Comrades of Bolesław the Dim]. Warsaw: Prószyński i S-ka.

Cohn-Bendit and Rüdiger Dammann (eds.). 2007. *1968: Die Revolte* [1968: The Revolt]. Frankfurt: S. Fischer.

Maruszewska Małgorzata. 2009. '»Pasażerka« wciąż żyje' ["The Passenger" Still Lives], *Gazeta Wrocławska* (Wrocław), 20 February 2009.

Medoff, Rafael. 2008. 'Schneewittchens Albtraum. Interview mit Dina Babbitt' [Snow White's Nightmare: an Interview with Dina Babbitt], *Süddeutsche Zeitung* (Munich), 7 September 2008.

Miłosz, Czesław. 1981. *The Captive Mind.* Trans. Jane Zielonko. New York: Vintage Books.

Mróz, Lech. 2009. 'Historia trochę wspólna' [A Slightly Shared History], *Midrasz*, 143.

Mróz, Lech. 2000. 'Niepamięć nie jest zapomnieniem' [Oblivion is not Forgetting], *Przegląd Socjologiczny*, 49 (2), 89-114.

Myśliwski, Wiesław. 2011. *Nagi sad* [Naked Orchard]. Kraków: Znak.

Nyiszli, Miklós. 2011. *Auschwitz: A Doctor's Eyewitness Account.* Trans. Tibère Kreme and Richard Seaver. New York: Arcade Publishing.

Okoński, Michał. 2005. 'Zderzenie symboli. Spory o Auschwitz po 1989 roku' [Clash of Symbols: Conflicts over Auschwitz after 1989], *Tygodnik Powszechny* (Kraków), 30 January 2005.

Olszewski, Michał et al. 2004. 'Miasto przedzielone drutami' [A Town Divided by Barbed Wire], *Gazeta Wyborcza Kraków* (Kraków), 21 May 2004.

Osęka, Piotr. 2005. 'Kłamstwa oświęcimskie' [Lies of Auschwitz], *Wprost* (Poznań), 22 January 2005.

Ostałowska, Lidia. 2000. *Cygan to Cygan* [A Gypsy's a Gypsy]. Warsaw: Czarne.

Ozick Cynthia. 2004. 'Prawa historii i prawa wyobraźni' [The Laws of History and the Laws of Imagination], *Literatura na Świecie*, 390-391: 81-94.

Polak, Grzegorz. 1992. 'Król czekał na ministra' [The King Was Waiting for the Minister], *Gazeta Wyborcza* (Warsaw), 24 November 1992.

Prot, Katarzyna. 2009. Życie po Zagładzie. Skutki traumy u ocalałych z Holocaustu. Świadectwa z Polski i Rumunii [Life After the Holocaust: Effects of Trauma on Holocaust Survivors. Testimonies from Poland and Romania]. Warsaw: Instytut Psychiatrii i Neurologii.

Rose, Romani et al. (eds.). 2003. *Zagłada Sinti i Romów: katalog wystawy stałej w Państwowym Muzeum Auschwitz-Birkenau* [The Holocaust of Sinti and Roma: Catalogue of the Permanent Exhibition of the Auschwitz-Birkenau State Museum]. Oświęcim: Stowarzyszenie Romów w Polsce – Romski Instytut Historyczny.

Rudnicki, Janusz. 2009. Śmierć czeskiego psa [The Death of a Czech Dog], Warsaw: WAB.

Saltzman, Lisa. 2004. 'Awangarda i kicz raz jeszcze' [The Avant-Garde and Kitsch Once Again], *Literatura na Świecie* 390-391: 210-2016.

Siedlecki, Janusz et al. 2000. *We Were in Auschwitz*. Trans. Alicia Nitecki. New York: Welcome Rain Publishers.

Smoleński, Paweł. 1999. 'Wobec końca' [Regarding the End], *Magazyn* (Warsaw), 16 December 1999.

Speer, Albert. 1970. *Inside the Third Reich: Memoirs*, trans. Richard and Clara Winston. New York: Orion Publishing Group.

Spitz, Vivien. 2005. *Doctors from Hell: The Horrific Accounts of Nazi Experiments on Humans*. Boulder: Sentient Publications.

Staszak, Kamilla. 2010. 'Wygrane bitwy' [Battles Won], *Polityka* (Warsaw), 16 March 2010.

Steinlauf, Michael C. 1997. *Bondage to the Dead: Poland and the Memory of the Holocaust*, Syracuse: Syracuse University Press.

Strzałka Jan. 2003. 'Filmowe zwierciadła Holokaustu' [Cinematic Reflections of the Holocaust], *Tygodnik Powszechny* (Kraków), 30 March 2003.

Strzelecka Irena. 2008. *Voices of Memory 2. Medical Crimes: The Experiments in Auschwitz*. Oświęcim: Publication Department PMAB.

Strzelecki, Andrzej. 2008. *Voices of Memory 1. The Evacuation, Liquidation and Liberation of Auschwitz*. Oświęcim: Publication Department PMAB.

Świebocki, Henryk (ed.). 2005. *Ludzie dobrej woli: księga pamięci mieszkańców Ziemi Oświęcimskiej niosących pomoc więźniom KL Auschwitz* [People of Good Will: A Book of Memory of the Inhabitants of the Territory of Oświęcim who Brought Aid to the Prisoners of KL Auschwitz]. Oświęcim: Publiations Department PMAB.

Szmaglewska, Seweryna. 1947. *Smoke Over Birkenau*. Trans. Jadwiga Rynas. New York: Henry Holt and Company.

Zaremba, Marcin. 2007. 'Oni mordują nasze dzieci. Mit mordu rytualnego w powojennej Polsce' [They're Mudering Our Children: The Myth of Ritual Murder in Post-War Poland], *Więź*, 588: 90-109.

Zertal, Idith. 2005. *Israel's Holocaust and the Politics of Nationhood*. Trans. Chaya Galai. Cambridge: Cambridge University Press.

Ziębińska-Witek, Anna. 2010. 'Kicz i Holokaust, czyli pedagogiczny wymiar ekspozycji muzealnych' [Kitsch and the Holocaust, or the Pedagogic Dimension of Museum Exhibits], *Zagłada Żydów*, 2010 (6).

Archival and Audio-Visual Materials

Radio broadcast by Wojciech Brodnik, *Ryte w miedzi* [Engraved in Copper] from the archive of Polish Radio.

Official correspondence related to the dispute over the watercolours of Dina Gottliebová-Babbitt in the possession of the Association of Roma in Poland in Oświęcim.

Dina Gottliebová-Babbitt's testimony recorded 20 May 1995 for the Jewish Museum in Prague, recorded by Anna Hyndarková.

Testimony of prisoners collected in the archive of the Collections Department of the Auchwitz-Birkenau State Musem.

Conversation with Dina Gottliebová-Babbitt, Association of Roma in Poland – unedited film footage by Marek Miller and Andrzej Jeziorek.

The position of the Auschwitz-Birkenau State Museum and the International Auschwitz Council in the case of the watercolours of Dina Gottliebová-Babbitt is available at: http://auschwitz.org/en/museum/news/museums-position-on-issue-of-portraits-made-by-dinah-gottliebova-babbitt,57.html

Helstein, Hilary. 2008. *As Seen Through These Eyes*, USA.

Internet Sources

The Center for the Documentation of Upper Silesian Medicine and Pharmacology, the Silesian University of Medicine in Katowice – Main Library: http://dokument.sum.edu.pl/index.asp

The Fritz Bauer Institute: http://www.fritz-bauer-institut.de/

Justice for Dina: http://www.justicefordina.com/

The Last Outrage: The Dina Babbitt Story: http://graphics8.nytimes.com/images/2008/08/09/arts/Babbitt_pages1-6.pdf

Animated version: http://www.youtube.com/watch?v=p8Q-7_ jLMs4&noredirect=1

Newsreel: 'Europa według Auschwitz' [Europe According to Auschwitz]: http:// www.terezin.europa-auschwitz.pl/

MacIntosh Bruce, "Super-Creator Team-Up: Neal Adams, Joe Kubert and Stan Lee Fight for Return of Holocaust Survivor's Art": http://www.comicon. com/ubb/ubbthreads.php?ubb=showflat&Number=532195#Post532195

The Auschwitz-Birkenau Place of Memory and Museum: www.auschwitz.org.pl

Walt Disney Studio Entertainment official website: www.disney.com

Sobelman, Michał, "Polacy–Żydzi: miłość, nienawiść i powrót do normalności. Między Antysemityzmem a antypolonizmem" [Jewish Poles: Love, Hate and the Return to Normalcy. Between Antisemitism and Anti-Polonism] http://fzp. net.pl/forum/viewtopic.php?f=1&t=3774

"Spotkania z Klio..." [Encounters with Klio]: http://www.kasztelania.pl/ historycznie.php/

Transcripts from the Nuremberg Trials: https://www.loc.gov/rr/frd/Military_ Law/Nuremberg_trials.html

Transcripts from the trial of Adolf Eichmann: http://nizkor.com/hweb/people/e/ eichmann-adolf/transcripts/

The David S. Wyman Institute for Holocaust Studies: http://www. wymaninstitute.org

United States Holocaust Memorial Museum: http://www.ushmm.org/

Waleczek Tomasz, "Od malarstwa do fotografii reklamowej" [From Painting to Photographic Advertising], undergraduate thesis:
http://www.strykowski.net/encyklopedia/ryszardhorowitzodpoczatku.php

Select Glossary of Historical Figures and Terms

Adenauer, Konrad (1876 – 1967): First post-war Chancellor of West Germany, from 1949 to 1963.

Arendt, Hannah (1906 – 1975): German-born, American Jewish political theorist. She reported on the trial of Adolf Eichmann for *The New Yorker* magazine.

Auschwitz Concentration Camp: A network of forced labour and extermination camps built by Nazi Germany in occupied Poland. The main complex was divided into three camps: Auschwitz I (commonly referred to as "Auschwitz" or "the main camp"), Auschwitz II-Birkenau (or simply "Birkenau") and Auschwitz III-Monowitz.

Bartoszewski, Władysław (1922 – 2015): Polish statesman, author, and Auschwitz survivor. He fought in the Resistance during World War II, was imprisoned under Communism, and after the restoration of democracy, served as Poland's Foreign Minister.

Begin, Menachem (1913 – 1922): Israeli statesman, founder of the Likud party, and Prime Minister of Israel from 1977 to 1983.

Ben-Gurion, David (1886 – 1973): Founder of the State of Israel, first Prime Minister of Israel from 1955 to 1963.

Borowski, Tadeusz (1922 – 1951): Polish author, journalist, and Auschwitz survivor. Best remembered for his collections of stories based on his time in Auschwitz, published in English as *This Way for the Gas, Ladies and Gentlemen* (Penguin Classics, 1992).

Brandt, Willy (1913 – 1992): Chancellor of West Germany from 1969 to 1987. Won the Nobel Peace Prize in 1971 for his efforts at reconciliation between West Germany and the countries of Eastern Europe.

Brezhnev, Leonid (1906 – 1982): Leader of the USSR from 1964 to 1982.

Cyrankiewicz, Józef (1911 – 1989): Polish socialist, Auschwitz survivor, and twice Prime Minister of Communist Poland, from 1947 to 1952 and 1954 to 1970.

Eichmann, Adolf (1906 – 1962): Nazi official and logistical overseer of the Holocaust, organizing deportation of Jews to ghettos and extermination camps. After the war, he fled to South America. He was captured in

Argentina by the Mossad in 1960, and put on trial in Israel. He was found guilty of war crimes and hanged.

Ficowski, Jerzy (1924 – 1906): Polish writer and poet. In addition to his own work, he is known for his writing on Polish Roma and his translations of Romani poetry.

Frank, Hans (1900 – 1946): Nazi official and governor of the part of German-occupied Poland known as the "General Government" (see entry below). Convicted of crimes against humanity during the Nuremberg Trials and executed.

General Government: Following the German and Soviet invasion of Poland in 1939, sections of the country were annexed directly by the USSR and the Third Reich. The remainder (largely central and southeastern Poland, including Warsaw and Kraków) was termed the 'General Government' and put under Nazi military rule from 1939 to 1945.

Gierek, Edward (1913 – 2001): Leader of Communist Poland from 1970 to 1980.

Goebbels, Joseph (1897 – 1945): Reich Minister of Propaganda in Nazi Germany from 1933 to 1945. One of Hitler's closest advisors.

Himmler, Heinrich (1900 – 1945): Nazi leader of the SS and main official responsible for overseeing the concentration and extermination camps.

Höss, Rudolf (1901 – 1947): Nazi SS official and longest-serving commandant of the Auschwitz concentration camp (1940-43 and 1944-45).

Kádár, János (1912 – 1989): Leader of Communist Hungary from 1956 to 1988.

Karski, Jan (1914 – 2000): Polish World War II resistance fighter. In 1942 and 1943, Karski delivered first-hand witness accounts of the situation in German-occupied Poland and the destruction of the Warsaw Ghetto to Allied governments in the United Kingdom and United States. After the war, he settled in the US, where he became a professor at Georgetown University.

Kiesinger, Kurt (1904 – 1988): Chancellor of West Germany from 1966 to 1969. Kiesinger joined the Nazi party in 1933 and during the war worked in the Foreign Ministry's radio propaganda department. In the 1960s, he was targeted by Nazi-hunter Beata Klarsfeld.

Levi, Primo (1919 – 1987): Italian Jewish author and Auschwitz survivor, renowned for his writings on the Holocaust.

Mengele, Josef (1911 – 1979): Nazi SS officer and lead doctor in the Auschwitz concentration camp. Part of the team that selected prisoners for murder by gassing. Performed inhumane medical experiments on prisoners. Evaded capture at the end of the war and fled to South America. He died of a stroke in Brazil in 1979.

NKVD: The People's Commissariat for Internal Affairs of the Soviet Union. Responsible for policing, domestic security, and international espionage. Oversaw the gulag, performed mass deportations and executions, as well as repressions and targeted assassinations in the USSR and abroad. Functioned from 1934 to 1946.

Nyszli, Miklós (1901 – 1956): Hungarian Jewish doctor and Auschwitz prisoner. Worked in the Auschwitz infirmary under the supervision of Josef Mengele.

Putrament, Jerzy (1910 – 1986): Polish writer, journalist, and politician. A former nationalist, he became a convinced Communist, and following the war, had a strong influence on cultural policy in Communist Poland. He became an ambassador, an MP, and finally a member of the Central Committee. He was profiled by Czesław Miłosz in *The Captive Mind* under the name 'Gamma'.

Selection: The process of sorting concentration camp prisoners into those fit to work and those who would be executed by gassing.

Speer, Albert (1905 – 1981): Nazi German architect and minister of Armaments and War Production. Hitler's chief architect and close personal advisor.

Theresienstadt: A concentration camp and 'model ghetto' constructed outside the city of Terezín in Nazi-occupied Czechoslovakia. Used in part as a way-station before deportation to Auschwitz.

Wałęsa, Lech (1943 –): Polish politician and trade union activist. Co-founder of the independent Solidarity labour union, winner of the Nobel Peace Prize in 1983, and President of newly-democratic Poland from 1990 to 1995.

A Guide to Polish Pronunciation

Polish is written in the Latin alphabet. Its spelling is phonetic but using certain accents and combinations of letters to express particular Polish sounds. The vowels a, e, i, o, and u are pronounced as in Spanish or Italian, and the emphasis falls on the second-to-last syllable. Most of the letters are pronounced roughly as in English, with the following exceptions.

Ą – a nasal *o* as in the French *on*, often pronounced *on* or *om*.

C – like the *ts* in *bits*.

Ch – like the German *ch* in *Bach*. Identical to *h* (below).

Cz – a "hard" ch as in *cheese*, made with the tongue curled back slightly.

Ć – a "soft" ch as in *cheese*, made with the tongue slightly forward in the mouth. Written *ci* before a vowel (e.g. *cia, cie*, not *ća, će*).

Dż – a "hard" *j* as in *jam*, made with the tongue curled back slightly.

Dź – a "soft" *j* as in *jam*, made with the tongue slightly forward in the mouth. Written *dzi* before a vowel (e.g. *dzia, dzie*, not *dźa, dźe*).

Ę – a nasal *e* as in the French *main*, often pronounced *en* or *em*.

H – like the German *ch* in *Bach*. Identical to *ch* (above).

I – like the y in *yes* when preceding another vowel (e.g. *bia* is *bya*, not *bi-a*).

J – like the *y* in *yes*.

Ł – like the *w* in *went*.

Ń – like the Spanish *ñ* as in *niño*. Written *ni* before a vowel (e.g. *nia, nie*, not *ńa, ńe*).

Ó – like the *oo* in *boot*. Identical to *u*.

R – trilled as in Spanish.

Rz – like the French *j* in *je*, but made with the tongue curled back slightly. Identical to *ż* (below). Pronounced like *sz* (below) when following a *k, p,* or *t*.

S – always "soft" as in *house*, never "hard" as in *lose*.

Sz – a "hard" sh as in *shake*, made with the tongue curled back slightly.

Ś – a "soft" sh as in *shake*, made with the tongue slightly forward in the mouth. Written *si* before a vowel (e.g. *sia, sie*, not *śa, śe*).

W – like the *v* in *very*.

Y – like the "short" *i* in *mix*.

Ż – like the French *j* in *je*, but made with the tongue curled back slightly. Identical to *rz* (above).

Ź – like the French *j* in *je*, but made with the tongue slightly forward in the mouth. Writen *zi* before a vowel (e.g. *zia, zie*, not *źa, źe*).